Broken Bonds

Book Three of the Barrington Family Series

Chris Taylor

LCT Productions Pty Limited

LCT Productions Pty Limited

18364 Kamilaroi Highway, Narrabri NSW 2390

ISBN: 9781925441031 (eBook)

ISBN: 9781925441048 (Print)

Broken Bonds is a work of fiction. Names, places, characters, brands, media
and incidents are either the product of the author's imagination or are used
fictitiously. Any resemblance to persons living or dead, events or locales is
entirely coincidental.

This book is dedicated to my daughter,
Imogen Taylor.
Happy Birthday, sweet nineteen!
Enjoy your final year of being a teenager!
I'm so proud of the
young woman you're becoming.
I love you.

And as always, to my husband, Linden. My best
friend, my soul mate. I
love you to the moon and back.

Other books by Chris Taylor

The Munro Family Series (in order)

The Profiler

The Investigator

The Predator

The Betrayal

The Deception

The Negotiator

The Christmas Vigil (A novella)

The Ransom

The Defendant

The Shooting

The Maker

The Sydney Harbour Hospital Series (in order)

The Perfect Husband

The Body Thief

The Baby Snatchers

The Final Bullet

The Debt Collector

The Lab Test

The Stolen Identity

The Cliff-top Killer

The Likeable Fraudster

The Sydney Legal Series (in order)

An Accidental Murderer

At the Hand of her Father

A Woman Scorned

Lies and Deception

Ordinary Evil

The Ties that Bind

The Perfect Crime

A Toxic Inheritance

Malicious Love

The Craigdon Family Series (in order)

Callum

Joel

Isabella

Nicholas

Sophia

Flynn

Noah

Logan

Elizabeth

The Barrington Family Series (in order)

Broken Lives

Broken Promises

Broken Bonds

Broken Spirits

Broken Minds

Broken Vows

Broken Hearts

Broken Dreams

Broken Homes

The Fairfax Family Series (in order)

A Cattleman in Disguise

A Cattleman's Quest

A Cattleman's Daughter

A Cattleman's Secret Baby

To Catch a Cattleman

The Doctor and the Cattleman

To Rescue a Cattleman

A Cattleman's Heart

For the Love of a Cattleman

Bachelors and Brides Series (in order)

Matilda

Austin

Farrah

Benjamin

Verity

Denver

Ebony

Tyrone

Willow

Books by Chris Taylor

Writing as Bella
Christian

This Is Where It Ends Series (in order)

Jessie's Story

Ryan's Story

Holly's Story

Sarah's Story

Veronica's Story

Love audiobooks? Check out Chris Taylor Books on audio

iTunes Amazon Audible

IX

Join Chris Taylor's Facebook reader group/fan page and be among the
first to receive news of book releases, read and review books prior to release
and other amazing offers.

Join Now!

Chapter One

Cassie Webster's stomach churned with dread. Tension kept her shoulders taut. She climbed out of her car and headed up the paved path that led inside the Broken Police Station. The air was crisp, a reminder that winter was on its way. The early morning sun hurt her eyes. They were sore and gritty, the result of a sleepless night. She squared her shoulders and shook off her fear as she climbed the steps. In all of her twenty-four years of living and growing up in Broken, she'd had no cause to visit the police station and she was eternally grateful for that. But now her run of luck had come to an end.

The squat, red brick building—*circa* 1970s—with its chocolate-brown tiled roof and wooden framed windows perched on a generous parcel of land. A decent-sized police station for a town with less than ten thousand people. Cassie noticed a couple of patrol cars parked alongside the building. A uniformed officer climbed out of one of them and scratched idly at his hair.

A fresh wave of nerves and dread washed over her. She felt intimidated being this close to a police station. She was a law-abiding citizen, but that didn't lessen the abject fear that threatened to overwhelm her.

Walk inside... That's all I have to do... One foot in front of the other...

The closer she drew to the front door, the more unreasonable her fear grew. If it weren't so imperative she speak to an officer, she'd turn tail and run. Her belly somersaulted on a rush of nausea. She gulped and clamped her lips closed, praying she'd hold on to the contents of her stomach.

I can do this... For Oscar I can do this...

Thinking of her brother spurred her on. She opened the glass door and went quickly up to the front desk. A young uniformed constable greeted her with a friendly smile.

"Hi. What can I do for you?"

"I-I need to speak to someone about a missing person. My brother."

"I see. Can I have your name?"

"It's Cassie. Cassandra Webster."

The constable jotted the name down on a notepad in front of her. "Take a seat and I'll have one of the officers attend you."

"Thank you," Cassie managed, her voice a hoarse whisper.

Turning away, Cassie sat down on one of the hard plastic chairs that were lined up in a row along the wall. Posters decrying drunk driving, domestic violence and a colorful, upbeat poster for a youth club run by the police filled a noticeboard that hung on the wall beside the counter. The place smelled of antiseptic, like it had been recently cleaned. Its astringent odor burned Cassie's nostrils.

With her fingers clutched tightly around her handbag, she dragged in a ragged breath and did her best to get her pulse rate under control. Her fear of the place lessened marginally once she walked through the door.

I did it… I'm here… Inside the police station… Now for the next challenge…

A side door she hadn't previously noticed suddenly opened and the space was filled with a tall and imposing man. She recognized him instantly. He'd aged well since the last time she'd seen him. Her heart went into overdrive.

He wore a suit and tie. This early in the morning, the tie was still crisply knotted. His shirt was a blinding white. He was a couple of years older than her, with short dark hair, blue eyes framed by impossibly thick dark lashes and olive skin that spoke of his Mediterranean heritage. He walked toward her and smiled without the slightest hint of recognition. She wasn't surprised.

Still, her stomach somersaulted on a fresh wave of nerves at his nearness. In her heightened state of awareness, she couldn't help but notice how the passing years had only accentuated his good looks. He could have been a leading man in Hollywood.

"Cassandra Webster? I'm Detective Trace Barrington."

She stood on trembling legs, her pulse wild and erratic.

Of course…Trace Barrington… *How many nights in high school did I fall asleep whispering your name…?*

Even as he drew closer, it was obvious he didn't recognize her. He extended his arm in her direction and her hand was swallowed up by his. His handshake was firm, his skin warm. She sensed a strength in him that gave her confidence. She blew out a shaky breath and squared her shoulders.

"Please, call me Cassie."

He acknowledged that request with a slight inclination of his head and then chuckled. "Relax. You look like you're facing your executioner. I won't bite. I promise."

She made a strangled sound in the back of her throat in response. It was all she could manage. He shot her another curious glance and then turned and headed back the way he'd come. He held the door open for her.

"After you."

She murmured her thanks, pleased that her inward terror and surprise at seeing him again hadn't displaced her manners. She found herself standing in a carpeted corridor with closed doors running the length of it on either side.

"Just in here," the detective said.

He moved to open the door nearest to them and once again indicated she should precede him. The room was small and claustrophobic. Not a single window in sight. A pale gray Formica table and two plastic chairs were the only furniture. A camera stood perched high on a bracket fixed to one wall.

"Take a seat," the detective offered.

Holding on to her courage, Cassie reached for the nearest chair. The large detective took the seat opposite. He dropped a notepad and pen on the table and then folded his long-fingered hands in front of him. His nails were clean and cut short.

"So. You're here to file a missing person report. Is that correct?"

She blinked and forced herself to concentrate on her reason for being there. "Yes." Her voice was barely above a whisper. She cleared her throat and tried again. "Yes. My brother. Oscar. Oscar Webster."

The detective wrote the name on the blank page and then looked back up at Cassie. "How long has he been missing?"

"About twelve hours. He hasn't been seen since around eight last night."

"That's not really enough time to formally consider him missing. How old is he?"

"F-fourteen, but he looks younger. He's small for his age and... He has autism."

"I see. Non-verbal?"

Cassie instinctively gave a brisk shake of her head. "No. He communicates well and he's exceptionally bright, but he... He has a rather simplistic view of the world. He sees the best in people. He's very trusting."

The detective made some more notes. "Has he disappeared like this before?"

Cassie bit her lip. "Yes, but he's never been gone this long."

"How long does he usually stay away when he takes off?"

"I don't know. A few hours. Never all night."

"How often does he disappear?"

"Every now and then. When things get too much for him. When he needs to get away to think and clear the noise from his head. Maybe once every few months. Lately it's been more often than that."

"So what changed?"

"I don't know," she said honestly. "He and our stepfather haven't been getting along so well lately. They've always butted heads, but it seems the older Oscar gets the more he irritates Malcolm. Don't get me wrong, Oscar can be a handful. But it annoys me that Malcolm loses his temper. I mean, *he's* the adult. And Oscar isn't exactly a normal teenager. He deserves to be cut some slack."

"What's Malcolm's last name?"

"Russell. Malcolm Russell."

"How long has he been with your mom?"

"They've been married five years."

"Do you think your stepfather might have something to do with Oscar's disappearance?"

Cassie stared down at the worn table. She hated having to air their dirty laundry in front of anyone, but if she wanted them to look for Oscar, she had no choice.

"Oscar and our stepfather got into an argument last night. Something about Oscar not doing his chores. I only caught the tail end of it, but Malcolm was furious."

"Do you think that's why your brother ran away?"

Cassie pulsed with irritation. "I didn't say he'd run away. I told you he was missing. We don't know whether he ran away or... If something terrible happened to him."

The detective eyed her steadily. "Is that what you think? That something terrible might have happened to him?"

Her frustration boiled over. "I don't know!" she cried. "That's why I'm here! I need you to find him!"

The detective continued to regard her calmly. He made a few more notes and then glanced up at her again.

"Tell me about Oscar's biological father. Is he still in your lives?"

Cassie stared stoically at her hands which were knotted in her lap. "We haven't seen our father for years. Not since Oscar was a baby. He... He went to jail a long time ago. We never saw him again."

"What's his name?"

"George Webster."

"Do you know where he is?"

"No."

The detective scrawled her father's name on the paper. "What about your mother? Is she concerned about your brother? Why isn't she here with you?"

Cassie tried not to squirm, but an automatic and deep-seated embarrassment about Marie Russell made it difficult. She dragged in a deep breath and stared at the detective defiantly.

"Of course she's concerned! The thing is, she's not well, and too upset to come with me. I'm an adult and she was happy for me to be the one to report Oscar missing."

The detective frowned but remained silent. Cassie saw the curiosity in his eyes but refused to elaborate.

"Have you called your brother's friends? People he hangs out with?"

"Of course I have. I've called everyone I can think of. The thing is, he only has one close friend. Joe was the first person I called. He told me he hasn't seen Oscar since school on Friday afternoon."

"They didn't see each other over the weekend?"

Cassie shook her head. "Apparently not."

"What's this friend's name?"

"Joe. Joseph Lahood."

"Any relation to the Lahoods who own the café on Main Street?"

"Yes. He's their son."

"What about a girlfriend?"

"Oscar doesn't have a girlfriend."

Once again, the detective made notes. Cassie clung to her patience.

This is taking so long! My brother is out there somewhere, cold, hungry, scared… He might even be hurt…

"Please. Are we nearly done? My brother's out there. We need to find him."

"Does your brother have a phone?"

"Yes. And before you ask, I've called him over and over through the night and again this morning. It goes straight to voicemail."

"Is it a smartphone?"

"Yes."

"Good. Those phones have built-in tracking apps. Do you have the "Find my" app downloaded?"

"Yes."

"Have you tried locating Oscar's phone with it?"

"No. I didn't think to do that."

"Do you have your phone on you now?"

"Yes." Cassie pulled it out of her handbag."

"Does Oscar have the app on his phone?"

Cassie felt a frisson on hope. "Yes."

"Open the app and let's see what it shows."

With her heart thumping with anticipation, Cassie did as he asked. It felt like an eon passed before the app loaded. They both stared at the screen.

Nothing.

Cassie bit back a sigh. The detective sat back in his seat.

"Can you give me Oscar's number and the name of the phone company he uses?"

Cassie supplied the detective with the requested information.

"Tell me more about your stepfather? What does he do for a living?"

"Malcolm's a park ranger. Works for National Parks." She paused and then added, "I haven't seen him since last night, either."

At the detective's raised eyebrow, she hurried to explain. "That's not unusual. He tends to take off for a few days after one of his outbursts."

"So you're not reporting *him* missing?"

She flushed with embarrassment. "No. He...um... Like I said, this isn't out of character for him. I'm sure he's just gone somewhere to cool off."

"When did you last see him?"

Cassie closed her eyes and willed away another wave of embarrassment. God, she hated having to do this... But she had no choice. If she wanted the police to help find Oscar, she had to answer their questions.

"I last saw Malcolm dragging Oscar by the ear up to the back shed. I'd just returned home. I'd stayed back late at work to catch up on some paperwork and prepare this week's lessons. As I said, I only caught the tail end of the argument."

"You're a teacher?"

"Yes. I teach history and geography at the high school."

"And you were at work on a Sunday?"

"Yes. My senior students have half-yearly exams coming up. I was doing some preparation."

"You said you caught the tail end of the argument between your brother and stepfather. What did you hear?"

"I didn't actually hear anything. I arrived as Malcolm was dragging Oscar up to the shed."

"So how do you know they'd been arguing?"

"Malcolm looked angry. That's not unusual when it comes to Oscar. The pair of them have a habit of rubbing each other the wrong way. I went inside and asked my mother what was going on. She told me Malcolm was upset with Oscar for not doing his chores."

"Why were they headed for the shed?"

Cassie drew in a ragged breath and let it out on a weary sigh. "That's where Malcolm takes Oscar to discipline him."

"In a physical way?"

She compressed her lips. "I guess."

The detective's gaze remained on hers. "Has he ever hit Oscar before?"

Familiar anger licked at her veins. "Yes. When he's had too much to drink. Or when he's stressed or had a bad day at work. Where Oscar's concerned, it doesn't seem to take much. It doesn't usually happen when I'm around. Malcolm knows I won't stand for my brother being punished in a physical way, but as I said, I arrived home late. It had already been set in motion before I got there."

"What did you do when you found out what was going on?"

"I took off up to the shed."

"Did you confront Malcolm?""

"No. I'd only come around the side of the house when Malcolm roared off in his truck."

"Was anyone else with him?"

"I don't know. I only saw the back of Malcolm's truck. I wasn't paying that much attention. To tell the truth, I was concerned about Oscar."

"What happened next?"

"I kept walking toward the shed. I wanted to comfort Oscar and make sure he was all right. He's usually upset after a run-in with Malcolm."

She drew in another ragged breath. "But he wasn't there. I looked around for a bit and called out to him, but he didn't answer. I thought maybe he'd gone off somewhere to be alone. But that was twelve hours ago. He's never stayed away so long and never on his own. I've called everyone I can think of. No one's seen him. Where can he be?"

Her voice cracked with emotion. To her horror, her eyes welled up with tears. She swiped at them impatiently with the back of her hand.

The detective regarded her compassionately. "Is there a special place your brother might go when he wants to be alone?"

"Not really. He likes the bush. The National Park backs onto our house. But he's afraid of the dark. I don't think he'd go there at night and definitely not alone."

"What time was the altercation with your stepfather?"

"About eight last night."

"It's awfully dark at that time of night. How did you see the two of them?"

She shrugged. "Our yard is well lit with security lights."

"What was your brother wearing last night?"

Cassie frowned in thought. "Blue jeans and a long-sleeved black T-shirt. Nike cross trainers. Oh, and a red waterproof jacket."

Trace wrote the information down. "Do you have a recent picture of him?"

"Yes." Cassie opened her handbag and reached for her phone. She scrolled through her photos until she found one of Oscar. "This was taken a couple of weeks ago, at my birthday. I can airdrop it to you, if you like."

The detective reached into his pocket and pulled out his phone. A few moments later, the photo appeared on his screen.

Trace Barrington gazed at the picture of the kid who filled his screen. Oscar Webster looked a lot like his older sister. Striking features made up of dark auburn hair, ivory skin, brilliant green eyes, freckles. A wide smile filled the boy's innocent face as he clowned it up for the camera.

Trace set his phone aside and focused again on the woman who sat across from him. She appeared genuine in her distress for her missing brother, but something didn't seem quite right. What was with the mother? Too upset to report her son missing? Too upset to turn to the people who might be able to help find him? His cop instincts told him something was awry.

He thought of Oscar. Several possibilities ran through this head: The kid had run away. It happened all the time. Maybe not so often in Broken where the total population was less than ten thousand people, but still... It happened. Second possibility: The prince of a stepfather might have taken him with him. Cassie couldn't say for certain that hadn't happened and the stepfather hadn't been seen by the family since last night either.

"Have you spoken to your stepfather? Asked him about Oscar?"

Cassie grimaced. "No. I tried to but his phone's either switched off or flat. The calls go straight to voicemail. I've left messages, but I haven't heard from him."

Trace asked for details concerning Malcolm's phone number and provider. He also asked for a description of Malcolm and his truck. Cassie supplied him with the information, along with a recent photo she airdropped to Trace's phone. He duly recorded her answers and then returned his gaze to her.

"Have you called any of Malcolm's friends? His work colleagues?"

"I don't have any numbers for his work colleagues or his friends. My mother doesn't either. His office doesn't open until nine."

Once again, Trace noted Cassie's responses on the paper in front of him. There was a third possibility and one he didn't particularly want to consider but had no choice. It was possible the boy could have run afoul of somebody else wherever he'd gone after the argument with his stepfather. The boy was small for his age, sweet, innocent looking. The sister had mentioned how trusting he was.

Despite the quaintness of Broken, it wasn't without its vices. There were two registered sex offenders living in the town. Not as many as some, but more than Trace was comfortable with. There was always the possibility one of them had come across Oscar and taken him. The thought weighed heavy in his gut.

Still, there was no point in getting ahead of himself, or worrying the family unnecessarily. He looked at Cassie.

"Thank you for coming in. You did the right thing. I'll speak to my superior and get onto this right away. What's the best way to contact you?"

She provided him with her phone number.

"It's a bit tricky to get hold of me on my mobile during the hours of nine and three. You're probably best to leave a message at the school office. I'll let them know what's going on so that if you need to speak with me, they'll send someone to find me right away. I'm on my way there now." She glanced at her watch and frowned. "In fact, if I don't hurry, I'm going to be late."

Her eyes met his. Hers were filled with storm clouds.

"I'm just so worried about him. I mean, please God he walks into our living room any moment, but what if he doesn't?" Her tone turned beseeching. "What if he *doesn't?*"

Chapter Two

Cassie climbed into her car and started the ignition. Though dread still formed a hard, cold lump in the pit of her stomach, she was relieved she'd gone to the police. There was something about the calm, tall, good-looking detective that instilled confidence. The fact she'd known him since high school was also comforting. Though it was obvious he didn't remember her, she could tell he'd taken her concerns seriously. She just hoped he'd find her brother.

Where could he be? Please, God. Bring Oscar home...

Looking over her shoulder, she checked for traffic approaching from behind her car and then pulled out onto the street. She made the journey to the high school by memory. Her mind was full of Oscar and what more she could do to find him. Trace had quizzed her about Oscar's favorite haunts and it shamed her to admit she really didn't know. He'd always been partial to spending time roaming the trails in the National Park that bordered the rear of their property, but that was only during daylight hours. She had no idea where he went after dark.

On those occasions when he'd taken off after a disagreement with their stepfather, he hadn't ventured far. Mostly they'd found him at his best friend's house. Joe Lahood only lived down the road. But she'd already checked with Joe. He hadn't seen Oscar at all last night. In fact, he hadn't seen him since school on Friday.

As she turned into the staff carpark, she realized she was going to be late for roll call. There was nothing to be done about that now. Hurrying, she made her way into the school building. During the first break, she intended to find Joe and ask him again if he'd heard from Oscar. Perhaps her brother had texted his friend overnight and Joe hadn't yet informed her. Or maybe Joe had come up with a better idea about where Oscar might be. It was worth asking the question again.

She'd also talk to Oscar's teachers. One of them might have some insights into where Oscar might have gone. She couldn't worry about how embarrassing it would be for her to admit to them she'd been out of touch with her younger brother for the last little while. She'd been so busy with work and running the household... She pulled herself up. No, there was no excuse for not paying closer attention to Oscar's needs. She'd set her pride aside for Oscar's sake and ask. She just hoped someone could help her find him.

After seeing Cassie Webster out, Trace picked up his coffee mug and headed for the tearoom. He'd just finished filling it with black coffee when his brother Zac walked in.

"How's it going?" Zac asked and reached for a mug.

"Not bad. You?"

Zac shrugged. "You know. The usual."

Two years younger than Trace, Zac was a junior detective who'd recently relocated from a position with the Drug Enforcement Agency on the central coast, to Broken. The sleepy rural town was far removed from the stress and adrenaline rush of working DEA in a busy metropolitan station. While Zac claimed to love small-town policing and Trace well understood that, he suspected Zac's return to their hometown had more to do with a certain woman who'd broken his brother's heart, than any real desire to spend his life dealing largely with DUIs and break and enters in Broken.

Zac and Emily Wilson had been high school sweethearts. As so many young romances did, theirs had ended in tears. Trace didn't know all the details but ever since the breakup Zac had been withdrawn and circumspect. Not at all like the cheeky, fun-loving brother Trace had grown up with. He hoped Zac moved on from Emily and found someone else to keep him warm at night—or go back and make things work with Emily. Either way, Trace didn't care. He just wanted to see his brother happy again.

Of course, it was also possible it was their mother's cooking that had Zac moving back close to home. It was a running joke in the family that Zac still ate dinner at home at least two or three times a week. Not that Trace could blame him. Their mother was a superb cook.

Still, Zac and his tumultuous love life wasn't Trace's concern right now. A child was missing. Though he didn't want to jump to conclusions, the fact was there were two registered sex offenders living in Broken: Charles Morley and Kevin Turner. Morley had been released from jail only a couple of months earlier. Convicted sex offenders were supposed to be monitored, but there were ways and means around that if the guy was smart and knew his way around the system.

From what Trace knew about Charles Morley, the man had the brains to do exactly that. Released from Long Bay Correctional Centre in March, Morley had once been a high-flying human rights lawyer living it up in Sydney's wealthy eastern suburbs before his spectacular fall from grace. As far as Trace was concerned, the man was a germ. Anyone who preyed on vulnerable children deserved to be put down. Some might find his attitude harsh, but that was the way Trace felt and he wouldn't apologize for it. Morley was the first person Trace intended to visit.

He regarded his brother over the rim of his coffee mug. "You busy?"

"Not really. I have to file some paperwork with the court on that Masters case. I've got a few statements I need to finish up. Why? Do you need some help?"

Trace filled him in on Oscar Webster.

Zac nodded thoughtfully. "Fourteen, you say? Are they sure he didn't just spend the night with friends?"

"Yes. The sister says she's called everyone she can think of. No one's seen or heard from him. I've called his number. Goes straight to voicemail. Same thing for the stepfather. The thing is, the kid's autistic. That puts this into a slightly more serious category."

"So, what's the plan?" Zac asked.

"I've put out a BOLO—be on the lookout—for Malcolm Russell, along with a description of his truck. Hopefully someone in one of the neighboring towns might have spotted him. I've also sent Oscar's photo to the local media outlets. It can't help having as many people as we can knowing he's missing and on the lookout for him. Right now, the plan is to go out and start asking questions. Charles Morley and Kevin Turner are at the top of my list."

Zac nodded. "Sounds fair. You want me to ride along?"

Trace tossed him a set of car keys that belonged to a police cruiser. "I thought you'd never ask."

Charles Morley lived in an average part of town that was popular with a mix of blue-collar workers, retirees and young families. Though Morley's rented house wasn't situated in the immediate vicinity of children, it was close enough to make Trace uncomfortable. Not for the first time, he wished the law allowed him to warn nearby families.

Zac pulled up outside the small weatherboard house. Though the paint was fresh and the corrugated iron roof was new, the place was surrounded by an air of neglect.

Trace and his brother climbed out of the cruiser. The front gate squeaked in protest when Trace pushed it open. Junk mail overflowed the mailbox. The lawn needed mowing. How Morley now spent his time was anyone's guess, but it wasn't spent in his front garden.

They walked up the cracked concrete path and climbed the steps that led to the front door. Trace rapped his knuckles against the wooden panel and then stood back to wait. A minute passed. Then another. Trace knocked again.

"Mr Morley? It's the police. We'd like to speak with you."

Once again, they were met with silence. Trace knocked a third time.

"Charles Morley? Is anyone home?"

"We should take a look around," Zac murmured.

They'd only just cleared the steps when their attention was captured by a man who'd sidled up to the dividing fence. Despite the late autumn chill, he wore nothing but a singlet and loose jeans that hung from his hips. His white hair was mussed, his cheeks grizzled.

"You lookin' for Charlie?"

Trace walked closer. "Yes. Do you know where he is?"

"He's gone."

Trace frowned. A registered sex offender was obligated to notify the police of their movements. As far as Trace was aware, no one at the station had been contacted by Morley.

"Gone?" he asked.

"Yeah. Up north. His mother's sick. Dyin', I think."

"Whereabouts up north?" Trace asked.

"Queensland. Gympie, I think he said."

"When did he leave?" Zac asked.

"'Bout a month ago. Asked me to keep an eye on the place."

"Did he say when he'd return?" Trace asked.

"Nope. I guess that depends on how long the old woman lasts." The man began to cough and wheeze. Trace waited him out. Then the man hawked up a globule of phlegm and lobbed it not far from Trace's feet.

Trace grimaced and ignored the man's unspoken insult. "And you haven't seen him in all that time?"

"Nope."

Trace thanked the man for his time and then headed back to the car. Zac followed.

"So, I guess that rules Morley out," Zac murmured.

"I guess...if he's telling the truth. I'll check in with Morley's parole officer. Let's see if we have better luck with Kevin Turner."

Zac put the cruiser into gear and headed in the opposite direction. According to Turner's file, he'd been employed as a technician by one of the electricity companies prior to his conviction for having sex with a minor. Trace wasn't sure what the man did for employment now but being on a register for sex offenders would definitely narrow his options.

In stark contrast to the neglect evident at Morley's place, Turner's front yard was neat and tidy. This late in autumn, the trees had changed color and provided a background of rosy reds and orange against the clear blue sky. Flower beds were filled with neatly pruned plants and shrubs in preparation for the oncoming winter. The grass was freshly mown.

As Trace and Zac made their way up the front path, Trace noticed the three-seater loveseat on the front veranda. The area was cool and shaded and provided a clear view of the street. Turner lived only two blocks from Oscar Webster. It hadn't escaped Trace's notice that the boy would have to pass by Turner's house every day on his way to and from school. Unless he caught a ride with his sister, which was always possible. After all, Cassie Webster was a teacher at the high school.

Turner answered Trace's knock after only the first attempt. He was dressed in T-shirt and jeans. Though faded and worn, his clothes were clean. His feet were bare. Through the screen door, he eyed them warily.

"What can I do for you?"

"Kevin Turner?"

"Yes."

"I'm Detective Trace Barrington. This is my partner. We want to talk to you about Oscar Webster."

The man frowned. "Who?"

"Oscar Webster. A young teenager. He lives not far from here. He's gone missing."

"Never heard of him."

Trace fished in his pocket and pulled out his phone. He found the photo Cassie had given to him.

"Here," he said, offering the phone to Turner. "See if this refreshes your memory."

Turner squinted at the photo. Slowly, he nodded. "Yeah. I've seen him. Didn't know his name was Oscar."

"How do you know him?" Zac asked.

"I don't *know* him. I've seen him pass by here every now and then on his way home from school. That's all."

Trace held his gaze steady on the man's face. Turner was clean-shaven. His hair was neatly trimmed. Though he had a slight belly protruding over the waistband of his jeans, he looked reasonably fit for a man in his late forties. No one looking at him would guess he was a sex offender.

That was the problem. These men—and the vast majority of them were men—went around in society with nobody the wiser about what went on in their sick minds. It was one of the reasons they went undetected for so long. There were two registered sex offenders in Broken, but Trace was under no illusion there weren't others who were yet to be caught. Sometimes that knowledge kept him up at night.

"When was the last time you saw this boy?" Trace asked.

The man shrugged. "I don't know. I don't keep records."

Trace bit down on his impatience. "Give us a ballpark. Did you see him come by here this morning?"

"No. I've been out back since I got up."

"What about over the weekend?" Zac asked.

The man paused as if in thought and then shook his head. "Nope."

Trace narrowed his eyes at the man. "Are you sure?"

Turner dropped his gaze. "Of course I'm sure. I haven't been out front all weekend."

"Where were you last night?" Zac asked.

"Here."

"All night?" Trace asked.

"Yeah."

"Can anyone verify that?" Zac asked.

"Yeah. My girlfriend. She was here, too."

"What's her name?" Trace asked.

"Mandy. Mandy Goodwin."

"Is Mandy home?"

"Yeah."

"Go and get her. We'd like to talk to her."

Turner disappeared. A few moments later, a thin woman of indeterminate age with brassy blond hair and a cigarette in her mouth met them at the door.

"Are you Mandy Goodwin?" Trace asked.

"Yeah. Who wants to know?" the woman replied in a belligerent tone.

"I'm Detective Barrington from the Broken Police Station. This is...Detective Barrington."

The woman looked from one to the other. "Are you shittin' me?"

"No, I'm not," Trace replied. "We're brothers."

They looked enough alike that Trace was sure she'd accept his explanation. She looked from one to the other and then nodded, seemingly satisfied.

"What can I do for you, Detectives?"

"What's your relationship to Kevin Turner?"

"He's my boyfriend."

"How long have you been together?" Trace asked.

"Five months."

"Do you live here with him?" Zac asked.

"Yeah. That's not a crime, is it?"

"No, of course not," Zac replied.

A sudden thought occurred to Trace. "Do you have any children, Ms Goodwin?"

She looked at Trace. "Not that it's any of your business, but yeah. I have two kids."

Trace's gut clenched. "Do they live here with you?"

Mandy stared at the ground. "No."

Trace hid his relief and posed another question. "Where were you last night?"

"I was here. With Kevin."

"All night?" Trace persisted.

"Yes. We had dinner, watched a movie and went to bed."

"What time was this?" Zac asked.

The woman took a drag of her cigarette and blew out a plume of smoke. "Let's see. We had dinner about seven. The movie went for a couple of hours. We were in bed by half-past ten."

She eyed Trace with curiosity. "What's this about, Detective?"

"We're looking for Oscar Webster. A young teenager. He's gone missing. His family's worried about him."

"Do you know Oscar Webster?" Zac asked.

The woman shook her head. "No. Should I?"

"He lives not far from here. Kevin said he's seen Oscar passing by here sometimes on his way to or from school."

"What does he look like?"

Once again Trace pulled out his phone. He showed her the picture.

The woman gazed down at the image for a few seconds and then shook her head. "Sorry. Can't say I've ever seen him before."

Trace eyed her steadily. "Are you from Broken, Ms Goodwin?"

"No. I moved here from Blacktown about six months ago. Needed to get out of the city. Too many people. Too much crime. I much prefer it out here in the country. I feel safer."

Trace nodded in acknowledgement. "We do our best to keep it that way. But right now, we have a teenage boy missing and we'd appreciate any help you can give us."

"Of course. I wish I knew more. I'll keep my eyes open and let you know if I see him."

"Thanks." Trace dug into his wallet for a business card and handed it over to her. "If you or Kevin think of anything else, or if you see Oscar, please give me a call."

She tucked the card into her cheap cotton bra. "Sure thing, Detective. You have my word."

Once again, Trace murmured his thanks. Together, he and Zac headed for their car.

Chapter Three

Kevin Turner's gut churned with nerves. He threw himself into his favorite armchair and tried to get his heart rate back under control. It was like that day all over again. The day his life had changed forever. Two detectives at his door, asking questions about a kid. Only this time it was a boy, and they weren't accusing him of raping him. At least, not yet.

Could the nightmare be happening all over again? If so, there was nothing he could do about it. A strangled sound of fear escaped his dry throat. From her position on the couch in front of the TV, Mandy turned to him and frowned.

"Do you know the kid they're talkin' about?"

He fought for nonchalance. "Yeah." His voice came out a squeak. He cleared his throat and tried again. "What I mean is, I recognized him. Like I told the police, he passes by here now and then. Seems like a nice boy. Friendly. We've talked a few times. He likes the flowers in the front garden."

Mandy's frown deepened. "How come I've never seen him?"

"I don't know. Probably because you're never out in the garden."

She gave him a dubious look.

Kevin's gut clenched. He tried to ignore the guilt that coursed through him. "Don't look at me like that. I've never hurt a child in my life."

She curled her lip up in disgust. "Don't be stupid. Why would I think that?"

Kevin drew in a deep breath and tried harder to slow his pulse. He was overreacting, seeing accusation where there was none. Of course she didn't suspect him of hurting the kid. Though she knew he'd done time, she had no idea why he'd been inside and that's how it was going to stay.

What he really wanted to do was tell the police about the boy's stepfather. That asshole was bad news. Oscar had shared enough about his troubles with the guy that Kevin knew the cops should be looking at Malcolm-bloody-Russell if they wanted to know why Oscar was missing.

But of course, he couldn't tell the cops anything because then he'd have to admit he'd done more with Oscar than see him pass by every now and then. He'd have to admit that the two of them had struck up a friendship over a mutual appreciation of flowers and that the kindhearted teenager was one of the few people in Broken who didn't judge him.

Though none of the townspeople knew he was on the register for sex offenders, a lot of them knew he'd done time. People looked at you differently when they knew you were an ex-con. They didn't trust you. They gave you a wide berth. But not Oscar. He'd treated him with kindness and respect. He'd always been pleased to see him. To stop in for a chat.

To discover his little mate was missing filled Kevin with concern. He wanted to join in the search party. He wanted to do what he could to help. But he couldn't do any of that. Just like he couldn't tell the police they were friends.

No, for his own sake, he had to stay the hell away from anything to do with Oscar Webster. As long as he convinced the police he had nothing to do with the missing boy, he'd be fine.

Cassie did her best to concentrate on her Year Ten history class, but it was difficult. She was trying to teach her students about the Freedom Rides, but her thoughts kept circling back to Oscar. She'd left strict instructions with her mother to call her if he returned, but so far, the few times she'd been able to check her phone, there had been no missed calls or messages. She bit back a sigh. She wished she'd gone to the police last night and not waited until the morning, but she'd kept hoping Oscar would get scared being out in the dark on his own and would come home.

She hated to admit she was also embarrassed to air their dirty laundry in public and draw unwanted attention to their family. Their mother especially took pains to stay out of the public eye. Cassie had honored that unspoken rule for as long as she could remember, but Oscar had never stayed away so long, and she was worried. Her mother would just have to cope with whatever attention the situation garnered. Cassie needed her brother found.

As soon as the bell went for recess, she hurried from the classroom. Kids streamed out of rooms and filled the hallways, talking and laughing and clowning around. On any other day, Oscar would be among them, grateful to be released from the confines of the classroom and into the play areas.

She sent a silent prayer heavenwards that her brother turned up safe and sound and headed toward the Year Eight area. Among the crowd of students, she sought out Joe Lahood. Like her brother, Joe was also small for his age, but instead of red hair and freckles, Joe had black hair and dark eyes and swarthy skin inherited from his Lebanese parents.

Last night, when she'd spoken to him, he'd been just as upset as she was that Oscar hadn't come home. She hoped Joe might have heard from him that morning, or thought of somewhere else they could look for him.

Spying Joe's dark head among a group of boys, she shouldered her way through the crowd and drew him aside, away from the other students so they could talk in private.

"Hi Joe."

"Hi Miss."

"Have you heard from Oscar?" she asked as casually as she could manage.

"No. Have you?"

Her heart sank. "No. Have you thought about where else he might be hiding?"

The boy shook his head. "No. The only place I can think of is the forest. We've been camping there before. Not all night, of course. Oscar would never stay out all night..."

His voice drifted off. Cassie could tell what he was thinking. She was thinking the same thing. Oscar was scared of the dark, even when he was with his best friend. And yet last night he hadn't come home. He'd spent the entire night on his own. She didn't want to think the reason he hadn't returned was that he might be hurt, but reality was fast setting in. She couldn't ignore the possibility any longer. It was the only thing that made sense.

"Are you sure you didn't speak to Oscar last night? Or even yesterday afternoon?"

"No. Like I said, the last time I saw him was at school on Friday afternoon."

"Did he talk about his plans for the weekend? Mention anywhere he was going?"

Once again Joe shook his head. "No Miss. Nothing like that. I'm sorry."

The boy looked so distressed, Cassie gave his shoulder a squeeze. Joe couldn't help her, and it wasn't fair for her to keep pressuring him to provide answers he didn't have.

She did her best to give him a reassuring smile. "Don't worry, Joe. I'm sure he'll turn up."

Joe's answering smile was just as strained. "Sure Miss. Of course he will. I promise to let you know if Oscar calls me. Or texts. Anything. I-I'll let you know."

It was all she could hope for.

It was mid-afternoon when Trace and Zac arrived at Cassie's house to interview her mother. The house was *circa* 1970s and was a traditional red-brick and tile, single-story house that blended in with the other houses of a similar age and style on that street. As they climbed out of the police cruiser, Cassie pulled up behind them in a late model Honda. In her hand she carried a leather briefcase bulging with papers. She joined them on the nature strip, looking wan and pale.

"Any news?" Trace asked.

"No, not as far as I know. I've been at school all day, but no one's called. What about you?"

Trace refrained from mentioning his visit to Kevin Turner. No sense in alerting her to the presence of a convicted sex offender when as yet there was no evidence Turner was involved. Instead he said, "I've put out an alert for your stepfather. Given he was the last person we know of to see Oscar last night, we need to find him. Hopefully someone might have seen him and will report back. I've contacted the media and provided them with a copy of Oscar's photo. Hopefully they'll run a story on tonight's news. I've also talked to a few locals. We're following all leads."

Her face flooded with hope. "So you have some leads?"

Trace grimaced. "Not leads as such. We're making enquires. You never know where they might end up."

Trace introduced his brother and then both men waited for Cassie to precede them through the front gate that led up to the house. The yard was neat and tidy. Native shrubs and bushes that were hardy and required little maintenance had been planted along the border in lieu of flowers. Not that Trace judged them for that. He didn't have time for flowers either.

Cassie walked up the three stone steps and crossed the concrete veranda and then opened the front door. It squeaked in protest. Trace saw her draw in a deep breath before she ushered them inside. Trace found himself in a long narrow hallway that ended in a modest kitchen at the back.

On either side of the hallway there were open doors. One of the front rooms was a bedroom. On the opposite side was a living room. They followed Cassie inside.

Trace pulled up short.

On the couch sat the most enormous woman he'd ever seen. She reminded him of some of the women he'd seen once on a reality TV show. *My Six-hundred-pound Life* or some such thing. The couch was a three-seater, but there wasn't an inch of space to spare. It sagged alarmingly. No wonder she hadn't made it down to the station. She probably struggled to move from the couch to her bedroom, let alone venture outside.

Trace fought to conceal his shock. He glanced at Cassie. Her expression was carefully blank. She kept her gaze fixed in the vicinity of her mother.

"Mom, the police are here. They want to talk to you about Oscar."

The woman on the couch let out a wail of despair. "My baby! Where's my baby! Have they found him?"

She turned a desperate gaze toward her daughter. The enormous rolls of fat that covered her stomach and arms jiggled alarmingly. Now Trace understood the weird vibe he'd gotten from Cassie when he'd asked her why she was there reporting her brother missing and not her mother.

Cassie moved closer to her mother. She stroked her mother's bare arm and made soothing noises.

"Don't upset yourself Mom. It's going to be okay."

The woman continued to gaze at Cassie, her expression beseeching. "Where's Oscar? Have they found him?"

"Not yet, Mom. But they will. I'm sure Oscar will be home any minute."

Trace stepped forward and introduced himself and Zac. The woman turned to look at him through eyes that were filled with confusion and pain.

"I'm Marie Russell. Oscar's mom. Please find him Detective. I need you to find him. I need my boy home."

"We're going to do all that we can to find him Mrs Russell," Trace assured her, "but first we need to ask you some questions."

The woman waved a plump hand in the vague direction of an armchair that stood adjacent to the couch.

"Take a seat. It hurts my neck to look up at you like that."

Trace glanced at Zac who'd parked himself in a corner. Trace perched on the edge of the armchair. The woman's gaze kept darting about, as if expecting to see her son jump out from behind the curtain or fill the open doorway. Trace cleared his throat.

"Tell me about Oscar."

A smile filled Marie's face, making her look almost beautiful. "Oscar," she breathed. "My baby. He was the most perfect child. Slept through the night almost from the time I brought him home from the hospital. So placid, so happy, so serene. Always smiling. He's still like that. Always has a smile on his face."

"What does he like to do? Are there any places he likes to hang out?"

"He loves going to the park and walking through the gardens. He loves flowers." She smiled. "He loves the way they smell; he loves their pretty colors. I told him when he grows up he could work in a nursery. He loves that idea."

Trace glanced at Cassie.

"We checked the park last night and again first thing this morning. He wasn't there. We talked to some children who were playing on the swings. No one had seen him."

Trace turned back to Cassie's mother. "What about when he hangs out with his friends? Where do they go?"

"His best friend is Joseph Lahood. They usually just hang out in Oscar's room or at Joseph's house. Sometimes they ride their bikes down the street or hike the trails behind our house." Her expression became more frantic. "You have to understand, Detective. Oscar's a homebody. He doesn't like being out for too long and even when he is outside, he never ventures far. That's why I'm so scared. He's been out all night. On his own. My poor baby must be terrified."

Huge tears filled the woman's face. Cassie moved over to her and patted her shoulder. "It's all right, Mom. Don't get upset. We don't know that he spent the night outside. He might be with a friend. Or anyone."

"He doesn't have any other friends!" her mother wailed. "He wouldn't just go with a stranger. He knows better than that."

From the look Cassie gave Trace, he could tell she also agreed. Trace cleared his throat.

"Tell me about your husband Malcolm. Have you seen or heard from him since last night?"

"No."

"I understand he and Oscar got into an argument last night," Trace said.

Marie nodded, her eyes downcast. Her double chins wobbled.

"Do you know what they were arguing about?" Trace asked.

"I think... I think it was something to do with Oscar not doing his chores. Malcolm got home late and was upset that Oscar hadn't done them." She lifted her gaze. "It's Oscar's job to feed the dogs and chop wood. We're stockpiling for the winter."

"Did you witness the argument?" Trace asked.

"Only the start of it. Malcolm came home and realized Oscar hadn't done his chores and started yelling at him. Malcolm knows I get upset when he yells at Oscar. They went outside. I didn't see or hear anything after that."

"Do you know why they went outside?" Trace asked.

The woman shrugged. The movement sent an alarmingly amount of fat wobbling. She kept her gaze directed at a point on the carpet.

"I don't know. Maybe they were going up to the wood heap."

Cassie glanced at Trace and shook her head. She'd already told him she'd guessed Malcolm was headed to the shed with Oscar so he could discipline him.

"How do Oscar and Malcolm usually get on?" Trace asked.

Another shrug.

"Please, Mrs Russell. We're not here to judge you or your family. We're here to find your son. We can't do that if you don't answer our questions."

At that, a fresh wave of tears filled the woman's eyes. She sniffed and swiped at them with the back of her hand.

"Malcolm's a good man. He's a good husband and father to my children."

"I'm sure he is," Trace agreed.

"He works hard to provide for us. He works such long hours. He comes home tired. I don't blame him for being irritable. That happens when you're tired."

"Of course," Trace said in a soothing voice. "Like I said, we're not here to judge you. We just want to find Oscar."

A few beats passed. Then Marie spoke again. "Malcolm and Oscar don't always get on. But it's not a malicious thing on Malcolm's part. Oscar... He can be difficult. You know he's...?"

"Autistic?" Trace supplied.

"Yes. But that doesn't hold him back. And he's as smart as a whip," Marie responded, her expression fierce.

"Of course. Your daughter told us he's a good communicator." Trace paused and then added, "Has Malcolm been violent toward Oscar in the past?"

Once again, silence fell in the small room. Trace saw Cassie regard her mother with a pleading look on her face. Finally, Marie responded.

"Violent sounds so ugly. It's not like that. Malcolm loses his temper sometimes with Oscar and... Sometimes it gets physical."

"Have you ever seen Malcolm hit Oscar?" Trace asked softly.

Marie shook her head. "No."

"Then how do you know Malcolm gets physical with your son?"

The woman heaved out a weary sigh, once again setting her enormous belly wobbling. "They go up to the shed. That's where they go when Malcolm wants to discipline Oscar. I know it sometimes turns physical because Oscar has told me."

"How physical? Had Malcolm punched Oscar before?" Trace asked.

"No, not that I know of. But sometimes he's hit him around the back of the legs."

"With his hand, or something else?" Trace asked.

"Just with his hand, I think."

"And Oscar told you this?" Zac asked.

The woman stared down at her lap. Once again, her eyes welled with tears. She gave a jerky nod.

"What about last night? Did you talk to Oscar after he went to the shed with Malcolm?" Trace asked.

"No. I saw them walk out of the house and that was it."

"What about Malcolm? Did he return to the house afterwards?" Trace asked.

"No. I only knew he'd left because I heard his truck roaring out of the driveway."

"How did that make you feel?" Trace asked.

Marie shrugged. Fresh tears glinted in her eyes and slid down her cheeks. "I don't blame Malcolm. He tries hard with Oscar. He really does. But like I said, sometimes he loses his temper. I hate it when he lashes out at Oscar, but I understand it. Oscar's not his son."

She lifted her gaze and stared at Trace almost defiantly. "It's not easy living with an autistic child. Malcolm's a good man. He takes care of his family. Sometimes he just...let's himself down."

"What about with you? Is he ever violent toward you?" Trace asked.

Chapter Four

Marie Russell shook her head vehemently. "No. Never. He loves me."

Trace's gaze shifted to Cassie. "What about with you?"

Cassie's eyes blazed. "No. He wouldn't dare carry on like that with me and he doesn't hurt Oscar either when I'm here, especially when he's like that."

"Like what?" Trace asked.

"Drunk."

Trace looked at Marie. "Was he drunk when he came home last night?"

With eyes downcast, she nodded. "Yes."

"Where's Malcolm now?" Trace asked. "We'd like to speak with him."

"I don't know," Marie replied.

"Is he at work?" Zac asked.

"I don't think so." Marie paused. "I called the National Parks office earlier this morning... They haven't seen him. They assumed he was out in the field."

"Did he notify them about that?" Trace asked.

"No."

"Okay," Trace replied evenly. "Have you spoken to him on the phone?"

"I called, but he didn't answer," Marie replied.

Cassie looked at Trace. "You might recall I told you earlier, this isn't the first time Malcolm's taken off. Sometimes... When he's drunk, he gets angry. He usually takes it out on Oscar. We all know he's an easy target."

She sighed and then added, "The thing is, this isn't the first time Malcolm and Oscar have gotten into a heated argument. Oscar usually hides out in the shed for a while afterward and Malcolm gets an attack of conscience and takes off until he's had a chance to cool off and sober up."

"Where does he go?" Trace asked her.

Cassie's lips twisted. "I'm not sure. He never says. When he turns up again, he begs forgiveness and all is forgotten... Until the next time." Her tone was filled with disgust.

"Why do you put up with it?" Trace directed his question toward Cassie's mother.

Tears glinted in Marie's eyes. "It's not as bad as you think. Malcolm works hard. Sometimes he gets stressed. We all do. Sometimes he drinks a bit too much. There's no crime in that."

Trace compressed his lips and merely nodded. "Tell me about Oscar's father."

Marie's shoulders slumped on a heavy sigh. "His name is George Webster. He hasn't been in the picture for years. Our marriage broke down when Oscar was only a baby. Malcolm and I got together when Oscar was nine."

A noise from the back of the house caught Trace's attention. "Does anyone else live here?"

Cassie nodded. "Yes. My other brother, Jeremy. He's seventeen."

Trace frowned. "You haven't mentioned him. Was he here last night when Oscar disappeared?"

"No. He was out until late," Cassie said.

"What time did he come home?"

"It was after eleven," Cassie said.

"Do you know where he was?" Trace asked.

"Yes. He said he was with his girlfriend."

"At her house?"

"Yes, I think so."

"What's her name?"

"Annie. Annie Leith."

"Where does Annie live?"

"On the other side of town. Near the old drive-in."

"Did you ask him if he'd seen Oscar?"

"Yes, of course. He hadn't. He helped me look for him when it was clear he wasn't in or around the shed and he'd been out way longer than usual."

"I'd like to talk to Jeremy," Trace said.

"Of course."

Cassie turned and headed down the hallway toward the back of the house. She returned a short time later with a tall, lanky teenager who was in that awkward stage – no longer a boy, but neither a man. Trace could see the resemblance to Cassie and Oscar – the same reddish-brown hair, green eyes, ivory skin. But whereas Oscar and Cassie's complexion was clear and blemish-free, puberty hadn't been so kind to Jeremy. His face was covered by serious acne.

Trace felt a wave of sympathy. On top of that, Jeremy's eyes were just a little too far apart, his mouth too wide, his chin too long. Altogether, he'd been robbed in the looks department, especially when compared to his physically attractive brother and sister. He wondered if that caused friction between the brothers.

Trace introduced both himself and Zac to Jeremy. The boy shook their proffered hands with a limp handshake. Trace eyed Jeremy quizzically and wondered if the older brother could have had anything to do with the missing boy.

"We'd like to ask you a few questions about Oscar," Trace said.

Jeremy stared down at the carpet, his hands jammed into the pockets of his school pants. Finally, he nodded.

"You go to Broken High School?"

"Yes."

"What year are you in?"

"Year Eleven."

Trace nodded. "Only another year and you'll be finished and out into the world. What do you plan to do once school is done?"

"I don't know. Maybe something in IT."

"You're good with computers?"

Jeremy gave a half-shrug. "I guess."

"What time did you arrive home last night?"

"I don't know. Around eleven. It was late."

"Kind of late to be out on a Sunday night with school the next day. Where were you?"

"I was at my girlfriend's house."

"Annie Leith?"

"Yes."

"Where does she live?"

He gave an address on the eastern side of town, confirming what Cassie had already told them."

"How did you get there?" Trace asked.

"I walked."

"That's a fair way."

Once again, all Jeremy offered was a shrug.

"How did you get home?" Zac asked.

"Same way. I walked."

"At eleven at night?" Zac asked.

Another shrug.

"No driver's license?" Trace asked.

Jeremy's cheeks turned an angry red. "No car."

"You're not allowed to borrow your stepfather's truck?" Trace asked.

"Hell, no."

Trace shot a look toward Cassie.

"He drives my Honda sometimes," she offered. "But like I said, I went into school yesterday afternoon and worked late. I needed my car to get home. I didn't know he'd gone to Annie's until after I arrived home."

Trace turned his attention back to Jeremy. "So you didn't think about calling your sister and asking her to pick you up?"

Once again, Jeremy's cheeks turned red. "My sister does enough for us already. I thought she'd be in bed at that hour, like she usually is. I didn't want to wake her. I didn't know about what had gone down with Oscar and Malcolm or that Oscar had taken off."

"Jeremy, you should have called me," Cassie protested. "I just assumed someone had dropped you off."

Trace kept his gaze trained on Jeremy. "Is that what you think Jeremy? That Oscar's taken off?"

Another shrug. Something flashed in Jeremy's eyes before he quickly averted his gaze. *Guilt?*

Trace continued to press. "Do you get on with your stepfather?"

"I don't know," Jeremy mumbled, his tone turning sullen. "What sort of stupid question is that?"

"Jeremy." Cassie's tone held a note of warning.

Jeremy shot her a belligerent look.

Trace cleared his throat. "How do you feel about Malcolm?"

Another shrug. "What does it matter how I feel? I'm not the one he hit."

"How do you know he hit Oscar?" Zac asked.

Jeremy's eyes flashed. "Because it's what he does. He gets mad and lashes out. Usually at Oscar."

"You've seen him hit Oscar?" Trace asked.

Jeremy eyed him briefly and then dropped his gaze. "Yes."

Cassie gasped. "Jeremy! Why haven't you ever said anything?"

Jeremy turned toward his sister, his expression belligerent. "Because what did it matter if I said anything? It's not like anything was going to change. You're never here most times when he gets like that. Angry and drunk and spoiling for a fight."

"When was the last time you saw him hit Oscar?" Trace asked quietly.

"About a month ago."

"Where did it happen?" Trace asked.

Jeremy hung his head. "In the shed."

"Were you in the shed too?" Zac asked.

"No."

"Where were you, Jeremy?"

Jeremy fell silent. Zac prompted him to answer.

Jeremy's eyes flashed with anger. "I was hiding outside, okay! I was hiding like a coward in the dark! I saw that asshole hit my brother and I didn't do anything about it. Because as much as I hate Malcolm, I hate Oscar even more. That little prick gets on my nerves! Always smiling, always laughing, always wanting to play. Everyone in this family bends over backwards for him, doing anything he wants while I have to beg for the slightest ounce of attention. It shits me to tears. Why couldn't I have a normal brother? Why did I have to be saddled with *him?*"

"Jeremy! You don't mean that!"

Marie's words were filled with pain. Cassie looked equally shocked by her brother's outburst.

Trace eyed the boy with speculation. Jeremy was jealous of his brother, that much was clear. But was he jealous enough for him to want to do his brother harm?

"Living with a brother like Oscar's difficult for you, isn't it?" Trace asked.

Jeremy stared at the carpet. "No shit, Sherlock."

"Have you and Oscar ever gotten into a fight?" Trace asked.

"Of course. We fight all the time. Like I said, he can be a prick."

"It annoys you when he's like that, doesn't it?" Trace asked.

"Of course. Who wouldn't be annoyed? Whenever he doesn't get his way, he carries on like a jerk. Or goes running to Mom or Cassie. They always take his side."

Both Cassie and Marie protested loudly. Trace kept his gaze on Jeremy. "What about Malcolm? Whose side does he take?"

Jeremy stared stubbornly at the floor and shrugged.

"Has Malcolm ever hit you?" Trace asked softly.

"Hell, no. Not anymore. I stay out of his way. I learned a long time ago it's best not to piss him off."

"Do you have any idea where Oscar is?" Zac asked.

"No."

"Have you tried to call him?" Trace asked.

"No."

Trace started in surprise. "No? Why not?"

"I don't know. I knew Cass had already called him a bunch of times. No sense in both of us doing it."

"You aren't concerned about where he might be?" Trace asked.

"Yeah, of course I'm concerned, but what the heck. He's fourteen. He's not a baby. A night out in the bush on his own won't hurt him."

"Jeremy!" his mother wailed. "Don't you dare say things like that! You know how much your brother hates the dark."

Jeremy merely crossed his arms over his chest and glared at the carpet.

"When was the last time you saw Oscar?" Trace asked.

"Around lunchtime, right before I left for Annie's house."

"He was here?"

"Yes. In the backyard. Kicking a football. He wanted me to play with him, but I wasn't interested. I had better things to do."

"Like visit your girlfriend," Zac said.

Jeremy shot a defiant look in Zac's direction. "That's right."

"Did Oscar say anything to you about going somewhere last night?" Trace asked.

"No. We didn't talk much about anything. I was mainly in my room yesterday playing on my computer. Then I grabbed some lunch and left. That's when I ran into Oscar."

"Do you care about your brother, Jeremy?" Trace posed the quiet question and watched closely for the boy's reaction.

"Of course I do. He just annoys me, that's all. That doesn't mean I want to see him hurt."

"Do you think he might be hurt?" Trace asked.

"I don't know. I was talking about him and Malcolm."

"What sort of relationship do you have with Oscar?" Trace asked.

Jeremy stared at the floor and shrugged. "Fine."

"So you think the resentfulness you feel toward him is normal?" Zac asked.

Once again, Jeremy merely shrugged.

"Are you concerned he hasn't come home?" Zac asked.

"Yeah, I guess, but really, I think everyone's overreacting. So he's been gone all night. Big deal. He'll turn up."

"Jeremy!" Cassie admonished.

The boy looked unrepentant. He glared at Trace and Zac. "Are we done here? I have homework to do." With that, he stalked out of the room.

Trace and Zac thanked Marie for her time and repeated their promise to do all they could to find her son. Trace left her with his business card and urged her to call him if she heard anything, or if Oscar turned up. Cassie saw them out.

"I'm really sorry about Jeremy," she said. "He's out of sorts. Oscar going missing has us all on edge."

Trace merely nodded, still unsure of what to make of Jeremy Webster. Still, he had no evidence that the boy was involved in his brother's disappearance and there was still hope Oscar could turn up again of his own accord.

They reached the front door and Cassie pulled it open. She turned back to Trace.

"Please, there's no way Jeremy has anything to do with Oscar's disappearance. I know him. When he's not feeling sorry for himself, deep down he loves Oscar."

Trace chose to reserve his opinion on that score. "Do you mind if we take a look in the shed?"

Cassie sighed and nodded. "Of course. It's up the back. The door's unlocked. Don't mind the dogs. They won't bite."

Cassie watched the two detectives walk around the side of the house and head further up the hill to the shed. She'd recognized Zac Barrington straight off. They were the same age, He'd been in her year at school. But like his older brother, Zac had shown no sign that he'd recognized her.

Was I really that invisible in high school? Obviously I was...

The two men looked enough alike that she'd have guessed they were related even if she hadn't known they were brothers. Though Trace looked slightly older and was a little broader in the shoulders, they shared the same imposing height, muscular chest and overall air of intimidation, even when they were trying to be polite. The dark hair and blue eyes were also the same. Trace had a dimple in his left cheek that was absent from Zac's, but the similarity was striking.

As they disappeared up the side of the house, she worried her bottom lip. Though they seemed to be taking her concerns about Oscar seriously, she wasn't sure if they believed her about Jeremy. She'd seen the expression on Trace's face when he'd questioned her brother. The same look of heightened awareness had been reflected on Zac's face. It wasn't exactly suspicion, but she could tell they were speculating about a possible role Jeremy might have played in Oscar's disappearance.

The problem was, they didn't know Jeremy. She'd known him all his life. Okay, so there might be some jealousy on Jeremy's part insofar as Oscar seemed to have been blessed with good looks and perfect skin, but there was no way her brother had done something to hurt Oscar. The two brothers might had occasional arguments, but Jeremy loved Oscar no matter what he said.

The same couldn't be said for Malcolm. He was a drunk and a bully with a short temper who often resorted to ugly behavior. She hated that her mother made excuses for him. Okay, so Oscar could be a handful at times and sometimes he could be a brat. There were no two ways about it. But that didn't give Malcolm an excuse to take out his discontent with his life on her brother.

Cassie accepted no one was perfect and Malcolm had moved in and done his best to take care of them all. It couldn't be easy helping to raise someone else's kids, but that didn't give him the right to lash out at them. She didn't care how remorseful Malcolm always was afterwards. He should have more self-control. She didn't honestly think Malcolm had seriously harmed Oscar, or had been directly responsible for his disappearance, but that didn't mean he wasn't behind Oscar taking off. Cassie wasn't privy to what had gone on in the shed, but it was possible whatever had occurred had been enough to send Oscar running. And now they couldn't find him.

She bit down on a sob of anguish and pressed her fist against her mouth in an effort to hold it in. The longer Oscar stayed away, the deeper her despair grew.

Please, Oscar… Please come home… Just come home… We all need you to come home… I miss you…

She hoped Malcolm would switch his phone back on and recharge it. Or maybe someone would recognize him and call the police. Either way, they needed to talk to him. While she was almost certain he was innocent of anything sinister when it came to Oscar, her stepfather might be able to shed light on what had gone on last night and where Oscar went afterwards. Anything to help them find her brother and bring him home. That's all that mattered.

Chapter Five

Two blue heelers tied up to chains barked as Trace and Zac approached the shed. Trace called out to them in an effort to reassure them and then opened the door to the shed. The hinges squeaked loudly in protest. The building listed to one side, like the foundation had begun to fail. Though the structure looked newer than the house, the red paint on the corrugated iron walls was cracked and peeling and the gutters were rusted through.

Pushing open the door wider, Trace felt around for a light switch. The sudden burst of illumination made them blink. Once their eyes had adjusted, they looked around. The shed was filled with the usual junk: a push lawn mower, edge trimmer, shovels, garden forks and a hoe. There was a shelf that was piled high with half-empty containers of weed killer, lawn fertilizer and kerosene.

Trace turned to survey the opposite wall. A peg board was affixed to it with nails. A variety of hand tools hung off the pegs. Set squares, pliers, hammers, screwdrivers, spanners, wrenches and various other tools. Trace scanned each hook. There were no blank spots on the board. It appeared all the tools were accounted for.

In one corner, a pile of cut wood was stacked up high against the wall. None of it looked freshly cut. They each silently catalogued what was there. Nothing appeared broken or damaged. The concrete floor was covered in dust, but that was all. No blood, no fluids of any kind. It was an ordered kind of mess. There were no signs of foul play.

"Nothing unusual here," Zac commented.

"You're right," Trace agreed. "Whatever went on between Oscar and his stepfather last night, there's no evidence they were even here. Let's go. We might have better luck with Oscar's schoolmate."

Hitting the light, he and Zac turned and headed back out into the sunshine.

Cassie stood by the window in the front room, watching as the detectives climbed into the police cruiser and drove away. Dread still sat like a cold hard lump in her belly. It had been there since last night when it had become clear Oscar had left the property. At the time, she'd hoped it was a temporary absence and that he'd be back just as soon as he felt better, but then the hours had stretched on and on and no one seemed to know where he was.

Her shoulders slumped on a weary sigh. She wanted to think positively, to keep imagining that Oscar was just licking his wounds somewhere. That at any moment he would come bounding back through the door, all smiles again. That's how it usually went. And Malcolm would eventually come home, apologize and life would return to normal once more.

Only Oscar still isn't home and no one knows where he is…

A sniffle from the direction of the couch pulled her from her thoughts. She turned and moved over to where her mother sat, hunched over a box of tissues. Her eyes and cheeks were red with tears. Emotion clogged Cassie's throat. She hated to see her mother like this. As much as Cassie wanted nothing more than to curl up in a ball and cry too, she didn't have the luxury of that. Her mother and Jeremy depended upon her to be strong for everyone. She wouldn't let them down.

Pulling up a chair beside the couch, she took one of her mother's hands. "Don't cry, Mom. We'll find him. He can't have gone too far. You know how he is. He hates being away from home for too long and he hates the dark even more. There's no way he's going to spend another night outdoors."

She peered toward the front window and prayed silently that what she'd said was true. The late afternoon light was fading fast. Soon another night would be upon them.

Where are you, Oscar? Why aren't you home? Please come home. We need to have you home…

From the corner of her eye, she spied Jeremy creeping along the hallway. He halted outside the door to the living room. She could see him hovering there, as if uncertain whether to step inside.

"Jeremy? Come in. I need to speak with you."

Her brother did as she asked and sidled into the room. He glanced at their mother who continued to sob quietly. His face was pale. His freckles stood out almost as much as his acne. His eyes reflected the same tortuous thoughts that filled Cassie's head.

"Jeremy, I need you to help me look for Oscar. Soon it's going to be dark. We can't leave him out there for another night."

"I thought we looked everywhere last night?" he replied, a little belligerently.

It was all she could do not to roll her eyes. "Obviously we didn't look *everywhere* because we haven't found him yet," she said in a tight voice.

"Well, where else am I supposed to look?"

She threw up her hands in exasperation. "I don't know! Talk to his friends, go to all the usual spots where Oscar hangs out. The skate park, the corner store, the football field, the cricket nets. I'll airdrop a picture to your phone. Show it to everyone you come across. Ask if they've seen him."

"What are *you* going to do?" Jeremy asked sulkily.

"I'm going to be out there, too. But first I have to organize dinner. Or do you think it's going to cook itself all on its own?"

She was disappointed in the sarcasm that had crept into her voice, but the truth was, if she didn't put the dinner on, there would be nothing for them to eat.

"Can't Mom do that?" Jeremy persisted.

Cassie bit her tongue to prevent another angry outburst. Everyone was on edge, including Jeremy. She understood that.

"Mom's too upset right now to do anything. We all need to pull together right now. Please, Jeremy? Will you go out and keep looking for your brother?"

"All right. I'll go," Jeremy offered grudgingly.

Cassie gave him a grateful smile. "Thank you." She paused a moment and then added, "What you said to the detective, about hating Oscar... I know you didn't mean that."

Jeremy stared at the floor. "Okay, so I don't hate him, but that doesn't mean he doesn't annoy the hell out of me most of the time."

Cassie moved closer and put her arm around him. He tensed, but she didn't release her hold.

"This is tough on all of us, Jer. But we need to stick together. We can't let this tear us apart. I know you want Oscar back as much as I do. We all need to do whatever it takes to bring him back. Okay?"

She pulled away slightly and looked at him. He gave a jerky nod. She hugged him again and then stepped away. "Go. Talk to everyone. I'll join you as soon as I can."

Before Jeremy left, she airdropped the photo of Oscar to his phone and after pulling on a baseball cap and filling up a water bottle, he left the house. Cassie sighed. Her mother's shoulders shook on a fresh wave of sobs. Cassie prayed for something more she could do to reassure her, but short of producing Oscar, she couldn't think of anything.

"It's all right, Mom. I'll see to dinner. Can I get you anything? A cup of tea, or a glass of water?"

"No thank you, honey. All I want is my boy."

Cassie compressed her lips. "What about your embroidery? Can I get that for you? Maybe it will take your mind off things. You're nearly finished that pillowcase, aren't you? It's looking beautiful. Mrs Marshall will be thrilled.

They're a wedding present for her daughter-in-law, aren't they?"

Her mother nodded. "Yes. I need to finish them before the end of the week." She cleared her throat and sat up straighter. "Pass me my sewing bag please, Cass. You're right. I can't just sit here and do nothing. Thinking about Oscar is driving me mad. I need a distraction."

Cassie did as she was asked and then left the room. She walked into the small, dated kitchen and set about putting together the makings of chicken soup. The temperatures had fallen these past few days, heralding the onset of winter. In her experience, hot chicken soup always brought some level of comfort. She only hoped that wherever Oscar was, he'd found something to eat. He always got out of sorts when he was hungry.

As soon as the soup was simmering, Cassie turned the heat down low and headed outside. She phoned Jeremy and arranged to meet him at the park.

"Any luck?" she asked when she saw him.

He shook his head. "No. I've shown his picture to everyone I came across. No one's seen him."

Cassie tried not to get disheartened. She refused to give up. Her brother was out there and she was determined to find him. They spent the next hour going from place to place, knocking on the doors of neighbors, speaking to kids. It was dark by the time they returned home. Tired and disheartened, they opened the front door and walked into the living room. Their mother raised hopeful eyes in their direction.

Cassie slowly shook her head. "I'm sorry Mom. We looked everywhere and spoke to everyone we came across. No one's seen him."

Marie Russell set aside the needle and pillowcase in her hands and let out a wail. Cassie's stomach clenched. She felt the same way.

Handing her mother a box of tissues, she quietly went into the kitchen. She served up three bowls of soup and took one to her mother. She and Jeremy ate in silence in the kitchen. All the while she prayed that Trace and his brother would have more luck finding Oscar.

The Café on Main was filled with kids buying milkshakes and ice creams after school. Large paper cups filled with hot chips smothered in tomato sauce or chicken salt were also popular. Trace and Zac waited for a noisy group of teenagers to leave before they approached the man who stood behind the 1970s-era, mint-green Formica counter. Joseph Lahood's father smiled a greeting.

"Trace. Zac. What can I do for you?"

Trace nodded in acknowledgement. "John. How are you? Busy as usual, by the look of it."

John Lahood's smile widened. "Always busy this time of the afternoon. By the time the kids get out of school, they're starving. You remember how it was, don't you?"

Trace glanced at Zac. They both chuckled. "Oh, yeah. We remember," Trace replied. "Your father used to have to put on an extra helping of hot chips just for the Barrington boys."

John chuckled. "Absolutely. Dad used to tell me, between you and your sisters, he made more money in a single afternoon than he did for most of the week."

"You're right," Zac added. "Our sisters were very partial to your father's strawberry milkshakes."

All three smiled fondly, caught up in their memories. Then Trace sobered. "Just wondering if Joe's around?"

John's expression also dimmed. "Sure. Got back from school not long ago. He's out back."

"Do you mind if we have a chat with him?" Trace asked.

"Of course you can. I suppose this is about Oscar?"

Trace compressed his lips. "Yeah. You heard. Been missing since last night. He still hasn't come home."

"I'm sure he's all right," John offered. "Kids disappear for a bit all the time. I remember when I was his age, I loved spending the night out in the bush."

Trace gave a non-committal shrug. John slowly turned and walked toward the back of the shop. He disappeared from view for a few minutes and when he returned, a dark-haired, dark-eyed teenager followed quietly behind him.

"Joe, these detectives are here to talk to you about Oscar," John said to his son.

Apprehension was clear on the boy's face. He looked from one detective to the other, his eyes wide with concern.

In an effort to reassure him, Trace went for a friendly smile. "Hi, Joe. I'm Trace and this is my brother Zac."

The teenager looked momentarily nonplussed. "You're both detectives?"

"We certainly are," Zac replied.

Joe continued to look scared. It was an understandable reaction. Most kids and even a lot of adults felt intimidated when confronted by the police.

Trace made another attempt to reassure him. "You're not in trouble, Joe. We just want to ask you a few questions. Is that okay?"

The boy shrugged and stared at the floor. "I guess."

"We understand you're friends with Oscar Webster," Trace said.

Joe nodded. "Yeah."

"You know he didn't come home last night?"

"Yeah. His sister, Miss Webster, called me last night to ask if I'd seen him. She also came and saw me at school this morning. She told me he's still missing."

"You're right. That's why we're here. We wondered if you'd heard from him."

"No. Like I told Miss Webster. The last time I saw him was in science class last Friday afternoon."

A sound from the back of the shop caught their attention. Trace watched as Joe's mother came into view, tying an apron around her trim waist.

"Trace! Zac! What are you two up to?"

"Hello, Noelene. It's good to see you," Trace replied.

Noelene and John were both of Lebanese descent. John had taken over the running of the café when his father had passed away a few years ago. Noelene also spent a lot of time there behind the counter.

The Lahoods had been in Broken for as long as Trace could remember. They were friendly people who always had a good word to say about their customers. They worked hard, were kind to strangers and went to church on Sundays. They could be counted upon to donate generously to any fundraiser and both John and Noelene were volunteers for the local State Emergency Services.

"Are you here about Oscar?" Noelene asked, her expression filling with concern.

"Yes," Trace said. "He didn't come home last night. His family is worried."

Noelene turned to her son. "Did you see him in school today?"

Joe shook his head. "No, Mom. I didn't."

"How long have you two been friends?" Trace asked, returning his attention to Joe.

"Since kindergarten," Joe's mother replied. "They seemed to click right away. I can remember that first day when Joe came home. All he could talk about was Oscar." A fond smile turned up the corners of her mouth.

"And you've been good friends ever since, haven't you Joe?" Noelene continued.

"Right," Joe muttered.

Joe kept his gaze fixed on the ground. Once again, Trace hurried to reassure him. "We're just trying to work out where he might have gone. Does he have a secret hideout? Somewhere he likes to go when he wants to get away from everything? Maybe somewhere the two of you like to hang out?"

"Not really," Joe replied. "We like to go camping in the bush behind his house. Of course, we never stay out all night. Oscar's scared of the dark."

Joe's voice hitched. His face had gone pale and he looked on the verge of tears.

Noelene moved closer and put her arm around his thin shoulders. "It's okay, Joe. I'm sure Oscar's okay. Any minute now he'll come bounding in here demanding an ice cream. I'm sure of it. I know you want to find Oscar as much as any of us. Just tell the detectives what you know."

Joe shook off her arm and moved out of reach. His face was flushed. "That's the thing. I don't know anything! I wish everyone would stop asking me!"

Noelene looked shocked at her son's outburst. From his position further along the counter, John also frowned. "Joe! There's no need for—"

"It's all right Joe," Trace soothed. "We understand. This is upsetting for everyone. We just thought you might be able to shed some light on where Oscar might have gone. That's all. Or maybe the two of you talked about him going somewhere, exploring another part of the bush. Has he ever talked about the caves over by Limestone Rock?"

Joe shook his head. "No. He wouldn't have a clue about those caves and even if he did, he wouldn't go inside. I already told you. He's scared of the dark."

"Right," Trace agreed. They were getting nowhere. He looked at Zac. His brother inclined his head, indicating it was time they got out of there. Trace gave an imperceptible nod. He turned back to the Lahoods to thank them for their time when Joe spoke again.

"That's not the only thing Oscar's scared of."

The ominous statement hung in the air. Trace replied in a quiet voice. "What else is Oscar scared of Joe?"

Joe stared at the ground, his eyes flashing with anger and contempt. "His stepfather. That's who. Malcolm Russell. Oscar hates him."

Trace kept his voice even. "Why does he hate him, Joe?"

"Because of what he did to him. He belted him when he was drunk. With a strap. Oscar told me. And it wasn't the first time."

Trace made a mental note. Oscar's mother and brother hadn't mentioned a strap. "Where does he go after a fight with his stepfather?" Trace asked.

"Sometimes he comes to my house. We don't live too far from each other. Other times he goes into the bush. There's a path that leads right to it from the back of Oscar's house."

"Do you know where it is?" Zac asked.

"Of course I do. We go there all the time."

"Can you show us?" Trace asked.

The boy gave a reluctant nod. "Yes."

Joe and his mother rode in the back of the police cruiser. They pulled up in the driveway of Cassie's family's house and climbed out. Joe led them up the hill, past the shed and into the bush. A faint path was evident among the groundcover and low shrubbery that covered the forest floor. It was no wider than an animal path but was easy enough to follow. Joe led the small group through the bush for a few hundred yards before they came out into a clearing.

"This is where we normally set up camp," he said.

Trace looked around. There were signs of an old campfire. Trace squatted beside it and poked at the ashes with a stick. They were cold. From the weeds that had begun to grow up among them, it was obvious the fire was long dead. If Oscar had been by this way recently, he certainly hadn't lit a fire.

"When did you last camp here?" Trace asked.

Joe shrugged. "I think it was during the last school holidays."

"When was that?"

"A couple of months ago."

Trace stood and brushed his hands off on his pants. He looked at Joe. "Did Oscar have any other friends? People he might turn to at times like this?"

Joe shook his head. "No. His only other friend was Kevin, and he wasn't really a friend. Just someone Oscar liked to talk to now and then."

"Does Kevin have a last name?" Trace asked.

Joe's face screwed up in a frown. "I think it's Turner."

Trace's heart stopped. He looked at Zac and then returned his attention to Joe. "Where does Kevin live?"

"The corner of West and Maitland Streets. The house with all the flowers."

Once again, Trace's gaze shot back to Zac. They stared at each other, both thinking the same thing.

Kevin Turner…registered sex offender…

Trace's gut filled with dread. At the same time, his heart began to pound with anticipation. They needed to pay another visit to Kevin Turner and this time they wouldn't be quite so pleasant.

Chapter Six

Trace dropped Noelene and Joe off at the café and after eliciting a promise from Joe that he'd call them if he thought of anything else that might help them find Oscar, Trace and Zac drove away. Trace headed toward Turner's address.

Zac turned to look at him. "You think Turner might have had something to do with Oscar's disappearance?"

Trace clenched his jaw. "I don't know, but it's a bit of a coincidence our missing teen just happens to be friends with a sex offender. Even more interesting that Turner played down his association with Oscar. The asshole told us he barely knew the kid and yet, according to Joe, they were friends. Something's off."

"I agree. Why didn't Turner tell us he and Oscar were friends?"

Trace narrowed his eyes. "I guess he knew exactly what conclusions we'd draw if he did. And he was right."

"Did you get in touch with Charles Morley's parole officer?"

"Yes. I left a message for him this morning. He called me back just as we were leaving to talk to Joe."

"Did he confirm the neighbor's story?"

"Yeah. According to Morley's po, he gave notice about a month ago that his mother was unwell. Asked and was approved to go and visit her in Gympie," Trace replied.

"So we can cross Morley off the list. Let's see how we do with Turner."

Flicking on the indicator, Trace turned into Turner's street. Two blocks further along and he'd come to Oscar's house. Turner had admitted to seeing Oscar pass by on his way to or from school. It would have been a simple matter for the pedophile to catch the boy's attention and strike up a conversation. Especially given Oscar's interest in flowers. Though the oncoming winter meant that the flowers in the Turner yard weren't so prolific as during the warmer months, that didn't mean Oscar hadn't been attracted to the colorful display in the past.

Zac pounded on Turner's front door. They didn't have to wait long before Turner appeared. He didn't appear pleased to see them.

"I've already said everything I have to say to you," Turner said as soon as he saw them standing on the other side of the screen door.

"We don't think so," Trace replied, his voice hard. "Get your ass out here, Kevin."

With an exaggerated sigh, Turner opened the screen door. It squeaked in protest. He stepped out onto the veranda and kept his distance. With arms crossed over his chest, he glared at them.

"I have nothing more to say to you," he said, his tone belligerent.

Trace stepped close, got in his face. "We'll decide when you're finished talking to us, Turner. There's a boy missing and it seems you know a hell of a lot more about Oscar Webster than you told us."

Turner shook his head slowly back and forth. "No. I swear. I already told you everything I know."

Trace glared at him. "We don't think so. See, the thing is, Kevin. You're a registered sex offender. You're not supposed to be talking to children. *Any* children. Not a single word. And yet, we heard today you've not only been talking to our missing boy, he actually thinks of you as his *friend*."

Trace took another step closer. Fear flashed in Turner's eyes. He took a step back and came up hard against the front door. He held his hands up as if to ward Trace off.

"I-I don't know what you're talking about! Why would I be friends with a young kid like that?"

"I'm not looking for an explanation," Trace snapped. "I want to know why you didn't tell us you and Oscar Webster are friends."

"We *aren't* friends! I don't know how many times I have to tell you!" Turner cried. "I see him walk by now and then. I might wave to him now and then. Maybe even say hello sometimes. That's it. I swear."

"Then why would Oscar describe you as his friend, Kevin?" Zac asked in a deceptively calm voice.

"How the hell would I know? The kid isn't the full quid."

Trace pounced. "How do you know that Kevin? If all you did was wave and say hello on the odd occasion, how the hell would you know something like that?"

Kevin's face turned red—with guilt or embarrassment, Trace couldn't be sure. The man sputtered a few moments longer and then eventually clamped his mouth shut.

"I'm not saying anything else. Not without my lawyer present."

Trace lowered his voice. "Why would you need your lawyer, Kevin? Have you done something wrong?"

Turner's face darkened to puce. His breath came fast. "No! No! No! I keep telling you! I hardly know the kid and I sure as hell don't know where he is. Now, if you don't mind, I'd like you to leave."

Unperturbed, Trace kept his voice even. "You want to hope that's true, Turner. If you so much as *look* at another kid, I'll have your ass back in jail quicker than you can blink. If you know *anything* about this missing child, you'd better start talking."

Turner remained silent, but the look he shot Trace's way was deadly. Trace returned the glare. The two eyeballed each other for a long, tense moment before Turner slowly averted his gaze. With a muffled curse, Trace turned on his heel and headed back the way he'd come. Zac followed in silence.

Kevin stood watching the detectives depart. He didn't move until the police cruiser had disappeared. Then he went back inside feeling more shaken than he cared to admit. The moment he closed the screen door behind him, Mandy started laying into him.

"You prick! You never told me you're one of those! A kiddy fiddler! Fuck! You'd better not have anythin' to do with that kid going missin', or I swear..."

She left the sentence hanging. Kevin lifted his arms up in a sign of surrender. "I didn't, Mandy! I'm telling you the truth!"

Her expression turned calculating. Her beady black eyes filled with malice. "'Cause I'm thinkin' I might have been a bit hasty tellin' the cops you were with me last night."

His gut somersaulted with fear. "No! Please, Mandy. You know I was here."

"How do I know? I fell asleep right after dinner. How do I know what you got up to after that?"

His panic ratcheted up another notch. "I had nothing to do with that boy's disappearance. You have to believe me."

Her expression turned mean. "You should have told me what you were. Keepin' that from me wasn't right."

He held up his hands in an effort to placate her. "Okay, okay. You're right. I should have told you, but you must understand how hard it is for me. When people find out what I did... They look at me differently. They treat me like shit. They whisper about me behind my back, they tell their kids to stay well away."

"And so they should!" she shouted, her face hard. "You're a fuckin' kiddy fiddler. A germ of the worst kind. I can't believe I lied to the pigs for you." She spun around and stormed away from him. He shuffled into the living room and threw himself down on the couch. He was still trying to come to terms with how quickly his world had been thrown off its axis when Mandy returned holding a red jacket.

"Who owns this?" she snarled.

Kevin peeked at the jacket and quickly averted his gaze. Nausea pooled in his gut. "I don't know," he mumbled.

"What's it doin' in our house?"

Anger ignited inside him. He jumped up off the couch. "I already told you! I don't know. I've never seen it before."

Mandy looked unconvinced. Throwing him a hard look, she once again left the room. He heard her stomping her way down the hallway.

All of a sudden, Kevin's legs gave out. He collapsed back on the couch. His gut churned with dread at the very real possibility she didn't believe him. Despair hovered at the edge of his consciousness.

God help me. If my girlfriend doesn't believe me, what hope do I have?

Trace was at his desk early the next morning, going over his notes about Oscar Webster. A quick call to Cassie confirmed the boy still hadn't returned. He'd now been missing roughly thirty-six hours. Though the nights were growing cooler, winter had yet to arrive and a night or two spent out in the elements wouldn't be too detrimental to a normal healthy teenager, but still, Trace felt an urgency to find the boy as soon as possible.

A junior constable tapped on the open door of his office. "Trace, there's a woman outside who says her name is Mandy Goodwin. She asked to see you."

Trace frowned and tried to place the name. And then he remembered. Kevin Turner's girlfriend. His heart skipped a beat.

I wonder why Kevin's girlfriend wants to see me...

Trace thanked the constable and then got to his feet. He reached for his jacket where he kept it on a hook behind the door and slipped it on. With his heart beating with anticipation, he made his way out into the public reception area. The woman he'd spoken to briefly the day before stood with her back to him. Today she wore skinny jeans and a floral printed blouse. Her hands were jammed into her pockets.

"Ms Goodwin?"

She turned at the sound of her name. Her gaze darted every which way. She looked nervous as hell.

"You asked to see me," Trace stated.

"D-detective. Yes. Thanks for takin' the time to see me."

"What can I do for you, Ms Goodwin?"

"It's Mandy."

Trace inclined his head. "So Mandy, what was it you wanted to see me about? Do you have information on the missing boy?"

She averted her gaze. "Er...yeah. Is there...somewhere more private we can talk?"

Trace led her into an empty interview room. She took a seat and he closed the door and then sat down opposite.

"What is it?" he asked.

From behind her back, Mandy produced a red jacket. It was made of some kind of nylon waterproof material and had the logo of a popular brand on one side. He carefully took it from her and held it up. It was a small size.

"What can you tell me about it?" he asked.

Mandy's smile turned calculating. "It's a boy's jacket. I found it in the mudroom at home."

Trace sat up straighter. His heart began to thump harder. He checked the label. No name. There was nothing to identify is as belonging to Oscar, but it sure as hell wouldn't fit Kevin and Cassie had said her brother had been wearing a red jacket the day he disappeared.

"Did you ask Kevin about it?" he asked.

"Course I did. He said he'd never seen it."

Trace looked at her. "You think he's lying."

The woman shrugged. "I never said that. But I did want to say somethin' else. You know when you asked me if I was with Kevin Sunday night?"

Trace nodded.

"Well, it turns out I forgot to include somethin'."

Trace forced himself to remain calm. "Oh?" he said in a nonchalant tone.

"Yeah, you see, Kev and I were home that night, like I told you. We had dinner about seven. But I fell asleep on the couch right after. I didn't sit up with him and watch a movie, like I said."

Trace stared at her. "You lied?"

Mandy squirmed on the chair. "I wouldn't say I lied. The thing is, I just forgot. I thought I watched a movie with Kev, 'cause we'd talked about doin' that right after dinner, but I fell asleep. The thing is, I'm not sure if Kevin was there all night or not."

Trace regarded her steadily. "Why are you telling me this?"

Her upper lip curled up with disgust. "Kevin never told me he was a kiddy fiddler. That's next level, you know. I've got two kids of my own. They're in foster care right now. Doesn't mean I don't love 'em or care about 'em. I'd never forgive myself if Kevin had somethin' to do with this kid goin' missin' and I didn't say anythin'."

"Do you think he's capable of something like that?" Trace asked.

Mandy pursed her lips. "I never used to think so. But who knows?"

"Have you ever seen Oscar Webster at Kevin's house?"

"No."

"Have you ever seen Kevin talking to him?"

"No. I've never seen him, but I know he's talked to that kid. Kevin told me."

Trace thanked Mandy for coming in. The minute the woman had departed the station, he was on his way out the door. He needed to show the jacket to Cassie.

Zac was out on another call and Trace didn't want to waste another moment waiting for him, so he climbed into the cruiser and arrived at Broken High School alone. He showed his police credentials to the woman in the front office and asked to see Cassie Webster.

"I'll let her know you're here, but she's teaching a class for another ten minutes. Is it urgent?"

"No, it's not that urgent."

"Very well. Would you like to wait?"

Trace tried to curb his impatience. He merely nodded and then proceeded to pace the small waiting area. Cassie had already called him earlier for an update. He hadn't been able to provide her with anything. Now he hoped the jacket might move the investigation along. After what seemed like an interminable amount of time, the bell went and kids poured out of classrooms and into the corridor. Cassie suddenly appeared before him out of the melee.

His gut clenched reflexively. She had the kind of beauty that stopped people in the street. He'd noticed it the first time he'd met her and every time since. She wore a tailored charcoal-gray skirt that fell just above her knees. She'd teamed it with a pale green, long-sleeved blouse that brought out the color of her eyes. Her auburn hair was pulled back into a simple ponytail. She wore minimal makeup, but that didn't detract from her attractiveness. He hadn't asked her age, but she didn't look much older than her students.

"Trace. What are you doing here?" Surprise and dread warred on her expressive face.

He held up his hand in an effort to reassure her. "I'm afraid we haven't found Oscar, but I wanted to show you something." He produced the red jacket that he'd placed in a clear plastic evidence bag.

"Do you recognize this jacket?" he asked.

She moved closer and picked up the plastic bag. When she looked back at him, her freckles stood out on her pale face. "Oh my God! It's Oscar's."

"Are you sure?"

"Well, no. But he has one just like it. He was wearing it the night he disappeared. Where did you find it?"

"A neighbor brought it in."

She frowned. "Which neighbor?"

"A woman by the name of Mandy Goodwin. She's Kevin Turner's girlfriend. He lives a couple of blocks away from you on the same street. Did Oscar ever talk about Kevin?"

Cassie shook her head, looking bewildered. "No."

Trace paused and silently debated about how much to tell her. "Joe told us Oscar knew him."

Cassie appeared surprised. "You've spoken to Joe?"

"Yes. He didn't have a whole lot to add, but he did show us a campsite where he and Oscar had camped before."

Her face lit up with hope. "Did you find anything?"

"No. I'm sorry. It didn't look like anyone had been there for some time. In fact, Joe said he and Oscar hadn't camped there since the last school holidays." Trace paused and then added, "Are you sure Oscar never mentioned Kevin? Joe said Kevin and Oscar were friends."

Cassie shook her head. A sad smile played around her lips. "That's the kind of person Oscar is. Friendly, outgoing. He'll talk to anyone and he thinks everyone's his friend. How did they meet?"

"I'm not sure, but Turner lives in that house on the corner of West and Maitland Streets. Oscar's route to and from school would have taken him right past Turner's house."

"I know the house you mean. It has a lovely garden. Well-tended. An abundance of pretty flowers. Not right now, of course. Winter's right around the corner. But in the spring and summer... It's lovely. Whoever lives there must spend a fair amount of time out in the garden. Maybe that's how they knew each other..." she mused. "Maybe Oscar stopped by for a chat on his way past? Oscar loves flowers. The bright colors, the perfumes. Sweet peas are his favorite. Especially the purple ones."

For an instant Trace considered telling her that Kevin Turner was a registered sex offender and then he decided against it. At best, the jacket was circumstantial evidence. They had no proof Turner was involved. The man was entitled to his privacy – for now at least. There was no sense in upsetting Cassie unless it was absolutely necessary, or for that matter, turning the town against a man who might very well be innocent.

Chapter Seven

After spending all afternoon after school putting up "missing" posters around the town and searching for Oscar with Jeremy, Cassie returned home disheartened and exhausted. Everywhere they went, they asked passersby if they'd seen Oscar and the answer had always been a negative shake of the head, followed by sympathetic looks. It seemed no one in the whole of Broken had caught even a glimpse of their younger brother.

It was now going on forty-eight hours since Oscar had disappeared. Though Cassie had continued to dial his phone, and that of her stepfather's, the calls continued to go unanswered. She was scared, tired and weighed down with dread. Her head ached and her thoughts were scattered. She couldn't concentrate on anything but finding Oscar. It had become a mantra in her head.

I need to find Oscar… I need to find Oscar… Find Oscar… Find Oscar…

She and Jeremy climbed the steps to their house, both feeling the weight of fatigue and disappointment. It was like the previous night all over again. Cassie dreaded having to face her mother with nothing positive to report. Again. Apart from putting up posters, they'd canvassed the neighborhood, traipsed along the trails behind their house, spoken to everyone they came across...and nothing. No one had seen Oscar. No one knew where he was.

As Cassie walked back into the living room, she braced herself. Her mother was in her customary position, sprawled on the couch. Cassie saw her mother's sewing bag nearby. The pillowcase she'd been working on was in her lap.

Cassie breathed out a silent sigh of relief. At least her mother had been trying to get her mind off things by working. That was a good sign. The TV was on low, a blue-and-white light in the dim room. Marie turned as Cassie entered, her face alight with expectation.

"Did you find him? Did you find my boy?"

Cassie shook her head. Tears of fatigue and frustration burned behind her eyes. "I'm sorry Mom. We looked and looked. He's nowhere to be found."

Her mother's lips trembled, but she managed to hold herself together. Cassie was grateful. She felt every bit as scared and worried as her mother. The longer Oscar remained missing, the greater the chance he'd come to harm. Then her mother gasped as if she couldn't hold back her pain any longer. Silent tears slid down her cheeks. Cassie bit her lip against a surge of emotion. She hated seeing her mother in such distress. She hated even more that there was nothing she could do to alleviate it.

With a weary sigh, Cassie drew up a chair beside her mother. "Please don't cry, Mom. It's going to be all right. We're going to find him. I swear."

Her mother turned watery eyes toward her. "You just said you looked everywhere. Nobody's seen him."

"True, but we've put up posters all over the town. Jeremy helped me. Someone's bound to have seen him. He's been gone two nights. He must be getting hungry. He'll knock on someone's door for food. Or he'll come home. Either way, we'll find him."

Marie buried her face in her hands. Her shoulders shook from the force of her sobs. Cassie's heart clenched with agony. She reached over and put a hand on her mother's arm and stroked it, murmuring mindless words of comfort. The same torrent of pain and despair tumbled inside her, holding her tense. It had been that way for two days and was only getting worse.

"What are the police doing?" her mother cried. "Why haven't they found him yet?"

Cassie refrained from replying. She'd also wondered why the police weren't doing more to find Oscar. Okay, so someone had turned in Oscar's jacket and the detective had obviously followed that up by bringing it to her and having her positively identify it, but what were they doing now? Had they gone back to the neighbor and asked more questions? And what about this Kevin Turner who had apparently been Oscar's friend? Had he been interviewed?

A photo of Oscar on the TV caught her attention. It was the same photo she'd provided Trace Barrington. Scrambling for the remote, Cassie turned up the sound.

The news anchor was introducing the story of fourteen-year-old Oscar Webster who'd been missing for forty-eight hours. Footage of their house flashed across the screen and then it was filled with file footage of the lead detective.

Her heart skipped a beat. Trace looked strong and steady and reliable—and impossibly attractive. He wore a dark suit and tie and appeared somber outside the police station. The reporter took up the story.

"Police have interviewed a registered sex offender who lives in close proximity to Oscar Webster's house and is believed to be known to the young teen. Detective Trace Barrington of the Broken Police Station has told us it is only one line of enquiry they are pursuing. At this stage, no one has been arrested. People are asked to come forward with any information that might help to find this missing child. Call Crime Stoppers on..."

Cassie stared at the TV, reeling with shock. *A registered sex offender? They've interviewed a registered sex offender who lives not far from here? It must be Kevin Turner... Trace had said the man lived a couple of blocks away on our street...*

A wave of anger so hot it was scorching, surged through her veins. Trace had interviewed a pedophile known to Oscar and hadn't bothered to tell her. Her breath came fast. She seethed with fury. Bolting from her chair, she stormed from the room and punched in his number. Out of deference to her mother, she continued out the front door and down the steps. She was halfway across the front lawn when Trace answered.

"How could you?" she cried without preamble.

"Cassie, you need to calm down."

"Don't you *dare* tell me to calm down! I just saw it on the news! Why didn't you tell me? You brought that jacket to me, knowing full well where it had come from and you didn't say a word, not even a *hint* that it had come from the home of a pedophile! I'm right, aren't I? Kevin Turner is a pedophile."

"Yes. I understand why you're upset, but we have no evidence—"

"He had my brother's jacket! Don't tell me you have no evidence!"

"You're right. At least, that's where our witness told us they found the jacket. We still have no proof Oscar was there, or that it's his jacket."

"The man's a registered sex offender! He didn't get on that register for nothing!"

"You're right. But the law doesn't work like that. We can't assume that just because he's been convicted of pedophilia that he's involved in Oscar's disappearance. So far, apart from the fact Oscar's missing, we have no evidence of foul play. I'm sorry, but I just can't go charging in there half-cocked, arresting someone on nothing more than hearsay and until we have definitive proof the jacket belonged to Oscar, there's nothing I can do."

His calm and methodical tone only served to infuriate her further. She continued to rant and rave at him, at the system, at the police department who didn't seem very interested in finding her brother. He took the abuse in silence. Finally, hoarse and out of breath, Cassie stopped.

"I understand how upset you are Cassie," he said in a calm and quiet voice. "But we are doing everything we can to find your brother. I know how much you want him back. So do I.

I'm in the process of submitting the jacket for testing. I'll need you to provide me with a sample of Oscar's DNA. A hairbrush or a toothbrush will suffice. Hopefully we'll find some of Oscar's DNA on the jacket that will prove conclusively it belongs to him. At this stage, we're proceeding on the assumption that it is his, but that doesn't give us enough grounds to make an arrest.

"We're also in the process of putting together a search party. The State Emergency Services, National Parks rangers. As well, I've put out a call over the local radio for volunteers. I've also called in the dog squad. I'll also need you to get me an item of clothing belonging to Oscar. Something that has his scent. We're going to start in the bushland behind your house."

"Jeremy and I have already looked there!" she protested.

"I understand. But Oscar's still missing. He might have fallen and hurt himself. Maybe he can't hear your calls. Whatever it is, we'll look again, and we'll keep on searching until we find him. You can believe that."

Cassie squeezed her eyes shut. She felt weighted down with despair. She was still furious at Trace for not telling her about the convicted pedophile living in their neighborhood and she chafed at every delay. She felt like charging into this Kevin Turner's house and demanding he tell her what he knew about her brother. He'd had Oscar's jacket, the same jacket Oscar had been wearing when he disappeared. There was no way she'd accept that was just a coincidence, she didn't care what Trace said.

"I'll get you an item of clothing and a toothbrush, but you'd better keep your part of the bargain and find my brother."

Trace ended the call from Cassie and scrubbed at his hair. It was regrettable the media had gotten wind of Kevin Turner. Even more unfortunate, the news would likely have spread like wildfire through the town. Every man and his dog would now know Turner was a convicted pedophile. There would be plenty among them baying for Turner's blood. The situation could very quickly get out of control.

Heading into the tearoom where most of the officers rostered on that day were taking a break, including his brother Zac, Trace quickly brought them up to speed and then issued orders that anyone who could make themselves available to meet up at Turner's house do so. Trace believed in the democratic principles all Australians lived by, including the freedom to get on with one's life in peace after they'd paid their debt to society, but he also understood the anger and fear and hysteria that could turn ordinary people into vigilantes when they thought their children were at risk. The situation with Turner was about to get very tense and Trace needed all the help he could get.

Too angry and overwrought to return to the house, Cassie shoved her phone in the back pocket of her skirt and jumped into her car. She started the ignition and threw the car into reverse. Stepping hard on the accelerator, she spun the tires on the gravel as she headed out of the driveway and onto the street. Throwing the car into gear, she turned the wheel and accelerated. She had no clear destination, just an overriding sense of urgency to get away.

She could still hear Trace's calm response to her angry accusations. Okay, so she might not have been acting rational, but the fact was, her brother was missing and a convicted pedophile lived on her street. What the hell was she supposed to think?

She made no apologies for shouting at Trace. He must know how she felt; how any rational person would feel upon hearing that kind of news. And to hear it from the TV reporter first, not the lead investigator! She deserved better. She prided herself on being just and fair with anyone who came across her path, but this was different. This was her brother.

Oscar…

Her heart clenched on a wave of emotion. She bit her lip against a rush of tears. She refused to believe he'd come to harm. No, he was out there somewhere, alive and well. She wasn't sure why he hadn't returned home, especially with another night encroaching, but she'd stay positive and hope for the best. Two nights away wasn't that long, after all. Anyone could survive a couple days away from home, even if they were outside and afraid of the dark.

Please be alive, Oscar… Please still be alive…

Without being consciously aware of her surroundings, Cassie suddenly found herself outside Kevin Turner's house. TV cameras, reporters, and an angry-looking crowd of people spilled off the front lawn and into the street. They were shouting out to Turner and calling him vile names. Cassie slowed. The anger among the crowd was palpable. Some of the faces she recognized. Bill and Carol who ran the 7-Eleven. Peter and Allison from the bakery. Monica who worked in the bank. All of them were screaming obscenities, their faces twisted with anger.

From out of her rearview mirror, Cassie spied the familiar red and blue and white strobe police lights. No doubt they were there to disperse the crowd and get things back under control. She thought of Trace, doing his job, defending Turner's rights. That made her feel angry all over again. She might not be of the same mind as the angry mob of locals, but that didn't mean she felt sorry for the man who lived behind the white paling fence.

With her stomach churning with anger and the ever-present dread, she checked over her shoulder then pulled back into the traffic. Slowly, she drove away, her mind now filled with Oscar.

Please, Oscar… Please come home…

Kevin peered through a crack in the front blinds and saw the crowd outside. His stomach lurched with fear. An angry mob had gathered on his front lawn and looked set to kill. He glanced at his girlfriend accusingly.

"You told them."

Mandy's eyes were cold black stones. "I had to. You had his jacket."

Kevin felt a surge of desperation. "I didn't do anything, Mandy! You have to believe me!"

Her expression remained unmoving. "You had that boy's jacket," she repeated.

Kevin scrubbed his hands through his hair. "It was an innocent mistake! He took it off and left it hanging on the fence. I didn't have a chance to give it back to him. That's all."

She looked unconvinced. "You told the police you barely knew him."

He shook his head in bewilderment. "What could I say?"

Mandy stood and came toward him, menace in her every step. "You should have told them the truth. Just like you should have told *me*. I had no idea you were in jail for kiddy fiddlin'."

A fresh wave of desperation washed over him. "It wasn't like that, Mandy! Please, you gotta believe me! I'm not like that. You don't understand." He paused and then dragged in a ragged breath.

"I-I thought she was older. She looked older. At least seventeen. How was I to know she was only thirteen? She was developed in all the right places. And she came on to *me*. She kept hanging around me, in the park.

"I used to go there to collect my thoughts. To have some time to think. My boss was on my back about not being productive enough and how he was going to have to lay me off. It was getting to me. This girl started spending time with me. Sitting with me on that bench. Asking lots of questions. Coming across like she was interested. Flirting. She told me she'd give me a blow job for twenty bucks. I thought, what the heck.

"That first time, she did it right there in the park. There was no one else around, but still... It was kind of exciting. The next time I invited her back to my house."

Mandy regarded him with distaste. "So, you had sex with her?"

"Yes. But it wasn't like that! She wanted it. That wasn't her first time. She knew exactly what she was doing. I paid her each time, but then she started whining that it wasn't enough. When I refused to give her anymore, she threatened to go to the police. I just laughed. I thought she was joking.

"Next thing I know the police are at my door and dragging me down to the station. That's when I found out she was only thirteen. I denied everything, but it turns out she was much more clever than me. She'd filmed the two of us going at it on her phone. I didn't even know."

He sighed wearily, feeling the horror of it all over again. "That was the end of me. I was gone. I had no choice but to plead guilty. Three years in the slammer and my life in ruins. Now I'm a registered sex offender and every time a kid goes missing, I'm going to be the first one in their sights. I moved here because I wanted to escape the city. I wanted a quieter life where I could get on with my life and keep out of everyone's way. Now that dream's been shattered..."

He peered once again through a crack in the blinds. "Look at the circus out there. I'm never going to get out of this alive."

Trace cursed long and loudly at the circus of media and well-meaning neighbors who were now spewing vitriol and trespassing in Turner's yard. They were angry, the tension hot, like a dry forest waiting for that first spark.

Just what I need...

He recognized Cassie's Honda in front of him and hoped like hell she didn't join the crowd. To his relief, though she slowed momentarily, after a few moments she continued forward until her lights were eaten up by the night. A handful of reporters had caught wind of the developing drama. TV camera crews were already there, filming the crowd.

Great.

The fact was, Turner might be a person of interest, but he wasn't the only one. Trace had put in another call to Malcolm Russell. Like all the other times, the call had gone straight through to voicemail. Either Russell had his phone switched off, or it was flat. Either way, the longer the man remained incommunicado, the higher he climbed on Trace's suspect list.

He'd also tried Oscar's phone again and had gotten the same result. Earlier, he'd requested a triangulation on both phones. Neither phone was pinging off any towers. That made their job of finding them all that much harder.

Pulling over to the side, he climbed out of the cruiser. He was relieved to see three other police cars in the street. He spied Zac and a junior constable standing at Turner's front gate, doing what they could to keep the angry locals in check. Trace joined them.

He nodded a greeting to both Zac and the constable. "Thanks for coming."

"No problem," Zac murmured. "Looks like you might need all the help you can get."

Trace compressed his lips, feeling grim. "You have that right. Let's hope we can talk some sense into them and avoid having to make any arrests. That's the last thing we need."

Lifting his voice above the crowd, Trace called for their attention. It took a couple of attempts, but at last the noise subsided.

"I'm asking you all to go home. This man is not under arrest. There is no evidence he's committed a crime. He's merely a person we spoke to, like we've spoken to a lot of you."

"He's a fucking pedo! A germ!" someone shouted.

"Let me repeat," Trace replied. "This man is no different than the rest of you whom I've spoken to. Right now, a young teenager is missing. Some of you know him. Oscar Webster. His family is worried. I'm asking you to put your efforts into finding him and leave this man alone. If we find evidence that somehow implicates him, I'll be the first person here with the handcuffs, but until that happens, he's entitled to live in peace and without fear for his life, just like each one of you."

"How can you defend him? He's nothing but scum!" A man near Trace spat a lump of phlegm at his feet.

"I'm not defending anyone," Trace replied. "I'm defending our democracy and those principles of justice we all hold so dear. We don't live in a society where people are convicted without an ounce of evidence—and thank God for that. You, me, all of us rely on that. Innocent until proven guilty."

He looked around at the mob, eyeballing as many of them as he could. "We're better than that. *You're* better than that. Everyone deserves their day in court. Right now, this man has nothing to answer for. How would you feel if this was your brother? Your father? Your uncle? He's paid his debt to society. He deserves to be left alone."

There was a grumbling among the crowd. Some of them had lowered their gazes and were shuffling their feet. Trace pressed home his advantage.

"Go home, all of you. Put away your anger. Let the police do their job. We'll find Oscar Webster and hopefully he'll be alive and well. In the meantime, if you really want to help, get together and start looking for him. I've organized a search party first thing in the morning with the State Emergency Services. Come and join us and do something constructive for Oscar and his family."

To Trace's relief, the crowd began to disperse. Those who continued to linger, he hurried along with threats of fines. When everyone had left, he drew in a deep breath and let it out on a weary sigh.

Zac came up to him and slapped him on the back. "You did good, big brother. Well done."

Trace grimaced. "Yeah. Until the next time. Now that this is out, it's only a matter of time before we're all back here again."

Trace stared toward Turner's house and saw a flicker of movement behind the blinds that covered the front windows. He narrowed his eyes. "That prick better be innocent or there's going to be hell to pay. "

Trace thanked his colleagues for answering his call for back up and after confirming they'd all be there first thing in the morning to kick off the search, he climbed back into his car. His thoughts went to Cassie Webster. He hated that she was upset and hurting and angry. He wished there was something he could do to make her feel better. The only thing he could do was find her brother. With determination surging through him, he put the car in gear and headed back to the station.

It was approaching nine o'clock when he arrived back at the station. Well past the time anyone else would be there working. In a town the size of Broken, the staff went home at six, including the officers. Police were rostered on-call after hours. If there was an emergency, they were paged. It wasn't ideal, particularly if time was of the essence, but that was the system in place for small country towns and most of the time it worked just fine.

Guided by memory and the faint flicker of security lights, Trace made his way through the dark police station. He switched on a few more lights and walked into the tearoom. After pouring himself what was left of some strong black coffee, brewed hours ago, he took his mug and went back to his office.

The meager information they'd gathered so far was spread out over his desk. He hated that they had so few leads. No leads, really. Just a lot of unanswered questions. It would help a lot if they could contact Oscar's stepfather. So far, the BOLO alert had given them nothing. That was frustrating the hell out of Trace. Where could the man be? How could no one have seen him, recognized him?

Malcolm Russell was the last known person to see Oscar that night. He could very well hold the key to the boy's disappearance and his whereabouts. Perhaps he and Oscar were together... But Russell's phone kept going to voicemail, keeping him out of reach. Trace hoped that now the story had made the TV news, Malcolm might be made aware of what was happening and make contact. That's if he wanted to be found...

Surely the man must turn up soon...

Trace had called the National Parks office on Monday. They'd confirmed that Malcolm Russell was employed in their office and that he'd been expected to show for work. They hadn't heard from him. They'd left phone messages and an email requesting that he contact them and let them know where he was.

When Trace asked if Russell's behavior was unusual, the woman he'd spoken to had reluctantly told him no. Malcolm had been known to go missing before. The longest had been for a week. When Trace dug even deeper, the woman admitted Russell had a drinking problem that sometimes interfered with his ability to show up for work.

This corresponded with what Trace had already been told about Cassie's stepfather. Still, it wouldn't hurt to try and obtain further insights into the man. With that thought in mind, Trace picked up his phone.

Wade Barrington lived in an even smaller country town about six-hours' drive north of Sydney, but he was also a park ranger employed by the same government body as Malcolm. It was possible the two had crossed paths. Trace was curious about the kind of man Russell was. From what Cassie and her mother had said, Trace had developed his own opinion of the man and it wasn't particularly flattering, but perhaps there was more to Russell than Trace realized. One thing he was certain of was that Russell had a temper.

Could he have lost control that night and caused Oscar serious injury?

Trace didn't know the man well enough to discount the possibility. It was definitely something he had to consider. With a sigh, Trace dialed Wade's number. It was late, but

Wade was a night owl, like him. He'd bet his brother would still be awake. He was right.

"Trace. What's up?"

"Wade. Thanks for taking my call."

"No problem. What can I do for you?"

"See, the thing is, we have a situation here in Broken. A missing boy. Well, he's fourteen, but he has autism. The way I figure it, he probably has a mental age closer to nine or ten."

"Does he communicate?"

"Yes. Apparently."

"How long's he been missing?"

"Forty-eight hours. Not long enough to start panicking, but long enough to feel concerned, particularly given his autism. I'm hoping you might be able to help."

"I'm a little confused. I live a six-hours' drive away. What can I do to help?"

"See, the boy's stepfather works for National Parks. I'm hoping you might know him. Maybe shed some light on his character."

"Is the father a suspect in the boy's disappearance?"

"Stepfather. We don't know that yet, but he was the last person we know of to see the child before he went missing. We haven't been able to contact him. According to our information, he got into an argument with the child right before Oscar went missing. Now he's gone AWOL and he's not answering his phone."

"I see. What's his name?"

"Malcolm Russell. You heard of him?"

There was a moment of silence on the other end of the phone. "Malcolm Russell? The name sounds familiar. He's from Broken, you say?"

"Yes."

"Malcolm Russell. Yeah, I know who you mean. Short and wiry, black hair, graying at the temples. Mustache. We've attended a few seminars together."

"Sounds about right. His stepdaughter provided me with a photo. If he's from Broken, he must be our man. I can't imagine there being two of them in a town this size."

Wade chuckled. "Right."

"What can you tell me about him? What kind of man is he?" Trace asked and sipped from his coffee.

"Well, I don't know him well and only from a work perspective, but I guess I'd say he's a decent enough bloke. I've heard he gets a bit out of control on the sauce, but other than that, I don't think there's anything sinister about him, if that's what you mean."

"What do you mean by out of control?"

"Oh, you know. Loud and obnoxious. Aggressive. Wants to fight everyone."

Trace made a note on the blank page in front of him. "I see. Do you think he's capable of hurting his stepson?"

"You mean, killing him?"

"Not necessarily. But okay. Do you think he's capable of doing something like that?"

"Look, I really don't know him all that well. We've only spent a day or two here and there at those boring seminars we're forced to attend every year."

"I understand and I don't mean he would have intentionally caused someone's death, but what if it was an accident? Do you think if he were angry enough, he could have lost it and maybe done something he didn't intend, and the boy ended up injured or dead?"

"Shit, Trace. I don't know. I really don't want to speculate about something so serious. Like I said, I hardly know the man. And who knows if he's like that when he's at home. Hell, for all I know he only gets on the grog when he's out of town."

Trace kept his mouth shut. It wasn't his place to besmirch the character of a man who could very well be innocent of any serious wrongdoing, at least insofar as it involved his stepson.

"What have you done so far to find the missing boy?" Wade asked.

"I've spoken to his family and friends. We've also canvassed the neighbors and others. No one's seen him. I've also organized a search party with the SES volunteers and the other local park rangers. We're gathering first thing in the morning to start the search. Oscar, that's the missing boy, likes to spend time in the bush. His house adjoins a national park. We're starting the search there."

"Sounds like a plan. Let me know how you do."

"Thanks. And thanks for your insights on Russell."

"I'm not sure if it will help."

Trace grimaced. "At this stage, everything helps." After thanking Wade for his time and wishing him a goodnight, Trace ended the call.

Chapter Eight

Cassie glanced at the clock that was fixed to the back wall of her classroom. From early that morning, the police, park rangers and State Emergency Service volunteers had been scouring the bushland, searching for any sign of Oscar. Cassie had wanted to join them, but at the last moment had decided to leave it to people who knew what they were doing. Instead, she'd gone to school and was doing her best to remain focused on her class. Her phone was in the top drawer of her desk, waiting for a call. A silent prayer that her brother be found alive, and okay, kept circling in her head.

"Miss, when were the pyramids built?"

Normally any sign of curiosity about history from her Year Eight students sent her heart soaring, but today it was all she could do to get through the class. She'd set up the lesson on the SMART board and had told the students to work in pairs through the set questions. It was a cop-out from her usual hands-on teaching style, but today that was the best she could manage.

The constant feeling of fear and dread that had been with her since the night Oscar disappeared had only grown more intense. She'd watched enough true crime shows on TV to know the longer he was missing, the more likely it was he'd met with foul play. Either that or he was so badly injured he was unable to get himself home. Neither possibility was reassuring and it was all she could do to force the negative thoughts aside. Instead, she concentrated on her unwavering belief Oscar would come home.

"Miss Webster, how do you spell Tutankhamun?" one of her students asked.

Grateful for the distraction, Cassie walked down the aisle and came to a halt next to the boy who'd asked the question. Max Jones was bright enough at learning, but he struggled with retention and spelling was nothing more than a memory test as far as Cassie was concerned.

She crouched down beside Max's desk. "Tutankhamun. Egypt's young pharaoh king. A tricky word, to be sure. Let's work through it together."

Letter by letter, she helped Max spell the word. When they finished, his grin split his face wide.

"Thanks for the help Miss."

His grin was infectious. A reluctant smile turned up her lips. "Anytime, Max."

She returned to her desk and took a quick peek at her phone. Nothing. She swallowed a sigh and forced herself to concentrate on her class. The day dragged on and her phone remained ominously silent. She clung to the thought no news was good news, but by the time three o'clock rolled round, her nerves were frayed. The moment the bell signaled the last lesson for the day, she collected her handbag from the staffroom and left. For the hundredth time that day she checked her phone to make sure she hadn't missed a call or a text from Trace, but there was nothing.

Climbing into her car, her anger and fear boiled over. She was desperate to hear from the police. A search had been going on all day and no one had bothered to call her with an update. Not a single call.

She headed toward the police station, intent on getting answers. Trace's police cruiser was parked outside the building, along with at least half a dozen others. Several TV vans also clogged the street. As she brought her car to a halt, Cassie saw several reporters jump up from where they'd been sitting and rush toward her, microphones extended.

"Ms Webster, can you tell us why you're here?"

"Cassie, have the police found Oscar?"

"Do you think your stepfather might have harmed him?"

"Where's Malcolm?"

The questions came thick and fast. Cassie ducked her head and pushed her way through the crowd. Half-running, she shouldered open the door to the station and strode into the reception area. An unfamiliar female constable sat behind the desk. Her eyes widened at the sight of Cassie.

"Ms Webster. Can I help you?"

Great. Just what I want. To be recognized by a junior constable...

Thanks to the barrage of media parked outside their house, Cassie's face had been all over the morning news. She hadn't even been able to make it out of her driveway without microphones and cameras being pushed into her face. Reporters from various news outlets had descended upon her the moment she opened the front door, throwing questions at her. In the end, she'd given them a few moments to take their pictures and get their sound bite. If it meant raising awareness about Oscar's disappearance, she was prepared to put up with the invasion of her privacy.

But that had been this morning. After a testing day at school and another day without word of Oscar, she wasn't feeling so amiable toward the press, or the fact she was now a household name. She gave the constable a tight smile.

"I'd like to see Detective Barrington."

"Trace or Zac?" the constable replied with a chuckle.

Cassie gritted her teeth. "Trace."

The constable smiled. "That's lucky because Zac's not here."

At the look on Cassie's face, the constable mumbled something about letting Trace know she was there. Cassie moved away while the woman spoke quietly into the phone. She chafed under the wait. After what felt like a lifetime—but in reality, was probably only a few minutes—the door opened and Trace appeared.

Lines of fatigue were etched around his eyes. His dark hair was unkempt, like he'd run his fingers through it more than once. Dark stubble shaded his chin and his cheeks. She felt a twinge of compassion but swiftly pushed it aside.

"Why haven't you called me?" she demanded.

Trace winced and then indicated for her to follow him. She pushed past him and headed into the interview room where he'd first spoken to her.

Has it only been three days since I was here, telling him about Oscar? It feels like a lifetime ago...

At least she'd made it all the way inside the station and even behind the scenes without having a panic attack. In fact, she'd barely given another thought to the bad memories. She guessed that was progress, at least.

Trace followed her inside and closed the door. He invited her to sit, but she was too wired to do that. Instead, she pushed her handbag higher on her shoulder and began to pace.

"My brother's been missing three days! Three days! And what are you doing, here at your desk? I dropped in a T-shirt and toothbrush belonging to Oscar first thing this morning. Did you even get them? You should be out there looking for him! You aren't doing enough to find him!"

He leaned back against a wall and crossed his arms over his chest. "I'm sorry I didn't call you," he said quietly.

She spun on her heel, intent on giving him another angry spray, but the look on his face stopped her. He looked worn out, defeated, bone tired. Before she could open her mouth, he spoke again.

"I've been out in the bush since first light, coordinating the search teams. Close to one thousand people have turned out. A wonderful show of support from the local community. I submitted the jacket and Oscar's toothbrush to the lab. Hopefully they'll find matching DNA. The dog team arrived here around nine. I gave them Oscar's T-shirt. They put the dogs to work right away. We haven't found him yet, but I want you to know, everyone's looking for him, including me."

Her anger subsided, but the fear and heartache didn't. A lump of emotion clogged her throat. "Then why haven't you found him? Why is it taking so long?" she cried.

"We're doing everything we can to find him," Trace replied, his voice low and steady. "But we have very little to go on. Apart from the jacket—which might or might not belong to your brother—we have nothing."

Trace scrubbed his fingers through his hair. "If only we could make contact with your stepfather, we might have something more to go on. As far as we know, he was the last person to see Oscar before he disappeared." Trace grimaced. "Unfortunately, Malcolm's phone is still switched off and all of my other efforts to find him have come to nothing."

"Mom and I have been calling him too. The calls go straight to voicemail," Cassie said dully.

"I'm sure it hasn't escaped your notice that we have reporters, photographers and TV cameramen from all the major media outlets filling every room in every hotel in this town. It's a pain in the neck to keep having to take time away from the investigation to answer their questions, but media attention can also be a good thing. It keeps your brother's face in front of people. You never know, someone might remember seeing him. Right now, we'll take anything we can get.

"The other good thing about the increased media presence is that Malcolm might see something on the news. Oscar's disappearance has become a national story, and though reporters can be obnoxious and rude, they have their uses. Raising awareness, getting the story out there to as many people as possible... That's going to help us. The more people who know about Oscar, the better. And like I said, there's a chance Malcolm might also catch the story on the news and come home, or at least contact one of us."

Cassie nodded, accepting his explanation, but his words didn't alleviate her dread. "It's been three days! We need to find him! Something's happened to him. I feel it in my heart. If he were able to, he'd be home by now."

She pressed a hand against her chest, as if she could hold back the pain. Her voice choked with emotion. Sympathy and compassion filled Trace's face.

"I understand your anger and frustration and fear," he said.

His sympathetic words only served to ignite her fury. As her anger flared hotter, she glared at him.

"How the hell can you understand how I feel? It's not *your* brother who's missing! It's not *your* brother who might never be found alive! Do you know how many people I've spoken to? How many posters I've hung? I've walked through the bush for hours, searching desperately for a sign Oscar's near." Her chest tightened on a surge of emotion. She gritted her teeth and tried to gain control.

I won't break down... I won't break down... I won't break down...

The pep talk seemed to work. She dragged in a ragged breath and spoke more calmly. "I understand you and your team have been working hard too, but none of you have found him! He's out there, Detective. He's hurt! There's no other reason he wouldn't have come home! We have to find him! We have to *find* him!"

Her voice cracked. Despite her best efforts, hot tears filled her eyes and spilled down her cheeks. The look of tenderness and compassion on Trace's face almost undid her. He made a move toward her and for a moment she thought he was about to take her in his arms, but he seemed to realize what he was doing and checked himself.

Digging around in her handbag, she pulled out a tissue and hurriedly swiped at her eyes. She abhorred any sign of weakness, especially such a public display. For a long time, she'd taken on the responsibility for her brothers, her mother too. Malcolm did his bit by providing for them financially, but everything else had fallen to Cassie.

She'd been the one they all turned to for advice, for help, for support, for answers when things got them down. She'd been the one to shop for groceries, prepare meals and clean the house. The boys had helped with the outside chores and had grudgingly helped inside when she prodded them to do it, but most of the time she was in charge of the household. She felt more like a parent than a daughter and sister.

Until now, she hadn't realized how heavy a burden all that had been. She'd stepped into the role when their father had left, and she'd never questioned it. At the time, her mother was locked away in grief and her brothers were too young to step up. So it had been left to Cassie, and so far she was proud of the job she'd done.

But now Oscar was missing, and she couldn't shake the feeling it was all her fault. She should have done more: protected him, looked out for him, made sure he was all right. Not just during those ugly episodes with their stepfather, but at other times. She'd gotten so busy with her career; she had paid less attention than she used to. And now Oscar was gone. The guilt was overwhelming. She hadn't even known he was friendly with a man who turned out to be a pedophile.

As if he could read her mind, Trace murmured softly, "Don't do that to yourself, Cassie."

She stared up at him defiantly. "Do what?"

Trace swallowed a sigh. The dark shadows beneath Cassie's beautiful green eyes gave her a haunted look. It was obvious she hadn't been sleeping well and who could blame her when her brother was still missing?

"It's no good blaming yourself," he said gently. "This isn't your fault. Oscar and your stepfather had an argument and that's all we know. It had nothing to do with you."

Her eyes flared with anger. "Please don't presume to know how I'm feeling."

Trace threw up his hands in a sign of surrender. "Okay. Whatever. I just hate seeing you beating yourself up like this. You don't know what went on in that shed. You don't know what was said. Hell, for all we know Oscar might be with Malcolm. Maybe they took off together? Who knows? That's why we're working so damn hard to find them. So that we know. Because regardless of whatever might or might not have happened, we still have no evidence of foul play."

He paused and drew in another breath.

"Yes, your brother is missing, and he's been away longer than usual. Maybe Oscar had had enough of the arguments with your stepfather. Maybe he hopped a bus? Caught a train? He could be halfway across the state by now."

"What with? He spent all his money on an Apple Watch and a PlayStation."

"Has anyone checked to see if they're missing money?" Trace asked.

Cassie frowned. "I don't think so. I certainly haven't. Then again, I wasn't at home the night Oscar disappeared. I had my purse with me, so he couldn't have taken any money from me."

"What about your mom and Jeremy? You should ask them. If it's gone it would give credence to the fact your brother might have left on public transport."

Cassie stared at the carpet. "I'll ask Mom and Jeremy," she mumbled.

"Has Oscar ever caught a bus or a train on his own before?'

"Yes. But only around Broken. Never out of town."

"But he understands how the public transport system works? That he can get on a bus or a train and go somewhere?"

"Yes."

Trace sighed. "I'm going to review all the CCTV footage around the bus and train station the night Oscar disappeared. This might be the break we need. In the meantime, let me know if your mother or brother are missing any money. He could have always gotten money from someone else of course—like a friend—but let's first start with the family."

Cassie crossed her arms over her chest. She drew in a deep breath. Trace could see the effort it took her to hold it all together. And then her bottom lip began to tremble. Fresh tears glinted in her eyes. Trace's gut clenched with sympathy.

Once again, he controlled his impulse to offer her physical comfort, though it wasn't easy. He felt for her. He hated to see her tears. But there was nothing he could do but keep looking for her brother and asking questions. And then he decided to share something personal that might help her understand.

"You said I didn't know what it's like to have a brother go missing, but that's not exactly true."

She looked at him, her eyes filled with cautious curiosity.

He went on. "I have a brother. Vaughan. He's forty. Quite a lot older than me. He was adopted by my parents when he was eleven. I don't know a lot about his early life, just that he was orphaned at a young age and put into foster care. He was passed around from family to family and... Let's just say, most of them weren't kind. It was tough for him growing up, but somehow, he managed to keep a positivity about him that shines through even today. He's a much-loved member of my family."

Trace drew in a deep breath and eased it out. He was surprised that talking about Vaughan had made him so emotional. Probably because nobody had seen his brother for so long. He glanced at Cassie. She had a dubious expression on her face.

"You're probably wondering why I'm telling you this."

She looked at him.

Trace blew out another breath. "See, my brother disappeared a bit over a month ago. No one knows where he is. He sent my father an email a week after he went missing, letting Dad know he was okay, but that's all we've heard from him. No one has a clue where he is or why he took off.

"It's not the same thing as Oscar because Vaughan's an adult and Dad did receive that email, but no one has heard from him since. The longer he's away, the more we can't help but wonder if the email's a hoax. If maybe something sinister has happened to Vaughan that no one knows about. What if all this time his life's been in danger and none of us have done anything to save him?" He paused and then added, "We're all worried about him."

Cassie's face filled with understanding. There was also a hint of compassion. He was glad she understood the reason he'd shared something so personal with her.

"I'm not telling you this to make you feel sorry for me or to take away from your situation in any way. But for what it's worth, I do know something about what it feels like to have a brother who's missing."

Cassie threw him a look filled with heartache and agony. "You're right. It's not the same. But thank you for sharing. Knowing about your missing brother somehow makes this easier for me. You might understand how I'm feeling. I'm sorry for giving you such a hard time."

As Trace stared into her beautiful eyes, something inside him shifted. A yearning to take away her sadness, to protect her from the ugliness of life. To make her smile, to make her life better, to see her overwhelmed with happiness.

His gaze grew more intense. "I'm going to find your brother, Cassie. You have my word."

Chapter Nine

Trace's words were still ringing in her ears when Cassie pulled up outside her house. She dodged a handful of reporters who were camped on the footpath and made her way inside. Her mother was sprawled out on the couch. It looked like she was putting the finishing touches on the pillow slip. Cassie greeted her softly and kissed her on the cheek.

"That looks lovely Mom. You're the only person I know who can form such delicate stitches as that." She traced the initials her mother had embroidered in white silk. "W and A."

"Yes. Wendy and Andrew. The bride and groom."

Cassie moved her finger over the delicate rosebuds that her mother had embroidered in soft pink. "This is beautiful Mom. I'm sure they're going to love them."

Her mother managed a small smile. "I hope so."

Cassie moved toward the kitchen. "Would you like a cup of tea Mom?"

"Yes, thank you honey." Her expression turned anxious. "What about the search party? Is there any news?"

Cassie compressed her lips and turned away. "Not yet Mom. But Detective Barrington told me they had nearly a thousand people out there searching for him. And a dog squad. I'm sure they'll find him Mom. After all, we're talking about Oscar. He couldn't have gone too far away."

She thought about what Trace had said about Oscar catching a bus or a train and hightailing it out of there. She turned back toward her mother.

"You aren't missing any money are you Mom?"

Marie frowned. "What do you mean?"

"You know. Money missing from your purse."

Marie's frown deepened. "No. At least I don't think so. Bring me my purse and I'll see."

Cassie reached for her mother's leather handbag and pulled out a small purse. She handed it to her mother.

Marie opened the clasp and dug around inside. "No. I only had about fifty dollars in notes and some loose coins. It's all still here." She looked back up at Cassie. "Why?"

Cassie blew out her breath and perched on the arm of the couch. "Detective Barrington asked me if it's possible Oscar caught a bus or a train out of Broken. He'd need money to do that."

Her mother's eyes went wide with shock. "The detective thinks Oscar ran away?"

"He's not saying that Mom," Cassie said quickly. "But we can't discount the possibility, can we? I mean, we taught Oscar how to catch the bus and the train, didn't we?"

"We wanted him to be independent!"

"Of course we did," Cassie reassured her, "and that's a good thing." She shook her head. "I just don't think he ran away. Why now? It's not like he hasn't had run-ins with Malcolm before."

Cassie sighed. Right now, they were all clinging to the fact he'd gone off somewhere to lick his wounds after a nasty run-in with Malcolm. As soon as he calmed down and got hungry enough, he'd turn back up at home. It was much better than any alternative.

Cassie stood and continued into the kitchen. She set the kettle to boil. "Would you like something to eat Mom?" she called out.

"A sandwich would be nice, honey. And bring me some painkillers too. I have a monstrous headache. I've had it all afternoon."

Cassie made a ham and tomato sandwich and seasoned it the way her mother liked. She left the sandwich on a plate and made a pot of tea. Along with two painkillers and a glass of water, Cassie placed everything on a tray and brought it in to her mother.

"Here you go Mom."

She sat the tray down on the small table her mother used for that purpose and then took a step back. Marie reached for the painkillers and tossed them back with a sip of water before starting in on the sandwich.

"Have you heard from Malcolm?" Cassie asked.

"No. I've called him over and over. He's still not answering his phone. He doesn't even know Oscar's missing!" She gulped on a sob. "I need him, Cassie. I need Malcolm home. I need him to reassure me everything's going to be all right. That my baby's all right."

Cassie felt a surge of unreasonable anger that her mother was so emotionally reliant on a man who could be so selfish as to disappear for days at a time and switch off his phone so no one could contact him. And now, when her mother really needed his support, he was nowhere to be found.

With a sigh of irritation, Cassie walked down the hallway toward her room. On the way, she saw Jeremy standing beside his dresser. He was still in his school uniform. He held a backpack in one hand and was stowing water bottles and energy bars inside, along with a torch.

"What are you doing?" she asked, stepping into his room.

"What does it look like?"

Her heart gave a little lurch of fear, but she eyed him steadily. "I don't know. Why don't you tell me?"

Jeremy shot her a wild look, his eyes flashing with defiance. "I'm going out there to find Oscar! Okay?"

"You're going looking for Oscar?"

"Yes! No one else seems to be able to find him."

A wave of relief washed over her. She leaned against the door.

Jeremy shot her a strange look. "What is it?"

She waved his question away. "Nothing. I... For a moment I thought you were running away too."

Jeremy's forehead creased in a frown. "What do you mean, *too*?"

"Nothing. Don't worry about it."

Jeremy advanced upon her, his expression filled with incredulity. "You think Oscar ran away?"

Cassie shook her head. "No, no. Of course not. Why would he do that?"

Jeremy looked unconvinced. "Then why would you say something like that?"

"It was silly. I shouldn't have. It was just something Detective Barrington said—"

"What did he say?" Jeremy cried.

"Nothing. He just said there isn't any evidence of foul play, and it could be possible... That is, he wondered if maybe... Oscar had run away."

Jeremy had started to shake his head from side to side before she'd even finished. "No way. There's no way he'd run away. He hates being on his own! Besides, where would he go? His only friend is still in town. And he had no money. He spent it all on that stupid watch. There's no way he hopped a bus out of here. That's the stupidest idea ever."

"You're right. But... Do you mind checking to see if you're missing any money?"

Jeremy shot her a dark look tinged with disbelief, but reluctantly strode over to his desk and picked up his wallet. He opened it and flicked through the notes and then dropped the wallet back on the desk.

"No. There's nothing missing." And then his anger got the better of him. His eyes blazed. "He didn't run away, Cassie! You know he didn't do that! We're talking about Oscar! He loves us! There's no way he'd leave Mom. He even cares about Malcolm."

Cassie started in surprise. "He does?"

"Yeah." Jeremy stared down at the worn carpet. "I heard him saying his prayers one night. He asked God to bless us all, including Malcolm."

Cassie blinked back a rush of tears. An overwhelming surge of emotion rushed through her.

Please, God. Bring him back. Please bring my brother home...

Jeremy returned his attention to his packing. He stowed the last water bottle inside and tightened the drawstring. Then he closed the clip and slung the backpack over his shoulder.

"You're not going to stop me, Cass. I owe it to Oscar to do whatever I can to find him."

"Of course I'm not going to stop you," she said. "But there are people out there who've been searching for him all day. SES volunteers, police officers, even a dog team. Detective Barrington said there were nearly a thousand people who showed up to help."

Jeremy shot her a hard look. "And have they found him?"

Cassie compressed her lips and remained silent.

"That's what I thought," Jeremy said, his expression equally grim.

Cassie sat down on his bed, feeling defeated. After a moment, Jeremy sat down beside her.

"No one knows the trails like I do, Cass. I *need* to do this. I need to do this for Oscar. I know we walked the trails already, but we must have missed something. Or maybe he took a different route? He's out there somewhere. He might be hurt. I can't sit here and do nothing, waiting for him to come back."

Cassie nodded. "I understand, Jeremy. I really do. But please don't stay out too late. Come home before it gets dark.

I couldn't bear it if I lost another brother."

Jeremy merely nodded, his face taut. Then he stood. She stood too. She threw her arms around him and hugged him tightly. "Good luck, Jeremy," she whispered. "Call me if you find anything, anything at all. I'll be waiting by the phone."

After dealing with some paperwork and returning a stack of phone calls linked to other cases that couldn't wait, Trace climbed into his cruiser and headed for Cassie's house. He felt bad about their earlier conversation, even though he'd done his best to remain calm and compassionate and had even shared with her something personal. Still, she was hurting, and he wanted to check in with her and see how she was doing.

The sun was low in the sky when he pulled into her driveway. At the sight of the police cruiser, the handful of reporters camped out near her house got to their feet and swarmed him. Knowing it was best to cooperate with them, he paused and braced himself for their questions.

"How is the search party going? Why are you here? Has something happened?" one woman shouted.

"We've had people from the SES, the police department, National Parks and many local volunteers out searching for Oscar Webster since early this morning," he said.

"Have they found anything?" another reporter asked.

"No. Not at this stage."

"Why are you searching the bushland? Do you think that's where Oscar is?" asked another reporter, pushing his mic up close to Trace's face.

Trace maintained his calm. "We understand Oscar liked to spend time in the bush. That's why we're searching there. If we find nothing of interest, we'll move the search elsewhere."

"It's nearly seventy-two hours since Oscar went missing. Do you think he's still alive?"

Trace cursed under his breath and eyeballed the reporter. The last thing he needed was for the media to start speculating about the likelihood of Oscar's death. He could just imagine Oscar's family watching his interactions with the press and wondering when he'd given up on finding their son and brother alive.

"Detective? Do you think Oscar Webster is still alive?" The young blond reporter with the heavy makeup repeated her question. She stared back at him, her gaze unflinching.

Trace stared straight down the camera. "We have no reason to believe otherwise. He's a fit and healthy fourteen-year-old. We might be in the last throes of May, but the weather is still mild despite winter being only a couple of weeks away. I want to thank all those members of the community who have volunteered and continue to volunteer their time to aid in the search for Oscar. Efforts will continue. We remain hopeful."

"What about—"

Trace blocked the question with a raised hand and turned his back on the gaggle of reporters. His long strides ate up the ground between the front fence and the steps that led up to the door. He knocked briskly on the wooden panel and waited for it to open.

Cassie met him at the door almost immediately. It was obvious she'd been watching his approach. Without a word, she stepped back and allowed him to enter, before quickly blocking out the sound of camera shutters and shouted questions. She ushered him past the living room where her mother was asleep on the couch. A half-eaten sandwich lay in her lap.

They went into the kitchen. It was small and cozy and overcrowded, but it held a warmth that told him this was the heart of the home. Reminders about various school events were pinned to the fridge, along with an assortment of photos, mostly of Oscar. In every one of them he was smiling.

"Can I get you something to drink? A cup of tea or coffee?"

"Thank you. A coffee would be great. Black, no sugar."

He watched her as she set about putting the kettle on to boil and fetching two mugs from a cupboard above her head. She was of average height and build, but she moved with the grace of a dancer. This evening her auburn hair was pulled back in a bun. The hairstyle would have looked severe on someone less attractive, but for Cassie, it highlighted her prominent cheekbones and drew attention to her mouth.

Her lips were a pink color, plump and looking pillow soft. He wondered what it would feel like to kiss her. The thought came from nowhere and made him blink. They were in the middle of a desperate search for her brother. Each day that passed without finding him made the possibility that something terrible had happened to him more real.

Still, Trace wasn't going to beat himself up about feeling attracted to Cassie Webster. She was smart and feisty. It was obvious how much she loved her family. He wanted to get to know her better, discover the real Cassie Webster. In the dying rays of sunlight that poured through the kitchen window, she seemed gilded in golden light. Her auburn hair looked like it was on fire. His breath caught.

She's so beautiful...

A reflexive clenching in his gut reminded him this wasn't the time or place. In different circumstances, he'd ask her out. Take her to dinner, or maybe the theater. Go to a football game. Whatever she wanted. But that would have to wait. Right now, the situation was complicated. He was certain the last thing on her mind was seeing him as a potential date.

As if privy to his thoughts, she turned just then and blushed. Her gaze immediately shifted to somewhere past his shoulder.

"D-do you take milk or sugar?" she stammered.

"No. I take it black."

Her blush deepened, spreading across her cheeks. She ducked her head and then turned her back on him, busying herself at the stove. "That's right. You told me that," she mumbled.

"Hey, don't sweat it. You have a lot going on."

She gave him a tight smile. "Yes."

She poured them both coffee and added cream and sugar to hers. She handed him a cup. Their fingers brushed. A tingling sensation started in his hands and traveled across his palm. It was a delicious feeling and something he hadn't experienced before. He peeked in her direction, but she was now leaning against the counter and seemed wholly absorbed in her coffee.

He took a sip of the black brew. It was hot and strong, just how he liked it. "How's Jeremy holding up?" he asked.

Cassie grimaced. "About as well as you'd expect. He's gone out to look for Oscar."

Trace merely nodded. He was as frustrated as anyone that they had no leads. The sniffer dogs had been out in the bush all day and had turned up nothing. Not a sign that Oscar had been there. Trace was acutely aware that the longer Oscar was missing, the more likely it was that he'd turn up dead. He didn't want to say that to Cassie, but she wasn't an idiot. He hoped like everyone else they'd find Oscar alive, and soon.

"I checked with Mom and Jeremy about the money thing. Neither of them are missing any. Of course, he could have gotten money from someone else. Like Malcolm."

Trace could see how much that admission cost her. He hurried to set her mind at ease. "I've spent the afternoon going through CCTV footage from the train station and the bus station the night Oscar was last seen. There was nothing. I also examined the footage for the following day, just in case he left town later. Again, there was no sign of him at either premises. It's doubtful someone gave him enough money for a cab, which means he's still here in Broken. I've also checked in again with Malcolm's employer. They still haven't heard from him."

Her eyes flashed with anger. "I just wish Malcolm would answer his damn phone! Of all the times to take off!"

"We have officers in all the nearby towns looking for him. Someone will find him."

Cassie knew the smile of reassurance Trace sent her way was meant to make her feel better and she appreciated his efforts. She'd treated him unfairly when she accused him of not doing enough to find her brother. She'd been scared and tired and overwrought—she still felt that way—but it wasn't Trace's fault. He was doing all he could.

She wished he wasn't so darn attractive. It made it so much harder to concentrate. She was ashamed to admit she'd even noticed that when her brother was still out there somewhere alone. But she was only human, and she definitely wasn't blind. Trace Barrington was sexy enough to front the covers of glossy magazines; leading-man, Hollywood-style sexy.

The look on his face when she'd turned from the window had covered her skin with heat. Warmth had spread to other parts of her body, parts she'd long denied. At twenty-four she was far from innocent, but she could count on one hand the number of sexual experiences she'd had and though they'd been pleasant, none of them had rocked her world.

But she had a sneaking suspicion Trace would be confident finding his way around a woman's body. He gave off an air of strength and reassurance she found enticing. In other circumstances, she'd be eager to explore things with him further... To feel something other than fear and dread.

Her face flamed at the thought.

How can I think such things when my brother is missing, likely cold, hungry and scared?

She needed Trace to focus on finding him. Sexy, confident, strong... Those things didn't matter. *Couldn't* matter. At least, not until her brother was found.

Chapter Ten

Jeremy's arms and legs were scratched from pushing through thorny bushes in his quest to find his brother. He suddenly wished he'd taken the time to exchange his school clothes for jeans and a long-sleeved shirt. Insects buzzed around his head. A bird cried out overhead. He looked up and saw the last rays of sunshine disappearing behind the trees. Night was closing in.

Another night without Oscar at home, safe and sound in his bed. Another night of not knowing where Oscar was. Another night listening to his mother's quiet sobbing. Another night of tension and underlying fear permeating the house.

As much as Oscar got on his nerves sometimes, Jeremy missed him. He missed the sound of Oscar's feet pounding up and down the hallway. Oscar calling out from one end of the house, shouting at the top of his lungs instead of just taking time to find the person and speaking to them in a normal tone. He missed the non-stop conversations only

Oscar could manage, careering from one topic to the next over the dinner table with hardly a break in between.

Now the house was like he imagined a funeral parlor would be. Hushed sobbing, silence and darkness. The curtains in the front room had been drawn ever since Oscar had disappeared. Jeremy had tried to concentrate at school. He was a senior, and every class mattered. But it was difficult. His mind kept veering toward Oscar, wondering where he was and if he was okay.

Is he cold? Is he hungry? Is he scared? Is he hurt? Where is he?

.And then there was the guilt. For all the times he'd yelled at his brother, told him to shut up. Refused to play ball. Called him stupid and other nasty names. For not being brave enough to stop Malcolm beating him. Shame washed over him.

Jeremy had never been a fan of church, but as he looked up at the darkening sky, he found himself pleading for help.

"Dear God. I'm sorry for all the nasty things I said. Please, please help me find him. He's my baby brother and I love him. We all do. I didn't mean it when I said I hate him. I don't. You know I don't. We need him back. Please God."

The sounds of other voices came to him in the distance. No doubt it was members of the search party, looking for Oscar further upstream from the spring-fed creek that ran through the forest. When Cassie had raised the possibility that Oscar had run away, Jeremy had immediately discounted it. But now, out in the forest with the dark encroaching, he thought back to the last time he'd seen his brother. The thought that Oscar might have run away and that Jeremy might have had something to do with it devastated him.

I should have just done the stupid chores… Then none of this would have happened…

With that thought, he continued to fight his way through the thick undergrowth, more determined than ever. He was well away from the more familiar hiking trails. Though he was doubtful Oscar would have gone so deep into the bush on his own, it was possible. Especially if he'd run off blindly after his argument with Malcolm and had kept running without thinking about where he was going.

Jeremy and Cassie had already walked the well-trodden bush tracks. This time, Jeremy had decided to try other, less-used trails. Every now and then, he called his brother's name, but so far he'd heard nothing. Still, he was determined to stay out there as long as it took. He wouldn't leave until he found him.

Pushing forward, Jeremy cried out when a low-hanging branch caught him across the face. Pain exploded in his cheek and brought tears to his eyes. He swiped at the branches, angry and scared and irritated that he'd been out there at least three hours and so far, he'd found no sign to suggest Oscar had been there. Taking a moment to catch his breath, he opened his backpack and pulled out one of the water bottles. He gulped down some water, wiped the perspiration off his brow and drew in a few breaths. At the same time, he planned his next move.

He could continue on the downward slope and end up at the creek. Or he could move higher and aim for the rocky outcrop not far from the caves. The detective had asked him if Oscar had ever gone there and Jeremy had told him no.

But what if I'm wrong? What if Oscar made his way to the caves? What if he's been there all this time?

If he was inside one of the caves, he wouldn't hear the searchers calling. Maybe that's why no one had found him?

With renewed resolve, Jeremy dropped the water bottle back in the pack and pulled out the torch. It wouldn't be too long and he'd need it. Already, the light was fast disappearing, especially this far into the forest. It would be as black as midnight in the caves. The thought gave him pause. He'd never been in the caves at night. They were spooky enough in the daylight. But this was about Oscar. Jeremy needed to find him.

Moving forward with determined strides, he adjusted the weight of the backpack on his shoulders. Picking up his pace, he stopped yelling Oscar's name in an effort to preserve his energy. The climb toward the caves was steep and it wasn't long before he was out of breath. Panting hard, he pushed on. The sense of urgency that had taken root inside him forced him to increase the length of his strides. He batted away branches and thorny bushes that tore at his legs, his only focus was getting to the top.

Moments later, his boot caught on an exposed tree root. Before he knew what was happening, he'd tumbled down the steep incline end over end, arms flailing, cartwheeling, legs flying until at last he came to a stop.

He gasped for breath, winded. A lump popped out on his forehead. He touched it gingerly and winced at the pain. It felt as big as an egg. Cautiously, he flexed his hands, stretched out his arms and legs. He was relieved nothing appeared to be broken. Pulling himself up, he gingerly got to his feet. Thankfully his legs held. He looked around and realized he was almost back where he'd started.

"Shit." Despair washed over him. He cursed again and then firmed up his resolve. It was a momentary setback. All he had to do was set out again and keep walking until he reached the top of the hill.

Come on… I can do this… I can do this for Oscar…

He looked around for his backpack. The torch had also gone. And then he saw a small yellow beam far below him. Picking his way carefully down, he found himself in the bottom of a ravine. The torch lay on its side, sending a thin beam of light along the ground. As he bent to pick it up, his gaze fell on a large bundle. It was covered in leaves and branches.

His heart skipped a beat. Training the beam of light on his discovery, he determined that the bundle was a sleeping bag. He inched closer. To his horror, he saw what looked like a pair of shoes protruding from one end.

Not just shoes. Nike cross trainers. The same kind of shoes Oscar wore…

With his heart thumping double time and his chest so tight he could barely breathe, Jeremy forced himself closer. He crouched and gingerly lifted the tiniest corner of the sleeping bag. He saw a jean-clad leg. And then the smell hit him, and he keeled over backwards, covering his nose and mouth, dry retching and gasping for breath.

Oscar!

As realization dawned, he screamed out his pain. *No, no, no! Oscar!* Tears poured from his eyes as he stumbled blindly in the dark, trying to get his head around the gruesome discovery. *What to do… What to do…* Finally, he fumbled for his phone.

Trace had finished his coffee long ago and no longer had an excuse to linger in Cassie's kitchen, but the truth was, he didn't want to leave. He enjoyed her company and sharing conversation with her, even when it touched on the painful subject of her missing brother. Still, it was getting late, and he had plenty to do before he'd have the luxury of turning in for the night—namely recapping with the boss of the SES and the head of the dog squad and going over anything they might have found. Then there was coordinating the search which would continue first thing in the morning.

The sound of Cassie's phone ringing interrupted his thoughts. He was in the process of rinsing his mug in the sink when he heard her gasp. He half-turned toward her and his gut clenched. She'd turned as white as a ghost. A second later, her phone dropped from her fingers and landed on the floor. It bounced once and then stopped. With dread flooding through his veins, Trace bent and picked it up.

Cassie still looked shell-shocked, so pale and still he felt another frisson of concern. He glanced down at the screen and saw her caller had been Jeremy. He handed her the phone. She took it blindly, not even looking at it. She ended the call and set the phone on the counter.

"What is it?" he forced himself to ask.

He saw her throat working, but no sound came out. He took a step toward her. "Cassie? Was that Jeremy?"

She gave a jerky nod.

He reached for her hands, unable to help himself. They were cold and clammy. He squeezed them reassuringly. "Cassie? Please. Talk to me. What is it?"

She turned haunted eyes toward him. His heart clenched at the pain in them.

"He... He found Oscar. He... He's dead."

Her voice cracked with emotion. And then she was sobbing like her heart was breaking. And no doubt it was. He winced at the devastation on her face. The sight and sound of her grief was so soul-destroying, Trace could no more stand by without offering her comfort than he could bring her brother back to life. With a muffled curse, he drew her in his arms and held her close.

Her whole body shook with the force of her grief. Tears poured down her cheeks. Within moments, his shirt was soaked. Though he wanted to hold her for as long as she needed, there was work to be done. Slowly, he released his hold and stepped back.

"I'm so sorry, Cassie. I'm so sorry." There was nothing more to say.

With the pressure of what he needed to do weighing heavily, Trace turned his back on her and moved further away. Using Cassie's phone, he called Jeremy and obtained details of his location.

"We'll be there as soon as we can," he assured the boy. "Hang tight."

He set Cassie's phone on the counter and pulled out his own. In quick succession, he called the station and requested officers attend the scene. He called the head of the SES and informed them Oscar had been found. The search would be immediately terminated. He also called the leader of the dog squad, who'd already called it quits for the day. Calls were made to the forensics team. Though Trace didn't yet know how Oscar had died, he wasn't taking any chances. He wanted to document and preserve any evidence in case it was needed. Then he organized mobile lighting and all the other things he thought they might need. Finally, he called the morgue.

Cassie walked on leaden feet through the thick bushland, following closely behind Trace. It was dark and hard to see, but she kept moving forward like a sleepwalker, one numb step at a time. Later, she wouldn't be able to recall the journey, just the incredible feeling of pain. She spied Jeremy at the bottom of the ravine and hurried toward him. The moment he saw her, he closed the distance between them at a run. Throwing himself at her, he clung to her gasping and sobbing, completely and utterly distraught.

She thought how it must have been for him, not only discovering Oscar's body, but having to stay with him, alone and in the dark, waiting for help to arrive. His whole body shook with the force of his grief. Her tears mingled with his as they mourned the loss of their brother.

All of a sudden, mobile lights were activated, bathing the area in so much illumination it looked like the sun was out.

There were people everywhere. Some had "Forensics" printed in yellow on the back of their overalls. Others were from the morgue. Then there were the police. Trace and his brother and at least five other officers, some in uniform, some—like Trace—in plain clothes. Finally, there were the reporters.

Somehow word had spread, and they'd flocked to the site like vultures. TV crews, photographers and reporters swarmed around, like blowflies on a carcass. No doubt they'd heard something over the police radio. Cassie hated the attention her brother's death was garnering, knowing the worst moments in her life would be all over the morning news to be picked over, analyzed, talked about... But there was nothing she could do about that.

Blue-and-white checked police tape cordoned off the site where Oscar lay. Cassie's gaze kept going back there, time and time again. She couldn't see much past the lumpy sleeping bag but knowing her brother's body lay inside was excruciating beyond anything she'd ever experienced.

She was hardly aware of releasing her hold on Jeremy. She took a step toward the body. Then another. She walked like she was in a dream. Or a nightmare. The noise, the crowd, the hubbub drifted away. Her vision narrowed to that bulky form. She took another step in that direction. A roar sounded in her ears. She kept moving forward, oblivious to everything around her. The only thing she was certain of was that she had to see her brother, had to see for herself that this was him.

And then Trace was there before her, blocking her path. His expression was somber, his eyes wretched and resigned.

"Cassie. Please. You don't want to see him like this."

Feeling tortured, she lifted her gaze to his. "I have to see him."

He touched her gently on the arm. "No, you don't."

Tears burned in her eyes. "Are you sure it's him?"

He nodded sadly. "Yes. It's him."

She stood frozen to the spot, unable to move, to breathe, to speak. She felt Trace take her by the elbow and lead her back to where Jeremy stood. Her brother put his arm around her shoulders and drew her close. She clung to him, taking comfort from his strong and steady heartbeat beneath her ear.

Cassie couldn't say how long they stood there, but at one point Trace approached them again.

"Jeremy? Do you mind if I ask you a few questions?"

Cassie dropped her arms from around her brother's waist and stepped away. Jeremy looked at Trace and nodded.

"What made you look down here? It's a long way off the trail."

Jeremy closed his eyes briefly and compressed his lips. "I tripped over a tree root and rolled all the way down the hill. I lost my backpack and torch somewhere along the way. I saw the torch shining in the ravine, so I went down to fetch it. That's...when I found him."

"Well, your brother was very lucky you had that fall. It's possible we would never have found him down here otherwise."

Jeremy stared at the ground, his eyes filling with fresh tears. Cassie moved closer and squeezed his arm.

"That looks like a nasty bump on your forehead," Trace said. "Make sure you let the paramedics check you out."

Jeremy touched the swelling on his forehead and slowly nodded. Cassie could tell he'd forgotten the injury was there.

"How did he die?" Cassie asked numbly.

Trace regarded her with compassion. "He was stabbed. A single knife wound."

Cassie gasped with disbelief. "Murdered?" It was like a horrible movie. She felt like she was on the outside looking in, like this was happening to someone else. It was someone else's brother who'd been murdered.

Trace nodded. "Yes. We also found his phone," he added quietly. "It was in the sleeping bag with his body. It was switched off."

"That's why it kept going through to voicemail," Cassie said, dazed.

"Yes."

She shook her head, bewildered, devastated. "Who could have done this?"

"We're following a few leads."

His tone was gentle, his words vague, slightly dismissive. Cassie could tell he'd only said that to appease her. It filled her with irrational anger. Heat suffused her cheeks. She glared up at him. "You need do better than that! You need to find out who killed my brother!"

He gazed at her and nodded once. "You have my word."

Until then, Cassie had clung to the hope Oscar had fallen and hurt himself, maybe hit his head, knocked himself unconscious and had died a natural death. Now that hope had been demolished. *Her brother had been murdered.* There was someone out there who'd hated him enough to kill him and leave him lying in a ravine where he might never have been found. He'd been left like refuse for the animals and birds to scavenge. It had only been luck that Jeremy had found him.

She couldn't think past the fact Oscar was never coming home. Never again would he come bounding through the front door, laughing and grinning and talking a mile a minute. Never again would he pick bunches of brightly colored flowers growing along the side of the road, thrusting them toward her, waiting for her smile. Never again would he burst into her bedroom waving his phone in the air, excited to show her his latest video. Never again.

"Can we go then?" she asked.

Trace nodded. "Yes. I'll get someone to escort you back to your car. I'll need you to formally identify Oscar. I'll stop by in the morning and let you know what time."

"Can't I do that now?"

Trace's voice was gentle. "Let's wait until morning."

As Cassie and Jeremy and a uniformed officer made their way back up the hill, they were approached by several reporters. The glowing red light on the TV cameras told her they were rolling.

"Cassie! Can you tell us whether it's your brother? Have they found Oscar?"

The officer shielded them with his arm and kept walking. Cassie and Jeremy followed. Cassie wanted nothing more than to turn tail and run without uttering another word and find somewhere dark and quiet to grieve, but then she paused. The TV stations had a wide audience. They could appeal to a large number of people with information to step forward. Getting Oscar's story out there might help find his killer. If there was even the slightest chance of that, she had to take it.

And so, she squared her shoulders and lifted her head and stared straight down the camera.

Telling relatives about the loss of a loved one was one of the toughest aspects of Trace's job. Though he loved everything about policing—especially in a small town where most people knew each other and there were often several generations of the same family living there—nothing prepared him adequately for having to bring tragic news.

He'd spoken again with Cassie. She'd assured him she wanted to be the one to tell her mother. Trace had offered to be there with her when she broke the news, but she'd been adamant she'd prefer to do it alone.

Trace had taken Jeremy aside before they left and had asked that he stay close by his sister. She was going to need his support. Trace would take Cassie to the morgue after the autopsy to formally identify her brother. Right now, it was going on for nine and everyone was beat, including him. He yearned for sleep, but the night was far from over for him yet.

As he drove through the quiet streets, it was obvious word of Oscar's murder had spread. Bad news had a way of doing that. Most houses were dark and still, like the occupants had already retired for the night. Perhaps the good people of Broken had retreated to the safety and security of their homes, locking out the evil that had visited their town that night. Though it wasn't public knowledge that Oscar's body had been found, Trace was certain the rumors to that effect had already spread.

The trip to the police station took him past the street where Oscar and his family lived. Trace instinctively turned his head in that direction and then cursed.

"Fuck."

A large mob was gathered outside Kevin Turner's house. Even from this distance, Trace saw the anger on their faces. There was no doubt they thought Turner was responsible for what had happened to Oscar.

Some of them held placards: *Pedophile. Monster. Get out of our town. Kill the pedo.* Trace's gut clenched. Reaching for the two-way radio handset, he called for backup, grateful when Zac immediately responded.

"I'm at the Turner house," Trace told him. "There's a mob here and they've decided Kevin's to blame. It's going to get ugly."

Zac assured him a contingent of officers would be there as soon as they could. Trace pulled the cruiser up to the curb opposite Turner's house and climbed out. Before he made it all the way across the road, someone threw a brick at Turner's front window. Glass splintered in every direction. The mob let out a cheer.

Feeling grim, Trace pushed his way through the crowd until he was at the very front. He eyeballed each and every one of them, calling to the ones he knew by name.

"Fred, you have no business here."

"Jack, go home to your wife and son. Hold them close."

"Peter, put down that placard. There's no place for that here."

He looked around at the rest of them. "That goes for all of you. I understand your need for justice, but this isn't the way to go about it. I promise you, there will be a full and transparent investigation. We have yet to formally establish how Oscar died, but we will and if someone was involved, we will find them. That's our job. *Our* job. The police. Understand?"

He gave the crowd a hard look. "Now, clear out before I arrest you for disorderly conduct."

"He's a sicko, a kiddy fiddler," someone shouted.

"Yeah! I saw it on the news!" someone responded.

"Don't tell me you're siding with a pedophile?" came another angry voice.

Trace resisted the urge to answer them. It didn't matter what he said, it wouldn't satisfy this crowd. They were angry and upset and they were baying for blood. They suspected one of their own had been murdered and they wanted answers. They wanted someone punished. They didn't care how Oscar had died, or the principles of justice or evidence. All they wanted was for someone to pay.

Anything Trace said would only further inflame the situation. He scanned the crowd again. He knew at least half of the people there. They were mostly good, law-abiding, church-going people. But tonight, they were angry and he needed to tread carefully.

He appealed to them once again. "Most of you know me. I was born and bred in Broken. My parents still live here. I went to school with some of your children. You know I'll do everything I can to get to the truth and find out what happened to Oscar Webster and whether he met with foul play. But I'll do it on my terms. By the book. Like I always do."

"Right now, we have yet to formally establish cause of death. But if there's evidence of someone's involvement, rest assured, we'll leave no stone unturned as we work to uncover them. So please, go home and hug your children. Tell them you love them and thank God you aren't in the same situation. The Webster family is going to need your support over the coming weeks. Focus on helping them and let the police do their job."

There was a grumbling among the crowd. Trace held his breath. At the same time, he stood his ground. From the corner of his eye, he saw Zac pull up in another police cruiser, followed by two more squad cars. The officers climbed out of their vehicles and formed a line behind the crowd. A silent, but threatening presence if anyone didn't do as they'd been told.

Slowly, grudgingly, people began to walk away. Some tossed their placards on the ground. Others tucked them under their arms and took them with them. Gradually, the crowd dispersed. Trace let out his breath.

He looked at Zac and the other officers who'd come to his aid. "Thanks, boys. Appreciate the help."

Zac patted him on the shoulder. "That's what we're here for."

"Do you mind checking on Turner? He might need some assistance securing that broken window."

"Sure thing," Zac said.

Trace merely nodded his thanks. "Now for the autopsy," he said grimly.

Chapter Eleven

It took Trace an hour to drive to the Lidcombe Morgue. He was grateful to discover chief forensic pathologist Samantha Wolfe was on call and was already gowned and gloved up in preparation for Oscar's autopsy. The boy's naked body had been laid out on a steel gurney. The single stab wound that pierced the boy's chest in the vicinity of the heart was now clearly visible.

Samantha looked up as he entered the autopsy suite. Her eyes crinkled in a grin. "Detective Barrington. It's nice to see you again."

Trace offered her a small smile. "We need to stop meeting like this, Doctor Wolfe. People will start talking."

She laughed. Happily married to another detective, his quip was taken in the way he'd intended. In fact, it had been more than six months since he'd been there. One of the benefits of living in a small country town was that homicides were few and far between. The last time he'd been at the morgue was for the autopsy of Arthur Miles who'd been found dead in his bed by his granddaughter. He was eighty-nine and there had been no signs of foul play. Trace hazarded a guess that Arthur had died from natural causes, but the old guy hadn't seen a doctor for more than twelve months and accordingly, the law demanded an autopsy.

As it turned out, Arthur had died from a heart attack. Case closed. Trace wished Oscar Webster's investigation could be wrapped up so easily.

While Samantha photographed and x-rayed the body, Trace stood off to one side and tried not to look at the small form on the table. Cassie had said her brother was fourteen, but physically he looked younger. Fine-featured, with skinny arms and legs, he was still going through puberty. His dark auburn hair reminded Trace of Cassie.

He thought of the pain she and her family were going through and a wave of anger washed over him. He clenched his fists. Someone had killed their brother and son and it was up to Trace to find who'd done it. His mind skittered to Turner. He was definitely on Trace's radar, but there would be no lynching on his watch. Like he'd told the angry mob, he did things by the book and he'd meant that.

"Nothing on the x-rays," Samantha murmured, gazing at the illuminated screen on the wall behind him.

She picked up a measuring tape and returned to the steel gurney. She placed the tape at one end of the small incision in Oscar's chest and measured the wound.

"Just over an inch wide."

"So, a decent-sized knife then," he said.

"Yes."

"Any idea how long?"

"Patience, Detective."

He shot her a wry look. "Any signs of sexual assault?" he asked when she bent over and made her way down the front of Oscar's body, closely examining every inch of his skin with a magnifying glass before turning him over and repeating the process on the opposite side, from the top of his head to the soles of his small feet.

Samantha remained silent a moment while she finished her inspection. At last, she stood and shook her head. "No."

Trace felt a surge of relief.

"But he has evidence of trauma and bruising on his left cheek which means he sustained a blow prior to his death."

"What kind of blow?"

"Blunt force trauma. If I had to guess, I'd say he was punched in the face."

"Do you have a time of death?"

"The cooler temperatures have slowed down decomposition. It's my guess he's been dead about three days."

Trace nodded grimly. *Three days.* That meant Oscar had been killed shortly after he went missing. Samantha picked up the magnifying glass again and this time peered closely at Oscar's face. A change in her body language made Trace tense.

"What is it?" he asked.

"It looks like we might have a foreign hair." She put down the magnifying glass and picked up some tweezers. Carefully, she extracted a single, short dark hair that appeared to have been snagged in Oscar's own. She dropped it into a stainless-steel dish.

Trace felt a frisson of excitement. It was possible they'd just found something to connect them with the killer.

"Anything else?" he asked.

Samantha shot him another wry grin. "What did I say about patience, Detective?"

Once again, she used the magnifying glass to closely examine Oscar's face. After a while, she stood and shook her head. "No. I'm sorry. That looks like everything."

Trace nodded. "At least we have something."

"Yes. I'll swab his mouth, his anus and his genitals for body fluids, just to be sure."

Trace watched as Samantha did as she'd said and stored the samples in pathology tubes to be sent to a lab for analysis. Then she picked up a scalpel and quickly and efficiently made the Y incision. Trace took a few steps back, content to watch from a distance. Though this wasn't the first autopsy he'd attended, they were always something to be endured, especially ones like this where a child was involved and the stench of decomposition hung heavy in the air. After removing and weighing several organs, Samantha once again reached for her measuring tape.

"The blade's gone between two ribs and entered into the upper atrium of the heart. My guess is the victim was stabbed with a medium-sized straight blade, between seven and eight inches long."

"Like a hunting knife?"

"Yes. Or a decent-sized kitchen knife. The kind that a lot of people have in their knife block."

"So, a single stab wound was the cause of death?"

"Yes. He would have died quickly. I've still to process his clothes and shoes and the sleeping bag in which he was found. If I find anything else, I'll let you know. Otherwise, it will be all in my report."

Any response Trace might have made was drowned out by the sound of the Stryker saw. Once again, he stood back while Samantha did her job. When she was done, Trace swallowed a sigh of relief. After thanking Samantha for her time, he pulled off his mask and dropped it in the medical waste bin on the way out of the room.

It was going on for midnight. He was beat. He thought of Cassie and her family and the awful pain they must be going through. He wished there was something he could do. He'd never felt quite so helpless. The fact they still had no clue who was responsible was frustrating and even though he was weighed down with fatigue, there would be no sleep for him tonight.

Blowing his breath out on a weary sigh, he climbed into his cruiser and headed for home.

The early morning sunshine peeked through Cassie's half-opened curtains, blinding her. She sat up and glanced at the clock. It was nearly seven. Her head pounded. Her eyes felt gritty and sore. She'd barely slept between dreams of Oscar— nightmares more like it.

He'd been calling for her, somewhere deep in the bush. She'd been searching for him, walking around in circles, getting more and more confused. The sky was dark purple and blue, like a fresh bruise. She heard him calling, but she couldn't pinpoint his location. Each time she started forward, his voice disappeared. Then he was there, standing in front of her, his face and hair caked with dirt. He held up his hands. They were dripping with blood. He started laughing and then his face crumpled into tears.

"Cassie… Help me… Please… Cassie…"

She'd woken with her heart beating so fast it felt like it would thump right out of her chest. Her hair was matted with sweat. The sheets and blankets were twisted around her legs and Oscar's voice still echoed in her ears.

The night was finally over, but guilt and pain and dread lingered in her veins. She felt weighed down by them, unable to move. There was a part of her, the more logical part, that knew she wasn't responsible for Oscar's death. But the other part—the emotional part—felt the complete opposite.

She was his big sister. She'd always looked out for him. There were ten years between them. She'd taken on the role of caring for him almost from the day he was born. And especially after their father was sent to jail. Oscar had only been a baby. Too young to understand. Cassie had taken it upon herself to make sure he never felt their father's loss. In some ways, she probably overcompensated. His autism had been another contributor to that.

As their mother's health had deteriorated, Cassie took on more and more responsibility for running the household. It hadn't been easy, but she'd done it. She loved her brothers fiercely and she loved her mother too. It fell to her to make their lives run as smoothly as she could.

But Oscar was dead—murdered. She hadn't been there to protect him when it mattered most. She didn't know if she'd ever get over the guilt.

She bit her lip in an effort to hold back a rush of tears. She'd cried on and off for most of the night. Her eyes were swollen and sore. No doubt she looked a mess. Not that she cared. It was a school day, but there was no way she could bring herself to walk into her classroom and carry on as if nothing had happened; as if her life hadn't fallen apart. And then she remembered she had to attend the morgue and provide a formal identification of Oscar.

The tears that had threatened now leaked from her eyes and slid down her cheeks. She turned her face into her pillow to muffle the sounds of her grief. A few moments later, the sound of car tires crunching on the gravel in their driveway registered in her consciousness.

Swiping at her eyes, she climbed out of bed and padded down the hallway. She pushed aside the curtains in the front room and saw Trace climbing out of his police cruiser. Though he walked tall with effortless strides, as he drew closer, she saw the grim expression etched into his features. Her heart clenched. She'd spent the past hours hoping it had all been a horrible mistake.

He's here to take me to the morgue...

She went back to her room and quickly threw on some clothes and opened the door before he had a chance to knock. Pulling it closed behind her, she stepped out onto the veranda. His expression remained grim, but concern and compassion filled his blue eyes.

"Cassie. How are you holding up?"

She gave him a half-shrug, aware that he wasn't really expecting a response. She hugged herself against the cool morning air. She wore jeans and a light cotton blouse, the first things she'd found when she'd reached into her cupboard. She hadn't given any thought to a coat when she stepped outside.

"Are you cold?" Trace asked, already pulling off his jacket.

She opened her mouth to protest, but he settled it around her shoulders and it felt so warm and comforting, she couldn't bring herself to part with it. With a soft sigh, she drew it more tightly around her and tried to ignore the spicy smell of his cologne that now surrounded her.

"Thank you," she murmured.

"How's your mother?" he asked.

Cassie sucked in a breath and blew it out. "About how you'd expect. As much as I dislike my stepfather, it would be better if Malcolm was here. Over the past five years, she's come to rely on him to get her through difficult situations."

"I'm surprised we haven't been able to locate him. It's like he's disappeared into thin air."

"No such luck, I'll bet," Cassie replied.

What she really wanted to know was what the autopsy had revealed and whether it had provided any clues to Oscar's killer. She dragged in another breath. "Tell me about the autopsy. What did you find out?"

Trace's expression softened. "The forensic pathologist confirmed he died from a single stab wound to the heart. It's estimated he was killed shortly after he disappeared."

She bit her lip on a fresh wave of pain and did her best to process that information. "So, all that time we were looking for him, he was already...gone?"

"Yes."

"Was it quick?" she rasped.

Trace seemed to know what she meant. "Yes."

Cassie's heart clenched. *Thank you Lord…*

"So what do we do now?" she asked.

"If you're up to it, we'll go to the morgue. I'll drive you there."

She nodded quickly, eager to get this over with and then thought of something else.

"Oscar's phone," she said. "Can we have it back?"

"Eventually," Trace said quietly. "Right now, it's with forensics. They're looking for fingerprint and DNA evidence. They're also checking the phone log and texts. Hopefully they find something that links the phone to the killer." He paused and then added, "You mentioned something about Oscar spending his money on an Apple watch. How often did he wear it?"

"He wore it all the time. Was he not wearing it when you found him?"

"No. The only thing he had on him was his phone."

She frowned. "He loved that watch. It cost him a lot of money. He saved up for a long time. He never took it off."

"I'll make a note and keep an eye out for it. What did it look like?"

"It had a silver face and a navy-blue band." And then Cassie remembered something else. "Did you find out anything about the red jacket? Did it belong to Oscar?"

"Not yet. I'm still waiting on forensics to get back to me. We're running some tests to determine if it definitely belonged to your brother."

Cassie closed her eyes against another wave of pain. It seemed every mention of Oscar had that effect on her. The magnitude of having to come to terms with her brother's death was overwhelming. She shivered, remembering her mother's reaction to the news. Marie Russell's howls of pain had sent a fresh rush of agony to Cassie's heart. She'd wanted to howl and wail and scream about the injustice of it, like her mother had, but she didn't have the luxury of grieving like that. Her family needed her, especially with Malcolm still absent. They were relying on her to be strong.

Her mother and Jeremy were in a worst state than she was. The minute she came to a stop in their driveway after returning from the scene, Jeremy had leaped out of the car and headed straight for his room. He'd been holed up there all night, refusing to talk, to eat, to come out. Their mother was just as bad, almost comatose with grief. Cassie had been forced to call the ambulance. A paramedic had administered a sedative. Her family was a mess. There was no way Cassie could fall apart, no matter how much she was inclined.

She looked up at the tall, broad-shouldered detective. His quiet strength was like a drug she needed, yet was fighting hard to resist. She wanted so much to lay her head on his muscled chest, even for a moment. What would it feel like if she leaned into him, let him take over her burdens for just a while? The feeling was overwhelming. She yearned to give into it...

She swayed toward him but pulled herself up just in time. If her grief hadn't been so consuming, she might have had room for embarrassment. To her relief, he said nothing.

"Are you ready?" he asked.

She gave him a jerky nod and followed him toward his car. They made the trip to the morgue in silence. An hour after they left Broken, Trace turned into the parking lot of the Lidcombe Morgue.

Cassie had never been to a morgue. She was filled with dread at the thought of walking inside the building and coming face to face with her dead brother. Still, someone had to do it and she couldn't expect Jeremy or her mother to front up. She was just glad she had Trace beside her to see her through it.

As if sensing her tension, he reached across the console and squeezed her hand. "It'll only take a few minutes and I'll be with you the whole time."

She nodded, beyond words. She climbed out of the cruiser and waited for Trace. They walked toward the building together. The concrete-and-glass structure that comprised the forensic medicine and coroners court complex looked deceptively inviting. A modern, architecturally inspired building with expansive grounds and neat hedges didn't hint at the depressing events that occurred within. A huge Norfolk pine tree grew near the entrance. Looking up at it, Cassie was weirdly reminded of the beach.

Inside, all references to the beach disappeared. The complex had been opened in 2019 and had cost more than ninety million dollars to construct. Everything was shiny and new and ascetically pleasing, but that didn't alleviate the hard lump of dread that had lodged itself in her stomach.

Trace shot her another quick look. Once again, he reached out and wordlessly squeezed her hand. "Wait here," he murmured.

She stood in the reception area and watched while he approached the woman who sat behind the desk. He pulled out his police credentials. The girl smiled and nodded. Trace turned and moved back to her side.

"We're right to go through." His gaze was reassuringly steady. "You ready?"

She drew in a shaky breath and nodded. "I guess."

She followed Trace and they were shown into a small room with a large glass window. She looked at Trace in surprise.

"So I don't have to...be in the same room?"

"Not if you don't want to," Trace said gently.

Cassie closed her eyes and drew in a breath. She eased it out, along with some of the dread that had held her taut.

"I... I don't want to. I'd rather remember him alive and happy and smiling..." Her voice drifted off. She looked at Trace. "Is that terrible of me?"

"Not at all," he assured her. "I'm not here to judge you, Cassie. We need a formal identification. That's it. We'll be in and out as quickly as that takes. I promise."

"Okay."

With that, Trace pressed a button. A few moments later someone dressed in hospital scrubs appeared on the other side of the window pushing a steel gurney. The body was covered in surgical drapes. The gurney was wheeled close enough to the window that Cassie could see the face was exposed. Her heart clenched with pain.

Oscar...

She must have made a sound, though she was unaware that she'd done so. Trace was beside her in an instant. His arm went around her shoulders. She leaned into his strength.

"Cassie, can you tell me who that is?"

Her chest was so tight she could barely breathe. Tears filled her eyes and slid silently down her cheeks. She brought her fist up to her mouth in an effort to hold back a sob.

"Y-yes. It's...Oscar. It's my little brother."

Unable to hold back the pain any longer, she turned blindly toward Trace and buried her face against his chest. His strong arms came around her and held her close. When her sobs had finally subsided, he released his hold. She pulled away. Her gaze was drawn back to the window. She almost sagged with relief when she discovered the body had been taken away again.

"You did so well, Cassie. So strong and brave. Let's get out of here."

She sniffed and swiped at her eyes and gave him a jerky nod. Together, they turned and left the way they'd come.

Chapter Twelve

Cassie had been silent for so long, Trace was concerned. He understood how traumatic it was to have to identify a loved one in the morgue, but in his experience, it was better to talk about it than to ignore what she'd been through. Her eyes were still red from her crying; her skin was pale; her lips taut. He could only imagine the thoughts running through her head. He tried to think of some way to distract her; to get her through the next hour before they returned to Broken.

"What made you become a teacher?" he asked.

She started at his question. No doubt her career was the last thing on her mind. Still, she seemed to give his question some consideration. The frown lines that had creased her forehead disappeared.

"I've always loved kids, loved being around them. At one stage I thought about doing something in childcare, but then I decided I wanted a different kind of interaction. I wanted to make a difference in someone's life."

She blushed, as if embarrassed by her revelation. Trace hurried to reassure her.

"I have nothing but admiration for teachers, especially high school teachers. These days that's a tough gig."

"Yes, we face a whole lot of different challenges than when we were at school, but kids haven't changed. They still have the same wants and needs and desires, the same trials and tribulations, the same insecurities..."

"Were you an insecure teenager?" he asked, curious.

She compressed her lips. "You really don't remember, do you?"

Trace frowned. "Remember what?"

Cassie closed her eyes briefly and then reopened them. She turned to look at him. "We went to high school together."

He blinked in surprise. "In Broken?"

"Yes. You were a couple of years ahead of me. Our paths never crossed, but I knew who you were. Zac was in my year. He doesn't remember me either."

Trace opened his mouth to speak, but she cut him off.

"It's okay. I don't blame either of you. You're Barringtons. You and your brothers and sisters were the most popular kids in school. I was invisible to most people. When they weren't ignoring me, they were giving me a hard time. That's another reason why I went into teaching. I wanted to create better memories of high school."

He felt like he'd been sucker punched. His head whirled with disbelief. He couldn't imagine not noticing a girl like Cassie Webster. And yet apparently, he had. And then another thought occurred to him. He froze, hardly daring to voice it aloud.

"Did I...?"

"No. And neither did Zac. But plenty did. I was teased and tormented mercilessly in the playground. I spent most of my time in the library."

Trace stared at her, still trying to get his head around the fact someone who looked like her had escaped his attention. At the same time, he felt a wave of anger that she'd been bullied at school. Nothing got him madder than knowing someone was being picked on.

"Why were you bullied?" he asked softly.

She blew out her breath on a sigh. "My father went to jail when I was ten. My mother was... Well, you know about my mother. I took on the responsibility of my younger brothers. Let's just say I provided them with plenty of fodder. I learned to ignore the taunts and teasing and focus on school. And I was good at it. I was smart. I had an excellent memory. I guess that's why I got along so well with my teachers."

She paused. "I had some great teachers. The best. They saw my potential and wanted to do all they could for me to realize it. And I wanted to please them. It worked for all of us. I graduated top of my class. By then I knew what I wanted to do. Follow in their footsteps, inspire a whole lot of other kids to reach for the stars and follow their dreams."

"Wow," Trace said, filled with admiration. "I'm so glad things worked out for you. Good on you."

She offered him a shaky smile. "So, what about you? Why did you become a police officer?"

Trace smiled. "Believe it or not, I wanted to help people too. Not just kids. Everyone. That's my idea of what policing is: helping the community to be a better place to live."

"By keeping people safe?"

"Yes, I guess. And reminding people of what's expected; that they're only letting themselves down when they break the law. The laws are there for a reason. Mostly to keep us safe. If we all follow the rules, life tends to be a lot more pleasant."

She grimaced. "You're right about that."

He cursed under his breath. He hadn't meant it to come out sounding like he was referring to what had happened to Oscar.

"I'm sorry Cassie. I didn't mean—"

"It's all right Trace. I know what you meant. And you're right. If everyone obeyed the law and played by the rules there would be far less heartbreak, less pain. We'd live in a utopia of love and peace and everlasting happiness."

He closed his eyes briefly against the bitterness in her voice. He understood she was hurting. She was allowed to feel like that. Hell, if someone had murdered his brother, he'd feel the same. He glanced in her direction. Her arms were folded across her chest, her expression distant. Looking at her, he was filled with a burning need to find Oscar's killer. He'd bring Cassie and her family closure if it were the last thing he did.

They traveled the rest of the way in silence. Trace dropped Cassie back home. She climbed out of the cruiser and murmured her thanks. He merely inclined his head and then reversed out of her driveway. She turned toward the house, dreading walking inside.

The crowd of reporters and TV camera crew had mostly dispersed overnight. Only a handful remained. Now that Oscar's body had been found, there was no longer a need to camp out at his house. From now on, any updates would be released by the police. No doubt Trace would have his work cut out for him dealing with that. For now, Cassie needed to be with her family and to help support them through what was bound to be the most difficult time of their lives.

She'd just opened the front door and stepped into the hallway when the sound of a car door slamming intruded on her thoughts. She turned and spied Malcolm striding toward her, a camera crew closing in quickly behind him. Her hands curled into fists. As he drew closer, she could see his eyes were bloodshot and puffy. His face was covered in whiskers. His hair was greasy, his clothes unwashed. An unpleasant odor emanated from his body. She didn't know where he'd been the past few days, but he looked like hell.

And then her anger ignited. For all she knew, he was responsible for Oscar's death. And even if he didn't have anything to do with it, he'd abandoned his family when they'd most desperately needed him. They'd all been going mad with not knowing where Oscar was and trying to find him. Now they knew and it was devastating and here was Malcolm, crossing the veranda and coming toward her like nothing had happened.

"How *dare* you show your face here now," she cried.

Malcolm stopped a few feet away. "What the hell are you talking about? What's with the press?" He turned and snarled at the cameraman. "Get that fucking camera out of my face."

Cassie fought to maintain control. "I'm talking about Oscar." Her tone was low and deadly as she pulled him across the threshold and slammed the door behind him.

Guilt flashed in Malcolm's eyes. He averted his gaze. "What about Oscar? What's the little prick saying I did now?"

Cassie's hard-fought control snapped. Her fury knew no bounds. "That little *prick*, as you so eloquently describe him, is dead. *Murdered!*" she screamed. "And it seems you were the last person to see him."

Malcolm's face leeched of color. His eyes bulged with shock and disbelief. "*What?*"

Cassie's lip curled upwards with disgust. "Don't pretend you haven't heard. It's been all over the news. You must have seen the coverage. Everyone's been calling you non-stop. Me, Mom, the police. Didn't it occur to you to pick up the phone and call one of us back? Or were you scared we might discover what you did?"

Malcolm's face suffused with guilt. "I... I didn't do anything! I don't know what you're talking about! I was on a bender. I haven't seen the news since I took off. And my phone went flat. I left in such a hurry, I didn't take a charger."

"Oh yes, you left in a hurry all right. So fast no one even knew where you went. Not even your wife," Cassie spat.

Malcolm's eyes went cold. "I don't know what you think I did, but you're wrong. You've always had it in for me, Cassandra. I was never good enough for your mom. But did you ever stop to think that didn't matter to us? We loved each other. Then and now. You couldn't handle that, could you? You've always been jealous of what we have. You—"

"Malcolm? Honey? Is that you?" Marie's cry of joy was choked with emotion and tinged with disbelief.

Malcolm moved so close to Cassie she felt his hot, fetid breath on her cheek. He glared at her menacingly. "I couldn't give a fuck what you think of me, little miss goody two-shoes. Okay, I might not be the perfect husband, but I keep food on this table, pay the bills and I damn well love your mother. I might get a bit rough with your brother every now and then, but so what? That doesn't make me a killer. Now, get the fuck out of my way. My wife needs me."

In a haze of anger and crushing defeat, Cassie stepped aside and let him in.

Trace was halfway through a much-needed cup of coffee when his phone rang. He pulled it out of the pocket of his jacket and checked the screen.

Cassie.

He'd not long ago left her outside her house. He wondered if she'd left something behind in the cruiser. Or maybe she'd remembered something that might help their investigation? Quickly, he answered the call.

"Cassie."

"Trace. I-I'm sorry to call you."

"That's no problem. Call me anytime. What can I do for you?"

"It's Malcolm. He's turned up, arrived home. Just now."

Trace's heart leaped forward. "Where has he been? Does he know about Oscar?"

"He said he's been on a bender. He denies even knowing Oscar was missing. Said he didn't have any charge in his phone."

"Do you believe him?"

"I don't know. He certainly looks like he's been on a bender, but that would have happened afterwards anyway... How do we know?"

"Do you think he's capable of doing this to Oscar?" Trace asked quietly.

She was silent for so long he wasn't sure she was going to answer. "I don't know what to think," she finally said.

"Where's your stepfather now?"

"He's here, at home. He's talking with my mom."

"Give me ten minutes. I'll be there as soon as I can."

Trace ended the call and dropped the phone into his pocket. He gulped down the remains of his coffee and pushed away from his desk. After having a quick word with his boss, he grabbed the keys to the cruiser and left. He dodged the handful of reporters still camped outside the station, ignoring their shouted questions and pushed the cameras out of his face.

Though the media had their uses during an investigation, right now he had nothing to say and until he had something concrete, he preferred to say nothing. Let the reporters interview neighbors and townsfolk, keep Oscar alive in the hearts and minds of their viewers. That would keep the pressure on the killer, whoever he or she was.

In the meantime, Trace would go about methodically getting answers.

A smaller contingent of reporters was also gathered outside Cassie's house. No doubt they were still trying to get confirmation that the body was Oscar's. Word might have also gotten out that Oscar's stepfather had arrived home. In an effort to preserve a modicum of privacy, Trace had deliberately kept any mention of individual family members out of the press but Broken had a population of less than ten thousand and there was always someone prepared to talk.

Rumors and information had a way of spreading fast. No doubt the media now knew Malcolm had gone AWOL about the same time Oscar disappeared. It wouldn't take them long to start drawing their own conclusions, no matter what explanation Malcolm provided. It didn't matter that the police had yet to formally announce the body was Oscar's. A body of a boy had been found. Oscar was missing.

As for Trace, he also held reservations about Cassie's stepfather, but he believed in the ancient tenet of criminal law that a person was innocent until proven guilty and he was prepared to hear Malcolm out. Trace's evaluation of the man as a suspect would depend on Malcolm's answers. It was as simple as that.

Trace grabbed a notebook off the passenger seat and climbed out. He checked he had a pen in his shirt pocket. Once again ignoring the barrage of questions lobbed at him from the reporters, he crossed the lawn and climbed the steps. He knocked on the front door and waited for someone to answer it.

Cassie met him there a few moments later. "He's in the front room with my mother," she said.

Trace followed her into the room. Marie Russell lay sprawled out on the couch. Her hair was a mess. Her eyes were red, her skin splotchy. She wore a flannel nightgown stretched tightly across her bulk. Trace wondered if she'd slept there.

Malcolm Russell sat on a chair next to his wife, holding her hand. He stood as Trace entered the room. Cassie made the introductions.

"Malcolm, this is Detective Barrington. He wants to ask you some questions."

Malcolm offered Trace a limp handshake. Trace guessed him to be in his late forties. Average build, average height, black hair and a mustache flecked with gray, but there was a wiry strength about him that didn't go unnoticed. Though he reeked of alcohol and unwashed clothes and his overall appearance was disheveled, there was a keen intelligence in his red eyes that Trace didn't underestimate.

"Mr Russell. I'm sorry for the circumstances that have brought us together. How are you holding up?"

Malcolm gave a brisk nod and compressed his lips, obviously not expecting any understanding or compassion from a cop who was there to question him over his stepson's murder.

"To tell you the truth, I'm still in shock," Malcolm admitted. "This is the first I've heard that Oscar went missing and now you tell me he's dead... That's the last thing I expected."

Trace nodded. "Is there somewhere we can talk?"

Malcolm's gaze slid to his wife and then returned to Trace. "Here's fine. I have nothing to hide."

"Very well." Trace pulled out his notebook and pen. "Let's start with the basics. Name, age and occupation."

Malcolm provided Trace with the requested information. "How long have you been with National Parks?" Trace asked.

"Twenty years."

"You enjoy it?'

Malcolm shrugged. "I guess. I was never one for a desk job. There's always paperwork demanding my attention, but park ranging gets me outside more often than not."

"You like the bush?" Trace asked.

"Yes. It's always felt like home to me."

"Are you from around these parts, Malcolm?"

"Yes. Born and bred not far from here."

"So, you know the National Park well?"

"All ten thousand hectares of it."

Trace whistled. "That must have taken some doing."

Malcolm shrugged. "You cover a lot of ground in twenty years. Besides, I had a head start. I used to spend a lot of time camping in the bush when I was a kid. That's why I wanted to be a park ranger."

"Tell me about the night you last saw Oscar," Trace said.

Malcolm stared down at the carpet. Shame or guilt—Trace couldn't tell which—tinged his whiskered cheeks. He drew in a deep breath and eased it out and finally began to speak.

"I'm not too proud to admit that night wasn't my finest moment. I'd had a hard day at work dealing with paperwork that had gotten out of control. My boss was riding my ass for letting my reports fall behind. Then there's the pressure we've been under ever since the bush fires. People are always looking for someone to blame."

He dragged in another breath. "Anyway, I got home and I wasn't in the mood for any recalcitrance."

"Is that how you saw Oscar? Recalcitrant?" Trace asked.

Anger flashed in Malcolm's eyes. "Look, I know what you're thinking. Oscar was autistic. I should have cut him some slack. But that boy's smarter than Einstein. He knew the rules here as well as anyone and some days he seemed to go out of his way to piss me off. Okay, I was the adult and I should have had more self-control, but when I got home that night and discovered Oscar had shirked his responsibilities, I went off."

"What do you mean by 'shirked his responsibilities'?" Trace asked.

"It's Oscar's job to feed the dogs and chop the wood. We've been stockpiling it for weeks. The winter's coming and no one likes cutting wood in the freezing cold. I got home and realized it hadn't been done. He also hadn't fed the dogs. I blew up."

"What did you do?" Trace asked.

"I started yelling at him. He started shouting back. He kept saying it wasn't his job, which was bullsh—nonsense. That only made me madder. I grabbed hold of him and hauled him outside."

"Where did you go?" Trace asked.

"Up to the shed."

"Is that where you usually go when you discipline Oscar?"

Malcolm looked grim. He glanced toward his wife and then looked back at Trace. "Marie doesn't like it when we argue in front of her."

Trace glanced at Cassie's mother. Tears welled up in her eyes and slid silently down her cheeks. He heard a sound of distress from Cassie's direction, but kept his gaze trained on Malcolm.

"What happened in the shed?"

"Nothing. I yelled at Oscar a bit more. He yelled back. I might have shoved him a bit."

"Did you hit him?"

Color blazed across Malcolm's cheeks. He stared at the carpet. "Yes."

Trace heard Cassie gasp. Marie cried out. They already knew Malcolm had gotten physical in the past when it came to disciplining Oscar, but Trace could understand how hearing the admission so soon after Oscar's death would be painful.

"How many times did you hit him?" Trace asked, his voice deceptively quiet.

A fresh wave of shame highlighted Malcolm's cheeks. "Only once. I swear. I... I punched him in the face. The little bastard... He kept giving me cheek... I was angry." He looked at his wife. "I'm sorry, Marie. "I shouldn't have done it. I lost my temper. I was so ashamed afterwards. That's why I took off."

Trace continued to regard him steadily. "That wasn't the first time you'd hit him though, was it?"

Malcolm hung his head. His voice hitched with emotion. When he looked back at Trace, his eyes were full of pain and remorse. "No. But it was the first time I'd hit him in the face."

The conversation halted. The only sound was of Marie quietly sobbing on the couch. Malcolm made a move to comfort her, but Marie held up her arm and stayed him.

"Don't! Don't you dare! This is all your fault! My baby ran away because of you and now he's *dead!*" She collapsed into another round of sobbing. The sound of it raised hairs along Trace's arms. She sounded like a wounded animal.

His gaze was drawn to Cassie. She stood a short distance away, looking pale and distraught. Silent tears ran down her cheeks. Her fist was pressed against her mouth.

Trace forced his attention back to Malcolm. "What happened afterwards?"

Malcolm sucked in a ragged breath. "Oscar left."

"Where did he go?" Trace asked.

"I don't know. He stormed out of the shed. The door closed behind him. I didn't see which way he went. I just assumed he was going somewhere to sulk for a bit. That's what he usually does."

Trace thought about the sleeping bag Oscar had been found in. "Was he carrying anything?"

Malcolm shook his head. "No."

"Are you sure?" Trace asked.

"Yes."

"So, after Oscar left, what did you do?" Trace asked.

"I was still mad as hell and I was hurting too. I was ashamed of my behavior. Hitting him was wrong. I knew the best thing I could do was take off too. I needed some time to cool off."

"Where did you go?"

"I got in my truck and started driving. I ended up several towns away. Got drunk, gambled, lost track of time. I spent a few nights in a cheap motel, passed out most of the time.

Finally, I decided to get my shit together and return home." He lifted his hands in a sign of surrender. "And here I am. Walking straight into a shit storm the likes of which I could never have imagined."

In the ensuing silence, Trace blew out his breath and then tossed the notebook toward Malcolm.

"Write down the names of the motel, the bar, the casino... Anywhere you went these past few days."

Malcolm nodded, his expression morose. "You don't believe me."

"I like to be thorough," was all Trace said. "I'll also need forensics to take a look over your truck. Do you have a problem with that?"

"No."

"Good."

"How long will they have it?" Malcolm asked.

Trace shrugged. "As long as they need. I'll also need a DNA sample." He pulled out a swab kit from his pocket and handed it to Cassie's stepfather.

Malcolm's expression turned anxious. "I didn't do it, Detective! I swear! I had nothing to do with Oscar's death!"

Trace's answering smile was devoid of humor. "Then I guess you have nothing to worry about."

After collecting Malcolm's DNA sample and bidding both Cassie and her mother a brief farewell, Trace showed himself out. Once again, he ignored the torrent of questions tossed at him by the reporters and climbed into his car. He headed straight for the station.

As soon as he arrived, he filled in the paperwork for the lab and packaged up Malcolm's sample. Then he started making calls. His first call was to the manager of the motel where Malcolm said he'd stayed. The man on the other end of the phone identified himself as Gary Brown. Trace gave him Malcolm's description and waited for the man's response.

"I don't remember his name, but yeah. He was here. Drives an F250. Cherry red color. I remember admiring it in the parking lot. He keeps it in good nick."

"How long was he there for?" Trace asked.

"Let me check the computer," Gary said.

Trace heard the tapping of a keyboard and then the man said, "Looks like he checked in late Sunday night. Checked out this morning. Paid his bill in full with a credit card."

"Do you have any surveillance cameras in the vicinity?" Trace asked.

"Sure do."

"Can you email me a copy of the footage from Sunday until this morning?"

"Sure thing," Gary replied amiably.

Trace thanked him and after providing the man with his email address, he ended the call. Next, he phoned the bar where Malcolm had said he'd spent most of his time. Trace went through the same routine as he had with the motel manager and received much the same response. The bartender remembered Malcolm. Yes, he'd been there the past several days. Yes, they had CCTV footage inside and outside the bar. Yes, he'd send it right away to Trace via email.

Trace ended the call and then leaned back against his chair and sighed. It seemed Malcolm had been telling the truth, at least about where he'd been. Of course, noting the estimated time of death, it was also plausible he'd murdered Oscar during their confrontation, loaded his body into the truck then dumped him in the forest before he'd taken off on his three-day bender. Trace would take particular note of Malcolm's arrival at the bar. The town was an hours' drive away. It had been around eight when Malcolm had left his house. Trace hoped for Malcolm's sake the time matched up.

Trace picked up his phone again and spoke to someone in the forensics department. They agreed to send a truck out right away to impound Malcolm's vehicle. They promised to get back to Trace as soon as possible with their findings.

With another sigh, Trace ended the call and set his phone down on his desk. His gut told him Cassie's stepfather wasn't the killer. The man had owned up to hitting Oscar when he could have just as easily lied. There had been no witnesses to the argument. No way of telling what had really gone on. And yet Malcolm had offered that piece of information, even when he must have known it wouldn't look good for him. That had taken courage. It also reinforced Trace's instinctive belief that Malcolm wasn't their man.

But he'd wait for the forensic analysis of Malcom's truck, the CCTV footage and the results from the DNA before he crossed him off the suspect list. Like he'd told Cassie's stepfather, he liked to be thorough.

Chapter Thirteen

It was Friday. Two days after the discovery of Oscar's body. Two days since Cassie's life had irrevocably changed.

She'd been home all morning, cleaning the house, cooking meals, trying to stay busy. As much as she wanted to be there for her senior students, there was no way she could manage fronting up to the classroom. Oscar's death was far too fresh, her grief still far too raw. She needed this time to try and come to terms with the tragedy and accept that her little brother was never coming back.

On impulse, she headed outside. She wasn't even sure where she was going until she found herself at the park. It was a place Oscar had loved to come. He loved the flowers, the freshly mown grass, the swings and climbing rock. He'd spend hours there, never getting bored. Not for an instant.

She smiled at the memory. She could almost hear him calling to her from the top of the rock wall.

"Look at me Cassie! I'm up so high! I can touch the clouds!" He'd give her his wide toothy grin and there was nothing she could do but smile.

Making her way further into the park, she noticed Joe Lahood sitting by himself on a bench, staring into the distance. Cassie's heart clenched. She went over to him.

"Joe?"

He didn't respond. She tried again. "Joe? Are you all right?"

He slowly turned his head in her direction and blinked. Once again, he remained silent. She crouched beside him.

"Joe? What are you doing here? Shouldn't you be in school?"

He grimaced. Tears glinted in his dark eyes. She wanted to draw him into her arms and offer him comfort but she wasn't sure how he'd respond and she was barely keeping herself together. Instead, she spoke again.

"I know how hard this is for you, Joe. It's hard for all of us. You and Oscar were such good friends. All the way back to kindergarten. He thought a lot of you, Joe. And you were always such a good friend to him. The best."

Joe's tears now fell in earnest. Cassie's eyes also filled. Unable to sit by and do nothing, she put her arm around his thin shoulders and hugged him to her side. She made a mental note to speak with some of his teachers and see if anyone had arranged for him to see the school counselor. Though the principal had informed her when she'd called to convey her sympathies that additional counselors would be provided for those children who felt the need to speak to someone about what had happened to Oscar, Cassie didn't know if anyone had spoken especially to Joe. He'd been closer to Oscar than anyone. It was little wonder he was feeling her brother's loss so keenly.

"Have you spoken to the counselor, Joe?'

He shook his head no.

"It helps to talk about it. What about one of your teachers? Would you speak to them about this?"

He merely sniffed and shrugged. And then he stood. "I have to go."

Before she could speak again, he left.Cassie also stood. She was too restless to sit. She glanced at her watch. School would be in recess. She pulled out her phone and dialed the deputy principal, Suzanne Crofter, grateful when the woman picked up right away.

"Cassie. I'm so sorry to hear about your brother. I can't imagine how you must feel. If there's anything I can do...?"

Cassie swallowed against the lump in her throat that threatened to block her breathing. The pain of losing Oscar was still so raw.

An awkward silence fell between them. Suzanne was the first to break it. "So, are you calling about anything in particular?"

Cassie drew in a fortifying breath. "Yes. I want to talk to you about Joe Lahood. I'm worried about him. Do you know if anyone's arranged for him to see a counselor?"

There was a beat of silence before the deputy responded. Yes. In fact, we'd referred him before this."

Cassie blinked in surprise. "Oh?"

"Yes. He's been acting out. Getting into fights. Being rude. It's not like him. I called his parents. They've been worried about him too. Apparently, he's been acting out at home as well. They've put it down to him being upset about Oscar going missing—and of course, Joe's devastated over Oscar's death. Noelene Lahood told me she's made an appointment with a child psychologist in Sydney. Doctor Zoe Parker. I haven't heard of her, but apparently she comes highly recommended."

"I see," Cassie replied. "Well, that's good. It's obvious Joe's struggling. I didn't know about the other, but things have just been made a thousand times worse with Oscar's death. I hope he gets the help he needs."

"Me too."

As Cassie ended the call, her thoughts turned to Jeremy. He was another kid who needed professional help. She made a note to call Noelene Haddad and get a number for the child psychologist.

Cassie ended the call and slowly returned her phone to her pocket. She stared at the empty bench where Joe had sat and hoped he found someone to talk to; someone who could help him through this terrible time. In fact, the more she thought about it, the more she was certain they could all do with some therapy. She, her mother, Jeremy... Perhaps there were group sessions on dealing with grief? She'd have to make enquires.

Her phone began to vibrate. She pulled it out of her pocket and checked the screen.

Trace.

Her heart skipped forward and then a wave of sadness overwhelmed her. She wondered if he had news of Oscar's case. With her chest so tight she could barely breathe, she quickly answered the call.

"Trace. Hi."

"Hi Cassie. How are you holding up?"

"I'm doing okay. Do you have any news?"

"I've been checking out Malcolm's story. It seems he's in the clear."

"Are you sure? We only have Malcolm's word about what happened in the shed that night. I didn't see him leave, I only heard him. When I checked the shed, Oscar was also gone. What if he'd already killed him by then? Malcolm could have thrown Oscar's body in the back of his truck and dumped him in the forest. Malcolm works for National Parks after all, and you heard him. He knows that forest better than anyone. He—"

"Cassie. Stop. It wasn't Malcolm. You don't really believe it was either. Forensics went over every inch of his truck. They also examined the shed. They didn't find anything. Not a speck of blood. Nothing. The chest wound your brother received would have bled considerably. Some trace of that would have been left behind."

Trace sighed. "Not only that, but CCTV footage from the motel and the bar where Malcolm said he went showed him there when he said he was. He was seen entering a bar at nine o'clock that Sunday night. It would have taken him an hour to get there from Broken. There's no way he could have gone into the forest, disposed of Oscar's body and been seen on the CCTV cameras in that time frame. I'm still waiting for the results of his DNA test, but I'm confident they will support the other evidence. I'm sorry, but he's not our guy."

Trace ended the call to Cassie and pushed away from his desk. He needed caffeine. Zac joined him in the tearoom, mug in hand.

"What's happening with the Webster case?" Zac asked.

Trace sighed and scrubbed a hand through his hair. He gave his brother an update.

"Anyone else in your sights?" Zac asked.

Trace grimaced. "Kevin Turner. He might not be our killer, but he hasn't been as upfront with us as he claims. He told us he barely knew Oscar, but Joe Lahood said Kevin and Oscar were friends. Then there's the red jacket. Turner's girlfriend said she found it in Kevin's house. At this stage we don't know if she's lying about that, but my gut tells me she's telling the truth."

"Has she given you any reason to believe she's being dishonest?"

"She lied about Kevin's alibi. She told us she and Kevin were home together all night, remember? Dinner, a TV movie, bed. When she came into the station with the jacket, she changed her story. Told me she'd fallen asleep right after dinner. She didn't know what Kevin had been up to after that."

Zac looked at him with surprise. "So she retracted the alibi she'd provided him?"

"Yes. At least for part of the night."

"Why?"

"Apparently he'd kept the bit about him being a convicted sex offender a secret. She only found out after our visit. That pissed her off. She said she had children of her own and couldn't stand the thought that Kevin might have harmed a child."

"She thought he was capable of that?"

"She didn't know, but she didn't want that on her conscience if he'd had anything to do with Oscar's disappearance."

"What did you think of her?"

"She came across as genuine, but who knows? She might have been trying to get back at Kevin for not telling her the truth about his past. It's a pretty big secret to keep."

Zac grimaced. "You're right about that."

Trace filled his coffee mug and headed back to his desk. Though Kevin had moved to Broken only a year earlier, that didn't mean he hadn't taken time to explore the forest. Like Oscar's house, Kevin's also backed up to the National Park. Trace was almost certain Turner had lied when he'd claimed to barely know Oscar. In fact, Trace had a growing suspicion the man had been quite friendly with the young boy. This was backed up by Joe Lahood and Joe had no reason to lie about that. It also accounted for why Oscar's jacket had been found in Turner's house—if Turner's girlfriend had told the truth.

Pulling his keyboard toward him, Trace tapped on the keys and accessed Turner's record. Within moments, the page loaded. Trace scanned the text. Turner had spent three years in jail for the rape of a minor. Trace dug deeper. He accessed the witness statements and discovered the victim had been a thirteen-year-old girl. The discovery gave him pause. Though it was unusual for a pedophile to switch between the sexes, it wasn't unheard of. The only glitch was, Oscar hadn't been sexually assaulted.

Apart from the single stab wound and a few defensive cuts on his hands, the bruising on his left cheek could be accounted for by Malcolm's fist. There was no other evidence of assault. This didn't feel like an attack by a pedophile. Still, Trace couldn't completely discount Turner. Not until he had a reasonable explanation about how Oscar's jacket had ended up in Turner's house. Trace had meant what he said when he'd assured Cassie and her mother that he'd do all he could to find her son's killer. The lack of leads might be frustrating as hell, but he wouldn't let that deter him.

Trace sipped from his coffee. His thoughts drifted to his brother, Vaughan. He'd been missing for nearly six weeks. Vaughan was an integral part of Barrington Mining. No doubt their father, Frank, was going insane. Not just over concern about Vaughan's whereabouts, but having been left to pick up the slack in the business. Frank had started Barrington Mining from scratch. There was nothing he didn't know about the business. But in recent years, Frank had taken a step back, only too happy to let Vaughan take a more active role. After all, Frank was sixty-five. He'd been looking forward to retirement, or at least slowing down.

Now he was back in the thick of it, dealing with the day to day stresses a billion-dollar business would bring. On top of that, they still didn't know where Vaughan was or when he might return. Frank had received a single email early on and nothing since. They had no way of knowing what had sent Vaughan running or if he'd since met with foul play. Nothing. It was doing Trace's head in.

He thought of Cassie and her family. In some ways it was a relief they now had closure. They could stop looking, wondering, questioning where Oscar might have gone and why. Though he wasn't coming home and that was devastating for all of them, at least the wondering and waiting was over. Trace could only imagine the angst his own parents were going through.

Where are you Vaughan? Get in touch, mate. Put our minds at ease… The people who love you are worried about you…

Elizabeth Craigdon stared out of the French windows that led outside to the pool and wished she didn't feel so tense. It had been weeks and she was desperate to hear news of Vaughan. After forty years, she'd finally found her son and now he seemed to have dropped off the face of the earth. To make matters worse, according to his brother, Christopher, he'd disappeared right around the time he should have received her letter. She had no way of knowing if that was the reason he'd taken off or if he'd even read it, and the not knowing was killing her.

She wrung her hands together and made a sound of distress. She looked around, relieved no one had noticed. Her soon-to-be husband, Archie, was upstairs taking a nap. He still hadn't fully recovered from the ordeal of his house fire. Thank God Christopher had happened by and rescued him in time…

She'd invited Christopher and his fiancée, Lexi, over for afternoon tea. In fact, they were due any minute. Best she get ahold of herself lest they sense there was an ulterior motive for her invitation… Because of course, there was.

They thought they were coming to share their engagement party plans. Even her children were abuzz with the news. Christopher seemed so happy. Elizabeth was truly pleased he'd found his soul mate. But she'd be even more pleased if he had news of Vaughan…

Christopher glanced across at his fiancée who sat in the passenger seat next to him. Lexi looked beautiful in a simple green blouse and white linen pants. Her luscious lips were painted in red lipstick and looked utterly kissable, but that would have to wait. They were on their way to visit his stepmother for afternoon tea. Though Elizabeth had already met Lexi during the gala dinner she'd thrown in the spacious grounds of Craigdon Manor to raise money for needy children, this was the first time either of them had seen her since their engagement.

Over the years, Lexi had been a foster mother to twenty-seven children. She still had the care of three foster kids at home, along with five she'd adopted. Elizabeth's generosity had brought the two women together. The plight of needy children was a cause also close to Elizabeth's heart.

Christopher took another peek at his fiancée. The beautiful sapphire-and-diamond peacock brooch she wore pinned to her blouse glinted in the sun. The blues and greens reflected the color of Lexi's eyes. It was a special piece, having been handed down by the women in her family. The only link she had to her birth family.

Despite the hardships she'd endured, she was just as beautiful inside as out. A kind and giving person who had such an ability to forgive that it often left him breathless. Even now, though she'd confessed to feeling nervous about the upcoming visit with Elizabeth, a soft smile of anticipation turned up her lips. His heart turned over with love.

How did I get so lucky?

As if she were privy to his thoughts, her fingers went to her brooch. Over the weeks they'd been together, he'd noticed she did this whenever she felt a little stressed. He reached over and squeezed her hand.

"Are you all right?"

She smiled again. "Of course. Just thinking how nice it is to be visiting your family. It's times like this I miss my own family. I never knew my father. I have no memory of my grandparents. The memories I have of my mother are so hazy I'm not sure what is real and what I've imagined. All I have is this."

Once again, she fingered the brooch. A look of yearning filled her face. Christopher drew in a breath and then asked a question that had been on his mind for some weeks.

"Have you ever thought about looking into your past? I mean, your mother might very well still be alive."

Lexi gave a soft sigh. "Yes. You're right. And I have thought about it. It's just that... Every time I think about it, I get scared."

"Of what?"

"Of what I'll find. What if she's alive and well somewhere and doesn't want anything to do with me? What if she hates that I've tracked her down? I couldn't bear it if she rejected me a second time."

Christopher's heart swelled with love and tenderness. If he could take away the pain of her childhood—being abandoned at the age of three by her mother and placed into foster care—he would have done it in an instant. Unfortunately, even he couldn't eradicate the past. What he could do was his best to make brilliantly happy memories, beginning in the present and for all the years that spread before them in the future.

"I understand," he said quietly.

She looked at him, her eyes filled with love. "I know you do."

He reached for her hand again. "I'm always here for you. If you ever want to do something about finding her, I'll be with you every step of the way."

"And that's why I love you, Christopher Barrington." She leaned over and kissed him softly on the cheek.

Chapter Fourteen

Elizabeth heard a knock at the door and stood to welcome her guests. A few moments later, her long-serving housekeeper, Amy, showed Christopher and Lexi into the music room. It had been called that because of the limited-edition baby grand piano that stood in pride of place at one end of the room. In her youth, Elizabeth had dreamed of being a concert pianist. Life had dealt her a different hand. She'd ended up married and a mother to six children, seven including her stepson, Christopher.

"Christopher. It's lovely to see you. Congratulations on your engagement." She pecked him on the cheek and then turned her attention to Lexi. "And you too, Lexi. I'm thrilled for you both. Welcome back to Craigdon Manor."

Lexi smiled. "Thank you, Elizabeth. It's lovely to be here. Thank you for inviting us."

Elizabeth waved away Lexi's gratitude. "You're family now. You're welcome in my home anytime. With or without an invitation."

"Thank you, Elizabeth. That's very gracious of you," Lexi said.

She and Christopher sat together on the couch. Elizabeth took her usual seat in the armchair opposite. Amy returned, bearing a tray laden with a silver coffee pot, cups, cream, sugar and a plate of fresh pastries. She set the tray down on the coffee table between them.

"Thank you, Amy. This looks lovely."

Amy beamed. "I baked your favorites, Christopher."

He gave her a wink and she blushed and quickly left the room. Christopher shot Elizabeth a bemused look.

"Amy's grown friendlier all of a sudden," he observed.

"She's always been friendly," Elizabeth replied.

Christopher raised an eyebrow. "To you, maybe. She was much more standoffish with me."

Elizabeth laughed. "Not without reason, no doubt. But ever since you saved Archie's life, she's had a change of heart where you're concerned."

Christopher grinned. "Well, I'm not sure I deserve her goodwill, but I'll take it just the same. These pastries look delicious." With that, he leaned forward and snatched a chocolate petit four and popped the morsel in his mouth.

"*Mm.* Ambrosia." He sighed.

Elizabeth poured the coffee and offered cups to her guests. She was dying to quiz Christopher about Vaughan, but she needed to bide her time. Only Archie knew Vaughan was her biological son and until she'd made contact with him and ascertained his attitude toward the news, she wanted to keep the relationship quiet. Although the longer the time went on, the more she suspected Vaughan didn't want to talk to her. The possibility broke her heart.

One thing she didn't want to do was to pique Christopher's curiosity about her sudden interest in his brother. He was a smart man. He would quickly work out that there was something unusual about her continued questions about Vaughan. After all, until recently, she'd never enquired much about his other family. Now she seemed to be asking him about Vaughan every chance she could. No, she needed to tread carefully if she didn't want to raise suspicion.

Christopher reached for another pastry and popped it into his mouth before sipping from his coffee. Patting away the crumbs from his lips with a napkin, he sat back against the couch.

"Tell me about the engagement party plans," Elizabeth urged.

Christopher and Lexi exchanged a tender look. He reached for her hand and entwined her fingers with his. They sat close together, their thighs touching. Their body language screamed their love. Elizabeth was happy for them. For a long time, Christopher had been angry and bitter about the hand he'd been dealt. It had taken a lot of soul searching and the love of a good woman to show him the error of his ways and set him on a better path.

"The date has been set for Saturday week."

Elizabeth smiled with surprise. "The second week in June! How lovely!"

Christopher grinned. "We didn't want to wait. Lucky for us, Mom is only too keen to host it for us and she's more than happy to do it on short notice." He paused and then shot

Elizabeth a concerned look. "I hope you aren't put out by that. I know how much you like to throw a party."

She smiled and waved his concern away. "No, of course not. Sometimes it's just as much fun to be a guest." She paused and then casually added, "I guess all the family will be there?"

"Yes. I think the guest list has blown out to more than two hundred. So much for a small and intimate gathering." He looked at Lexi and gave her a wink, followed by a tender smile.

Elizabeth smiled too. It was lovely to see them so in love. But she needed to know if anyone had heard from Vaughan. She reached for her coffee and took a sip. Setting it back down, she posed another casual question.

"So, Vaughan will be there, too?"

Christopher merely shrugged. "Who knows? No one's heard from him since that first email he sent Dad. I sent him a text to tell him about the celebration, but I didn't hear from him. I don't even know if he's checking his phone. Every time I call it goes straight to voicemail."

Elizabeth's spirits plummeted. "I see. It's like he's dropped off the face of the earth," she forced herself to joke.

Christopher grinned. "You have that right. Perhaps that's his plan? To drop out of life for a while. Although I can't for the life of me think why. As far as I know, he was happy with his life. He certainly didn't give any indication of any troubles at his birthday party."

Elizabeth wished she could share with Christopher her suspicions that Vaughan's sudden disappearance might have everything to do with her, but she lost her courage. She needed to respect Vaughan's right to keep that news a secret —or not. Until she spoke to him, she had no idea how he felt about the fact she was his biological mother, no matter her growing suspicions.

She swallowed a sigh and forced another smile. All she could hope was that Vaughan would show up for Christopher's engagement party. Then she'd know for sure how he felt.

Cassie rubbed at the ache in her shoulders and thought longingly of a hot cup of coffee that might give her the boost of energy she needed to get through the work in front of her. She'd gone into school after hours to mark papers. They were only revision papers, but she felt guilty about not being there for her senior students. She wanted them to get feedback on them before their upcoming exams. Thankfully she didn't have to field any well-meaning questions. Apart from the cleaners, the place was deserted.

On a weary sigh, she set her pen down and stretched her arms over her head. The ache in her shoulders was from sitting bent over her desk for so long. Lucky for her, she was almost done. She peered out of the window opposite her desk. Night had set in. She should get home, check on her mother, see to dinner, check on Jeremy. She'd barely seen him since Oscar's body had been found.

But right now, she didn't have the energy to face another family meal. Another round of sadness and disappointment, heartache and agony that Oscar was dead and his killer still hadn't been found. She wanted to feel angry at Trace, but she knew he was doing everything he could. So far though, it hadn't been enough.

On a surge of determination, she marked the final papers and then gathered them into a neat bundle. She left them on her desk, along with a note to the substitute teacher that they were ready to be handed back. It was Friday night. She ought to be out somewhere, unwinding with a drink. Hanging out with friends. Having fun. *Fun.* She could barely remember what that felt like. With Oscar's death still weighing heavily, she couldn't imagine being that carefree again.

She thought about Joe and the trouble he'd been in recently. She understood his need to act out. She wanted to act out too. She wanted to scream and yell and swear. She wanted to punch something. Hard. She wanted to rail at the injustice of it. Her beautiful brother, filled with sunshine, dead. Not just dead. *Murdered.* She still couldn't believe it.

Who could have done such a thing in Broken? Why?

On another sigh, she pushed back from her desk and gathered her handbag. She dropped her phone into it and reached for her car keys. She was halfway to the staff carpark when she decided to hell with it. She was going out for a drink.

Trace massaged the knot in the back of his neck and tried not to feel so defeated. He'd been working hard all day and getting nowhere. It seemed no one had seen or heard from Oscar Webster in the hours after his argument with Malcolm Russell. The boy had simply disappeared into thin air. One thing they did know was that he'd ended up in the National

Park. Whether he'd gone there beforehand and met up with someone who'd eventually taken his life, or whether the deed had been done somewhere else and he'd been dumped there, Trace had yet to figure out.

He was still waiting for the report on the single black hair that had been found on Oscar's body, along with the results of the other samples Samantha Wolfe had taken. Forensics was in the process of examining the sleeping bag and the clothing Oscar had been wearing, along with the red jacket. Trace hoped like hell they found something the killer had left behind. *Maybe another hair?* Something else to link Oscar to his killer. Trace would take anything at this point. They needed a break. Something to point them in the right direction, any direction. He needed something to take back to Cassie, offer her some hope.

Cassie.

So beautiful, so strong, so resilient. A firecracker. He still couldn't believe they'd been at school together. He had no memory of her. They'd obviously run in different circles. He felt a pang of disappointment that he hadn't known her back then.

It wasn't hard to work out she was the backbone of the family, the one who kept things running, made sure everyone was doing okay. Understandably, Oscar's death had hit her hard. Trace could see she blamed herself for his death, for not keeping her youngest brother safe. She wasn't the first relative of a murder victim to feel that way. He wanted to comfort her, reassure her this wasn't her fault, but his words would sound hollow. She needed time to come to terms with her grief.

The station was quiet and dim. The rest of the staff had gone home for the night. Trace should go home too. Get some sleep. If he could. With that thought in mind, he shut down his computer. The phone near his elbow rang, piercing the silence. He reached for it automatically.

"Broken Police Station. This is Detective Barrington."

"Detective, it's Roger White at the morgue. I work with Samantha Wolfe. She asked me to call to let you know she's finished with Oscar Webster's body. She's still waiting on DNA results from the various samples she took, but she instructed me to let you know the boy can be released to his next of kin for burial."

Trace closed his eyes briefly on a surge of emotion. Thanking the technician for his call, Trace hung up the phone. He blew out his breath. Another difficult call to make. He thought about doing that but decided against it. It would be better to give her that kind of news in person. He'd call in on his way to work in the morning. In the meantime, he was going to stop in at his favorite bar. It had been a tough week and he sure as hell needed a drink.

Cassie was on her second glass of wine when the door behind her opened and let in a fluttering, cool breeze. Idly, she half-turned on the barstool and, to her surprise, she spied Trace. His bulk filled the doorway. Her stomach took a nosedive. Her pulse leaped wildly out of control.

Their gazes locked. She saw the flare of surprise in his blue eyes and a moment of hesitation. Unwilling to examine her motives, she sent him the briefest smile of encouragement. He acknowledged it with a nod and then closed the distance between them. He took the vacant stool beside her.

"Hi," he said and smiled.

The smell of his spicy cologne reached her nostrils. She'd always found him attractive with his rugged good looks and blue eyes framed by ridiculously long dark lashes. The dimple in his left cheek. The high-wattage smile. Of course, he'd been way out of her league. They might as well have functioned on different planets in high school. No wonder he hadn't remembered her.

The current circumstances hadn't changed the way she felt about him, how she was drawn to him. Preoccupied with Oscar's whereabouts, she'd been more intent on the air of strength and confidence that surrounded him, rather than his undeniable physical attractiveness. That had given her hope in their search for Oscar; that this giant of a detective might be able to find him.

But now she became aware of so many other things. Like the way his eyes crinkled when he smiled. The little lines around his mouth. The five o'clock shadow that covered his cheeks and somehow made him look even sexier. Her traitorous heart skipped a beat. Ignoring the acceleration of her pulse and in an effort to put them on a more formal footing, she asked him if he had any news concerning the investigation.

He compressed his lips and shook his head. "No. I'm sorry. We found a foreign hair on Oscar's body, but we're still waiting on lab results."

Her heart leaped with excitement. "A hair?"

"Don't get your hopes up. It could be anything. Maybe even from an animal. He was found out in the bush."

Cassie nodded her agreement and tried to slow her racing pulse. Trace ordered a beer. She glanced at him sideways, taking in his strong profile. He gave off such a quiet air of reassurance. She was sure she wasn't the first person to feel comforted by his sheer presence.

As if sensing the direction of her thoughts, he turned to her, his eyes intense. "I'm going to find Oscar's killer."

"I believe you," she said. And she did.

Their gazes held. Time stood still. The noise of the bar dimmed, evaporated. All Cassie could hear was the rush of blood in her ears and the pounding of her heart. It was good to feel something other than never-ending pain.

With difficulty, she dragged her gaze away and took refuge in her wine. "Let's talk about something else," she suggested.

Trace saluted her with his beer glass and took a mouthful. "What would you like to talk about?"

"I don't know. Tell me more about your family. I might have been in the same year as Zac, but I never really knew him. Or any of you."

His lips quirked upwards in an adorable smile. "Oh, I'm pretty sure you don't want to hear about my family."

His mood was contagious. She smiled back, intrigued. "Why not?"

"Because there's so many of them!"

She laughed. "That's right. I remember there were a few of you. How many are you talking?"

"Nine."

Her eyes widened with surprise. "Wow. I don't think I remember that many."

He looked sheepish. "Actually, there are eleven counting my parents."

Now she was shocked. "You have *eight* brothers and sisters?"

Trace grinned, unabashed. "Yep. Five brothers and three sisters." He paused and grinned again. "Oh, and I'm also a triplet."

She clapped her hands in delight and laughed again. It felt so good after the dark shadows that had filled her every waking moment this past week. "A triplet? That's right! I vaguely remember that."

"Yeah. There's Charlotte, Molly and me. Charlotte's now a cop. Molly's a paramedic. I'm the oldest by a minute or so. Then Charlotte. Then Molly."

Cassie relaxed on her stool. She reached for her wine and took another sip. "Tell me more."

"Well, my oldest brother is Christopher. He's actually a half-brother. My mom had him before she met my dad."

"I don't remember Christopher at all. How old is he?"

"A fair bit older than us. He just turned forty-one."

"Wow. Is he married? Does he have any kids?"

"No and no. But he got engaged a week ago. Everyone's excited about that. I think my parents had almost given up hope that he'd ever settle down."

"Are they happy for him?" she asked.

"Yes. Absolutely. Everyone loves Lexi. She and Christopher were made for each other."

Cassie felt a yearning so strong it almost snatched her breath. How wonderful it would be to find her soul mate.

Someone to love her, protect her, support her. Keep her safe and warm on a cold winter's night...

She cleared her throat. "Who's next in the lineup?"

"That would be Vaughan. You probably don't remember him either. He's forty. And before you ask: no wife, no kids."

"Another Barrington who's trying to avoid the marriage noose?" she joked.

"I don't think so," Trace said thoughtfully. "I don't think Vaughan has anything against marriage and he loves kids. It's just that he's spent a lot of his time dedicated to my father's business. It's a big concern and takes up a lot of his time. Well, it did until recently. Right now, he's AWOL."

Cassie nodded slowly. "I remember you telling me about him. So, you still haven't heard from him?"

Trace compressed his lips. "No."

"I'm sorry," she said quietly.

Trace's answering smile looked forced. "Don't be. I'm sure he's all right. No doubt he'll turn up and take right up where he left off. I just wish he'd let us know where he is."

The wistfulness and underlying note of concern in his voice wasn't lost on Cassie. Her heart clenched. She knew all about how it felt to be worried about a missing brother. She hastened to change the subject.

"What about your other brothers and sister? Tell me about them."

Trace took a gulp of his beer and then replied. "So, after Vaughan comes Lincoln. He's twenty-seven. He was a few years ahead of you in school."

She frowned and tried to call on long-buried memories. "I can't picture him. What does he do for a living?"

"He's recently been discharged from the army. Did three tours of Afghanistan."

"Wow."

"Yeah. He's finding it a little hard to adjust to civilian life."

"I bet."

"Charlotte, Molly and I are next in line. We're twenty-six."

"Nice. In case you're wondering, I'm twenty-four."

"Nice."

They both smiled. Their gazes caught and held. Awareness arced between them. Confused and unsettled, Cassie looked away and reached for her glass. After taking a fortifying sip of wine, she spoke again.

"Okay, we're getting to the pointy end of the Barringtons. Keep going."

"Well, Wade comes next. He's twenty-five."

"What does he do?"

"He's a park ranger with the National Parks."

Cassie bit her lip, taken by surprise. "Like Malcolm."

"Yes."

She took refuge in her drink. "Okay, so I know Zac comes next. We were in the same year. Of course he was completely besotted with Emily Wilson the whole way through high school. No one else existed. Are they still together?" she asked, curious.

"No. They split up shortly after they graduated. I've never asked him for the details."

"So, did you inspire him to enter the police force or was it the other way round?" she teased.

"Definitely not the other way round. I went into the academy straight out of high school. So did Charlotte. She's a cop too, remember? She works in homicide."

The word hung between them, reminding them about the circumstances that had brought them together.

"That must be tough," Cassie whispered.

"You bet," Trace replied, his voice sounded equally strained.

Cassie swallowed against the lump of emotion that was lodged in the back of her throat. Determined to lighten the mood, she quipped, "So that leaves just one. Hannah's the baby of the Barrington family, right?"

Trace smiled softly. His eyes telegraphed that he understood her motive for switching the subject—this time to less painful topics.

"Right. Hannah's just turned twenty-three and you've never met a more spoiled brat."

Cassie grinned with surprise. "Really?"

Trace laughed and shook his head. "No. Not really. But she's been slow to find direction in her life. She only recently took on fulltime employment. For years she's lounged around the house telling anyone who'd listen how she was clueless about what she wanted to do with her life. Mom and Dad have always been supportive of our career choices, and they were happy to have her at home, but they also made it clear to all of us they expected us to achieve something with our lives."

"So did she finally come up with something?" Cassie asked, genuinely interested.

"As a matter of fact, yes. Although I don't know if it was her idea or whether Dad just got tired of her lounging around. He gave her a job as a manager in one of his mines."

Cassie blinked with surprise. "A mine?"

"Yes. A coal mine. In the Hunter Valley. By all accounts, Hannah's loving it."

"Wow. She sounds amazing! She's pretty young to be a manager of anything, let alone a coal mine."

"Yep. Dad threw her in the deep end. Sink or swim. I think he knew she'd take to it like a duck to water. And she has."

"Good for her," Cassie said approvingly.

They both took a moment to sip from their drinks. Cassie thought about how wonderful it would be to have so many siblings and parents who obviously cared deeply for their kids. And then she felt a stab of shame. Her mother loved her children without question. It was just that she'd lost her way. When their father had been sent to jail, Marie had allowed herself to become overwhelmed with grief and was still trying to find her way back. Cassie had almost given up on that ever happening.

"What is it, Cassie?"

The gentleness in Trace's tone undid her. Tears burned in her eyes. "I was just thinking about my family."

"Oscar?" he asked quietly.

"No. My mother. And my dad," she added softly.

"Tell me more about him," Trace urged.

Cassie grimaced. "You already know he went to jail, and we never saw him again. What else is there to know?" She heard the bitterness in her voice but was helpless to prevent it. She glanced at Trace. He regarded her with eyes filled with compassion.

"I remember you telling me his name. George Webster."

"Yes."

"How old were you?"

"Ten."

"What was he convicted of?"

She shrugged. "I don't know. My mother never said. We never talked about him."

"Have you ever tried to find him?"

"No." It came out in a ragged whisper.

Once again, Trace's expression was filled with kindness and understanding. Their gazes meshed. They shared a long look, as if there were only the two of them in the world. Cassie's heart thumped. Her mouth went dry. Her tongue stole out to moisten her lips.

Trace's gaze zeroed in on her mouth and she was filled with a rush of heat. The sensation was so unexpected, so foreign it took her by surprise. Flustered, she looked away. She fiddled with the straps of her handbag, suddenly feeling uncomfortable.

I want to kiss him…

The realization shocked her. She couldn't believe she was thinking about something like that when every other waking moment had been filled with tortuous grief. Her brother hadn't even been dead a week…

What the hell am I thinking? I need to get out of here…

The thought evolved into action. She slung her handbag over her shoulder and climbed off the barstool. Trace looked like he wanted to protest but said nothing.

"I… I have to go," she said."

"Of course. I'll walk you to your car."

"No. It's fine. Please."

"Are you sure?"

"Yes."

"Well, okay. Thanks for keeping me company. It was nice talking to you."

She'd already turned away when she heard him call her name.

"Cassie?"

She turned back to face him. "Yes?"

"Sorry, I just remembered something."

"What is it?"

He drew in a deep breath and blew it out. "I'm sorry. I was going to wait until the morning, but seeing as you're here..."

"What is it?" she repeated.

"I had a call from the morgue this evening. They're ready to release Oscar's body."

The words hit Cassie hard. She gasped, feeling a rush of nausea. Trace stood and reached for her, his face filled with concern. He guided her back to the barstool and insisted she sit down. The realization that she'd now have to make funeral arrangements made her lightheaded. All of a sudden, there was no skirting around the reality of Oscar's death. Her brother was dead and needed to be buried. Her baby brother was dead. He was never coming home...

The thoughts crowded her head, filling it with noise and pressure until she wanted to scream. Trace's brow furrowed.

"Cassie? Are you all right? You've gone very pale."

She looked up at him with all the pain and devastation that cascaded inside her. "No. I'm not."

With a muffled curse, he put his arms around her and drew her close. It was awkward on the barstool, but she was grateful for his support. She closed her eyes and rested her head against his chest. She breathed in his quiet strength and tried to recover her equilibrium. After a moment, she lifted her head.

He dropped his arms.

"I'm sorry. I didn't mean to do that," she whispered. He stroked a rough finger down her cheek. Her belly filled with butterflies.

"You don't need to apologize. I should have waited for the morning. I—"

"No," she interrupted him. "I'm glad you told me. I'll go home and start making preparations…" Her voice drifted off as she was overcome with another surge of pain. To her horror, hot tears filled her eyes and spilled over.

Trace moved as if to take her in his arms again, but she stopped him.

"No. Please." Any more kindness and compassion from him and she'd break down altogether. She was barely holding it together as it was. Once again, she climbed down off the barstool and made to leave.

"Would you like me to come with you? To the funeral home?"

Cassie blinked. His offer had taken her by surprise. And then she was filled with an overwhelming feeling of gratitude and relief. "Would you?"

"Of course," he said without hesitation.

She closed her eyes against another rush of emotion. "Thank you," she whispered. That was all she could manage.

Chapter Fifteen

The day of Oscar's funeral was filled with sunshine. The sight of the clear blue sky and white fluffy clouds flooded Cassie with hope. It was the kind of perfect, late autumn day that made her grateful for being alive. At the same time, it was the saddest day of her life. Three days earlier, she'd spent a painful two hours at the funeral home, making decisions about the coffin, the flower arrangements, the music, the slideshow, the service. There had also been a mention of spreading a basket of rose petals and releasing a dozen white doves.

She'd sat there half-frozen with shock, the words raining down on her head. Never could she have imagined herself sitting there in the funeral parlor, being forced to make decisions about her little brother's burial. The whole thing was surreal and she would never have gotten through it if it hadn't been for Trace.

He'd taken time off work to be with her. He'd been her rock. Strong, silent, reliable. He'd helped her with suggestions when she felt overwhelmed, interpreting the questions that were lobbed at her by the funeral director, fielding others. By the time they'd finished, she was a wreck and if Trace hadn't taken her in his arms and held her until the trembling stopped, she wasn't sure it would have.

He'd dropped her back home to her family and had assured her he'd be at the funeral. Now she searched for him among the crowd. It should have been easy to spot him. After all, he stood head and shoulders above most men. But it seemed like more than half the town's people were there, crowding into the church, and she struggled to see him.

The students, in school uniform, and teachers from the high school had formed a guard of honor on either side of the hearse. They had been there saluting their fallen classmate when his coffin had been carried into the church. Cassie had been reduced to tears, sobbing quietly as Oscar's casket was escorted inside. She'd remained outside, waiting for the rest of her family.

Her stomach was tied up in knots. When her mother had announced she'd attend the funeral. Cassie and Jeremy had looked at her in shock.

"How are you going to get there? It's a long way to the church from here, Mom. Are you sure?" Cassie asked.

Marie and Malcolm shared a look. "I'm going in Malcolm's truck," she announced.

Cassie frowned, her mind trying to work out how her mother was going to fit inside the cab.

"I'm riding in the back," Marie added. "*Right* in the back."

Cassie gaped. She tried not to sound as appalled as she felt. "You mean, in the *tray?*"

Her mother gave her a defiant look. "Yes Cassie. In the tray."

Now Cassie waited on the steps of the church for her family to arrive. When she'd left home about half an hour earlier, her mother was still getting ready. For all Marie's earlier determination to be at the funeral, she seemed to have lost some of her drive. When Cassie left, she wasn't sure if her mother was going to make it or not.

Please, Mom… Please get here… Do it for Oscar… Do it for all of us…

And then she spied Malcolm's truck pulling up to the curb. A murmur rose from the crowd that milled outside. Cassie didn't have to look to know why. Her mother sat sprawled inelegantly in the tray of Malcolm's vehicle. She had her arms spread over the tailgate, holding on for dear life.

She was dressed in an enormous purple silk tent that floated lightly over her body. Cassie had no idea where her mother had found it, but she teared up at the sight. Purple had been Oscar's favorite color. Cassie wore purple too. Even Jeremy had found a lilac-colored shirt. Marie Russell hadn't been seen out in public for years. Now she was there, in all her glory, letting the crowd look their fill. And then Malcolm and Jeremy climbed out of the truck and went around to the back.

While Jeremy supported their mother, Malcolm eased the tailgate down. With the two men on either side of her, Marie hopped and shuffled and rolled off the back of the truck. The crowd gasped as one. Cassie held her breath. Her fingernails dug into her hands, her heart beat fast.

Please don't fall over… Please don't fall over…

Reporters scrambled, eager to get close. They'd never seen anything like it. The TV cameramen moved quickly, frantic to capture every moment of the spectacle. Marie wobbled for a moment, but then appeared to find her feet. She stood straight, her shoulders back, flanked by her husband and son. People stared and whispered behind their hands, some stifled laughter, and yet Marie withstood the shame and humiliation and held her head high.

Tears rolled down Cassie's face. She'd never been prouder of her mom. Marie was well aware of the spectacle she made, but she faced down the crowd anyway. For Oscar. Her beloved son. She took a step forward and then another. Sweat popped out on her forehead from the strain, but she continued on, one excruciating step at a time. When she made the top step of the church, a loud cheer went up from the crowd. More tears stung Cassie's eyes and ran down her already-damp cheeks. Cassie moved to stand beside her mother and hugged her as hard as she could.

"Thank you for coming, Mom. I love you so much."

"I wanted to be here for my baby, and for you and Jeremy too." She looked from Cassie to her son and then to Malcolm. "You're my family. Nothing could have kept me away."

From the corner of her eye, Cassie finally spied Trace. He looked splendid in a tailored, black suit. Her eyes widened at the sight of his glossy, deep purple tie.

"How did you know?" she whispered as he made it to her side.

"You told me. The sweet peas. Remember?"

Cassie could barely speak over the lump of emotion that lodged itself in her throat. She reached for Trace's hand and squeezed it, loving the feel of his strength and warmth. When she went to pull her hand away, he tightened his hold. Their gazes met. The depth of emotion in his eyes took her back. She felt an answering response in her heart.

She was so glad for his solidness, his strength and quiet support. He was a decent guy, a man she could fall for. And then the priest was ushering them inside and she blinked and turned away. Trace released her hand, but as she made her way toward the front pew of the church, she was grateful for his presence. She felt him behind her every step of the way.

It was a beautiful service. One after another, people from the town came forward and spoke about Oscar. Many of them Cassie didn't even know, but somehow her brother had gotten to know them and had touched their lives. There were also stories recalled by some of his classmates. Funny stories that made everyone laugh. Even some of his teachers spoke. Their tributes to Oscar brought tears to Cassie's eyes.

She looked around for Joe, wondering if he would say something. She spied him sitting flanked by his parents. He was hunched over, his head in his hands. It was obvious he was sobbing. A fresh burst of pain tightened her stomach.

Poor Joe.

As she watched, Noelene Haddad put her arm around her son's shoulders and drew him close. He turned and buried his face against her side. Cassie was grateful he didn't have to battle through this all alone.

She turned her head slightly and saw Trace. He sat a few pews behind her. His expression was somber and sad, his jaw clenched. But there was also a light of determination in his eyes. It gave her comfort that he'd meant what he said when he'd assured her he'd find Oscar's killer.

As the slideshow came to an end and the church swelled with Oscar's favorite song, the congregation stood as the pallbearers carried his coffin outside. Cassie's mother began to sob uncontrollably. Her immense grief was like a physical thing, a palpable pain that almost brought Cassie to her knees.

Tears poured freely down her cheeks. She sobbed for the loss of her brother and for the life he'd been robbed of. Through her tears, she looked at Jeremy seated beside her. His lips trembled with the effort to hold in his emotion. His girlfriend, Annie, sat on his other side. They held hands, their fingers entwined. And then the priest gently touched her on the arm and indicated that she and the family should precede him out of the church.

Pulling herself together as best she could, she quietly urged Jeremy to help Malcolm with their mother and then slid from the pew and began the long journey back down the aisle. The whole time her gaze was fixed on the cherry-wood coffin that bore her brother's body.

Somewhere in the distant recesses of her mind, she catalogued the enormous bouquet of gerberas that were spread over the top of Oscar's casket. Gerberas in every color. While purple sweet peas had been his favorite, this late in the season they would have been impossible to come by. Still, the funeral home had done their best. In the absence of sweet peas, Cassie had put in one simple request: The display of flowers, whatever it was, needed to be as bright and colorful as they could manage. She was glad they'd honored her request. She was sure Oscar was looking down on them now, grinning from ear to ear. The thought almost made her smile.

The funeral procession traveled down Main Street, past the butcher's, the pharmacy, the supermarket, Lahood's café and then took the turn that led to the cemetery on the edge of town. Once again, Cassie's mother put on a show for the townspeople when she climbed in and out of the back of Malcolm's truck. Cassie felt their stares, but she didn't care what they thought. Her family had suffered the most devastating of losses. Everything else paled in comparison. Overriding all of that was the overwhelming pride she felt in her mother for again subjecting herself to what was undoubtedly a humiliating experience and doing it for her son.

When it was over and the crowd had dispersed, Cassie waited quietly with her family. Her mother stood by the grave, crying. Malcolm was there, offering his support, holding her steady, murmuring words of comfort in her ear. Jeremy stood by—now dry-eyed—a stoic expression turning his face to granite. Annie stroked his back and spoke quietly to him. From the corner of her eye, Cassie saw Trace. He stood a little way away from them, but the care and concern in his gaze left her in no doubt how he felt.

She took a few steps toward him, wanting to thank him for being there. He met her halfway.

"How are you holding up?" he asked quietly.

She could only manage a shrug. She was pleased for her dark sunglasses that shielded her from his gaze. Her eyes felt hot and swollen. No doubt she looked a mess. But somehow, she sensed Trace wouldn't care. From what she knew of him, he went far deeper than that.

"It was a lovely service," he said.

She gave him a shaky nod. "Y-yes. It was. So many people said so many beautiful things about him. Oscar would have been thrilled."

Her voice cracked on a surge of emotion. Without hesitation, Trace stepped forward and folded her in his arms. She tensed momentarily, aware that there were still people around, but he felt so strong and sure and secure, she relaxed against him and savored the comfort he so generously offered. More tears filled her eyes and leaked down her cheeks. After all the tears she'd cried, she was amazed they kept flowing, but she was helpless to stop them. Trace didn't seem to mind. He held her close, saying nothing, letting her grieve.

Finally, the tears subsided and she slowly pulled away. He released her immediately, his arms falling to his sides.

"I-I'm sorry," she stammered, scrambling around for a tissue in her handbag.

"Don't be sorry. Here." Trace offered her a neatly folded linen square.

"Th-thanks." She took the handkerchief and dabbed at her eyes. Then she blew her nose. She thought about offering the handkerchief back to him, but then decided against it. She tucked it into her handbag and sighed.

She looked at him. "Are you able to come to the wake? We're holding it at the bowling club."

Trace nodded. "I have a few things to do back at the station, but I'll stop by when I can."

She kept her gaze on his. "Thank you. For everything."

"Don't thank me yet. I'm not done yet. Not by a long shot." His eyes flared brightly with determination. "Not until your brother's killer is behind bars."

She nodded slowly with acceptance and gratitude. "I'm counting on that."

Trace left the cemetery with Cassie's distraught family front and center in his mind. He was more determined than ever to find the person responsible for Oscar's death. It infuriated him that they had so little to go on. He'd studied those attending the service, looking closely for anything out of the ordinary, anything that revealed guilt. A plain clothes detective had videoed the service, tucked away in a discreet nook of the church. They'd examine the footage afterwards, looking for anything or anyone out of place.

He felt like they were clutching at straws. There were no eyewitnesses, no evidence indicating who the killer might be. All they had were some flimsy pieces of physical evidence that might or might not be relevant. He slammed the steering wheel, his frustration boiling over, wishing there was something concrete they had to go on.

He thought about Marie Russell. Her husband had been sent to jail, forcing her to raise three young children alone. She'd suffered terribly for it. Her physical appearance was testament to that. And what of Cassie and her brothers? Oscar and Jeremy had been too young to have any memories of their father or what it felt like for him to be absent from their lives, but the same couldn't be said for Cassie.

She'd been ten when her father had been sent to jail. Old enough to feel his loss. Even worse when he didn't come back. It made Trace curious about the crime George Webster had committed and how long he'd spent doing time. He also wondered about what would cause a man to turn his back on his family—his wife and kids. Malcolm had only arrived on the scene five years ago. Trace could only assume Marie had been on her own before that.

So why didn't George return home after his jail term came to an end?

Pulling the cruiser to the curb outside the police station, Trace climbed out and headed inside. He sent a vague wave of acknowledgement in the direction of the general duties officer manning the reception desk and headed through the doorway that led out back to where the interview rooms and the detectives' offices lay.

Not even bothering to stop for coffee, Trace sat behind his desk and pulled his keyboard toward him. He tapped on keys to access the police database and then entered George Webster's name. Thirty-nine entries filled the screen. He cursed under his breath. He didn't know the man's date of birth, but he guessed Cassie's father was probably somewhere around her mother's age. Late forties, early fifties, perhaps.

He was able to eliminate all but three possibilities. He clicked on each name and scanned the additional information provided on each criminal. He found Cassie's father a few minutes later.

George Jeremy Webster was now fifty-one years old. He'd been convicted of assault occasioning actual bodily harm and had been sentenced to five years in jail, with a non-parole period of three years. Webster had no previous convictions which told Trace the assault that had sent him to prison must have been severe. Five years was a long time for a first offender.

Trace clicked on another tab and opened another file. This one usually contained information on the address Webster had provided to the Department of Corrections on his release. Trace scanned the information and then blinked in surprise. The address given was in Broken.

So, he'd returned to his hometown after his release... Why didn't he make contact with his family?

And then Trace had his answer. About halfway down the page he noticed the word "deceased." Trace read the account of George Webster's death. According to the police report, upon Webster's release from prison, he'd headed straight for a nearby bar. After drinking heavily for several hours, he told the bartender he was going home to his wife and kids in Broken. Unfortunately, he never arrived.

After staggering down the street toward the taxi stand, he ended up stumbling onto the road and was hit by an oncoming car. He was killed instantly. It was standard procedure that the next of kin be notified. Trace could only guess Marie had decided to spare her children further pain and had kept the news to herself. After all, they'd already gotten used to not having him around...

With a heavy sigh, Trace leaned back against his chair and scrubbed his hands through his hair. He couldn't imagine how it had been for Cassie all these years. Never knowing what had happened to her father, not knowing if he were alive or dead. If he'd cared about her and her family. If he ever thought about them and wanted to see them again.

Now Trace had the answers. He debated silently about whether to tell her. His main reason for looking into her father was so that she might discover what had happened to him. Now he knew the truth, he wasn't sure if he should keep the news to himself.

As quickly as the thought developed, he dismissed it. Cassie deserved to know. Discovering her father had been on his way back to them when he was killed might be the very boost she needed right now. It would also provide her and her family with closure. Everyone deserved that.

Mind made up, Trace shut down his computer and left.

Chapter Sixteen

Cassie moved through the crowd of mourners who filled the bowling club's auditorium to capacity. Her mother was safely ensconced on a comfortable couch big enough to hold her and was being waited on by both Malcolm and Jeremy. Cassie noticed many of the townspeople came up to her mother to pay their respects. They treated her with courtesy and appeared genuinely upset about the loss of her son. It was all Cassie could have hoped for and she finally felt a lessening of the tension that had held her in its grip from the moment she realized her mother was going to attend the funeral.

Every now and then, she looked around for Trace, disappointed when she didn't see him. It was ridiculous how quickly he'd come to mean something to her and how much she depended upon his quiet strength. No doubt when the investigation came to a conclusion, they'd go their separate ways. After all, that's what had brought them together and as much as she wanted to think they'd grown closer—were friends—there was no guarantee he saw her as anyone other than a grieving relative connected with his current case.

But what about when he drew me close and whispered words of comfort against my hair?

So, he was a good and decent person. That much was obvious. He was a detective. He'd sworn to protect and serve. His choice of occupation demonstrated how much he cared for others. Being kind in a professional way, that's all this was.

"Cassie. How are you doing?"

At the sound of her name, she turned and found the high school principal regarding her through concerned eyes. Jacquie Harper had been so supportive through all of this. Not only had she urged Cassie to take off as much time as she needed, but Jacquie had also arranged for additional counselors to attend the school in the days after Oscar's death.

Now Cassie offered Jacquie a strained smile. "I'm doing all right. This is a tough day for everyone, but we're getting through it."

Jacquie gave her a gentle smile. "Yes." She paused. "Take some more time off. As much as you need. We can cover your classes."

"Thank you. I really appreciate that. I'm feeling a little guilty about my seniors... They have exams next week... I feel like I've let them down by not being there..."

Jacquie eyed her steadily. "Don't be silly. Everyone understands. You saw the show of support from the student body outside the church today. Your students think very highly of you." She paused and then added, "You're a wonderful, dedicated teacher Cassie. Don't ever doubt that. Broken High is lucky to have you."

"Thank you," Cassie replied.

From the corner of her eye, she saw the door to the auditorium open. Trace's broad shoulders filled the space. Without volition, her heart leaped forward. Her stomach swarmed with butterflies.

Get a grip, Cassie. He's the detective investigating your brother's murder. That's all.

But as he drew nearer and her pulse raced faster, it was all she could do to mumble a few words of farewell to her boss and turn and walk toward him. He spotted her almost immediately and emotion flared in his eyes. Her knees went weak from the intensity in his face. He stared at her as if there were only the two of them in the room. She knew exactly how he felt.

It was like the parting of the Red Sea. The crowd of people disappeared. The murmur of conversation became a background noise, no longer registering with her. There was nothing and no one but him. She walked like a sleepwalker toward him, feeling dazed but also feeling the inevitability of it. She couldn't have stopped herself from closing the distance between them if she'd tried.

Trace had searched for and found Cassie in the crowd and started walking toward her. At one point, as if sensing his scrutiny, she turned and saw him. She said something to the older woman beside her and then began moving toward him.

Her gaze remained fixed on his. There was nothing in the world that could have made him look away.

What a sap I am… If my brothers could see me now… They'd kill themselves with laughter…

Trace wasn't known for his big romantic gestures. He'd dated on and off in high school and during his time at the police academy and even after being posted in Broken. But none of his relationships had been serious. He was the perennial bachelor. Footloose and fancy free. He loved to play golf in his spare time, hang out with his mates and have a beer with his friends and family. He'd never felt the need to have a woman in his life. Until now, he'd never been in love.

In love? What am I talking about? How can I be in love? I hardly know her…

But that didn't seem to matter. The amount of time they'd known each was immaterial in this instance. What was more important was how quickly they'd connected. Okay, so being so closely involved with a murder investigation certainly had a habit of hastening things along. People spoke about and shared details and information they never would have in normal circumstances. But this thing with Cassie—whatever it was—was more than that.

It transcended the investigation and went to the very heart of who they were. She saw him in a way not many people did. She believed in him. Only his family knew how much he cared about the people he served and how his quiet and reserved character hid a deeper personality. Someone who often cared too much. Maybe not at first, but through these difficult times, she'd learned the man he really was.

Some would call his sensitive nature a drawback in the kind of work he did, but Trace didn't see it that way. The more he cared, the greater his desire was to see justice done. He only hoped and prayed that same determination held him in good stead in Oscar's case and that one day he'd bring the case to a satisfying conclusion.

As Cassie drew closer, he saw the nervousness and excitement warring on her face. It made him feel good to have proof she was happy to see him. He sensed that there was something special between them, something more than the investigation of her brother's murder, but he didn't know for sure.

Her smile widened. When she drew close enough, it seemed natural to take her in his arms and hug her. She hugged him back. Her sweet curves felt so right against his hardness. She was all soft, sweet-smelling skin and glossy auburn hair. Most of her freckles had disappeared under a layer of makeup, but the odd one had escaped. He liked them. They gave her a uniqueness he found appealing. No doubt she didn't see them the same way.

"Thank you for coming," she said.

He smiled softly at her breathless tone, pleased that he wasn't the only one feeling a little out of his depth.

"I told you I'd show."

"So you did. Would you like a drink?"

"A beer would be great." At her brief look of surprise, he added, "I'm off duty today. I only went back to the station because there was something I wanted to do."

She lifted a single eyebrow in silent query.

"I'll explain later," he said.

They went up to the bar and Trace ordered a beer. "What are you having?" he asked her.

She drew in her breath and eased it out, letting her shoulders fall. "I might have a glass of white wine. Sauvignon Blanc if they have it."

Trace put her order in with the bartender and a few moments later, the man returned with their drinks. Trace handed the man enough money to cover both. He handed the glass of wine to Cassie. She murmured her thanks.

The bar situated on one side of the auditorium was crowded with mourners and the noise level had risen to where it was almost impossible for them to have a normal conversation. Trace leaned down toward Cassie.

"Let's go somewhere we can talk."

She nodded. He led her through a passageway that ended in a small courtyard. The sun was low in the sky and long shadows filled the space. Downlights in the ceiling provided sufficient illumination, but their soft golden glow also cocooned them, provided an air of intimacy. A cool breeze drifted in from the carpark. Cassie shivered. Her black dress was stylish and fit her well, but it didn't look particularly warm. Trace shrugged off his jacket and handed it to her.

"Here."

Her gaze flicked up to his. Her eyes were filled with shadows. He could tell she was thinking about the last time he'd done that. "Thanks," she murmured and slipped it over her shoulders.

They had the space to themselves and the din from the wake barely reached them there. Trace led her to a table in one corner and pulled out a chair for her. Once again, she murmured her thanks.

Trace took the seat opposite and sipped from his beer. Cassie regarded him over the rim of her wineglass. Purple smudges of fatigue shadowed the skin beneath her eyes. No doubt she hadn't been sleeping well. The thought sent a surge of protectiveness rushing through him.

And then he remembered his gift. He'd wanted to give it to her at the funeral, but it hadn't arrived in time. The courier had turned up at the police station just as he'd been leaving for the wake. He pushed away from the table and stood. Cassie frowned up at him.

"Is something wrong?" she asked.

"No, but I just remembered... I have something for you. I forgot to bring it in. It's in my car. I won't be a minute."

With that he retraced his steps and strode across the carpark to the cruiser, a short distance away. The bouquet of flowers still lay across the back seat. He collected them and hurried back to Cassie.

"These are for you," he said, feeling almost shy.

Her eyes widened with shock at the sight of them. "Sweet peas? You bought me *sweet peas?*"

He shrugged. "You told me how much Oscar liked them..."

She buried her nose in the fragrant bouquet and drew in a deep breath. When she looked up, her expression was still dazed.

"I don't believe it! I tried to order some for Oscar. Purple ones, just like these. But no one could help me. They all said the same thing. It's nearly winter... Sweet peas aren't available this time of year... Impossible... In the end, I settled for the gerberas."

"And they looked stunning," Trace hurried to reassure her. The last thing he wanted was to make her feel inadequate over the arrangements she'd made for her brother.

"They did," she agreed softly, "but these are just beautiful. And they smell divine. Oscar would have loved them."

She looked up at him and her eyes were shiny with tears. "How did you manage it?"

He shrugged, feeling a little uncomfortable. At the same time, he was thrilled that she was pleased.

"I called my mother," he admitted.

Cassie's eyes widened in surprise. A smile played around her lips. "Your mother has a hothouse?"

Trace blushed. "No. What I meant was, I called my mother to ask where I might find some. She gave me the name of a few exclusive florists in the city. I made some calls and impressed upon them how important it was that they find me purple sweet peas."

He flushed again. No doubt he'd just revealed way too much of what he was feeling. He didn't want to scare her off. He peeked at her and was relieved when he saw she was smiling again.

She looked at him. Her eyes were wide and luminous. His heart thumped.

"You went to so much trouble."

Her voice was heavy with emotion, almost breathless. He was glad he wasn't the only one having difficulty breathing. He sat down beside her and reached for her hand. It felt so small and soft in his large one. Another wave of protectiveness washed over him. It was the same kind of feeling he had for his sisters. But as that morphed into something else, heat throbbed through him and centered in his groin. All thoughts of his sisters evaporated.

"Trace. I don't know how to thank you," she whispered.

He looked at her with all the emotion he felt inside. "You're an amazing woman, Cassie Webster. I can't tell you how proud I am of you, how much I admire your courage, your strength."

She shook her head, as if disagreeing with him. "If you'd seen me a few hours ago, you wouldn't say that. I'm neither strong nor brave."

He held up his hand. "Stop. Please. I won't have you talking like that. You've been through so much in your life. I'm not just talking about this—" He waved his hand around. "You're the bravest person I know. And you've been through a devastating and traumatic event which continues."

He took her hand and stood, bringing her upright. He rested his hands on her shoulders and stared down at her, trying to make her see.

"It's okay not to be strong all the time. I get that you feel you need to be that way for your family. They've relied on you for so long. You're afraid that if you show them any weakness, they'll fall apart. I understand. I really do. Plenty of people rely on me, too."

He softened his tone. "But you don't need to pretend with me. If you ever feel the need to fall apart, or you need someone to lean on, lean on me. I have broad shoulders. I won't judge you. I promise."

The mountain of grief that had been building inside Cassie ever since the night Oscar had failed to return home suddenly reached its summit. Though she'd cried at the funeral and earlier, it seemed there was still plenty more tears to come. It was like a dam breaking, gushing over the sides, destroying everything in its path. She threw her arms around Trace's waist and clung to him like he was a life raft in the middle of a terrible storm. His arms came around her and he drew her close: strong, safe, secure.

She closed her eyes and with great gulping sobs, let the torrent of emotion fall. She could no sooner hold it back than she could restore her brother's life. Trace was right. She'd been so strong for everyone—her mother, her brother, Joe. It was a relief to let it all out. To release her tightly held self-control. To cry like she'd never stop. And all the time, Trace held her close, stroked her hair and whispered words of comfort.

Finally, she lifted her head, her eyes still wet with tears. He stared down at her with such tenderness, her heart stopped. With his gaze still locked on hers, he reached out and swiped her bottom lip with the soft pad of his thumb. Fire trailed in the wake of his touch.

Without conscious awareness of what she was doing, Cassie reached up and brought his head down to hers. Their lips touched. Softly, so softly, but an instant later it was like a tinder had been struck. Heat seared her mouth.

She tightened her hold around his neck and kissed him for all she was worth. He kissed her back with an answering passion that stole her breath. And then slowly, slowly they both became aware of their surroundings. Trace lifted his head. Cassie eased herself out of his arms. They were both breathing hard.

"Wow," Trace said.

Cassie laughed nervously and tried to slow the pounding of her heart. "Yes. Wow."

They both started talking at the same time. Embarrassment flared across Cassie's face. She averted her gaze, feeling awkward. At the same time, her nerve endings sung.

"How about we return to our seats?" Trace suggested.

Cassie nodded and sunk into her chair. Reaching for her wine glass, she took a grateful sip. Trace sat down opposite and likewise took refuge in his drink. They were silent for a moment, each caught up in their thoughts.

Cassie was still dazed from their kiss. She'd been kissed plenty of times before, and yet she'd never been kissed like *that*. Trace Barrington took kissing to a whole new level. She wasn't shocked to realize she wanted to do it again.

She snuck a glance in his direction and was pleased to see he still looked as flushed as she felt. It felt good to know he'd been as affected by their kiss as she was.

"Did you get finished with your business at the station?" she asked for want of something better to say.

He cleared his throat and nodded. "Yes. I wanted to speak with you about that."

The gravity of his tone sent shivers of alarm running along her spine. "Oh?"

"Yes. I... I pulled your father's name up in our system. I was curious about what he'd been sent away for and... I thought I might be able to find him... Or at least get you that answer and his last known address..."

Cassie's heart stopped cold. She stared at him in shock. "You... You looked up my father?"

"Yes. I hope you don't mind?"

Cassie didn't know what she thought. It was the last thing she'd expected him to say. "I... I don't know what to say... Wow... I'm totally taken aback..."

She saw the concern in Trace's eyes and hastened to assure him. "I'm not upset or angry. I'm just surprised. I never expected you to do something like that. I've lived for years with not knowing where my father is."

"Fourteen years, in fact," Trace said.

Cassie nodded slowly. "You're right. It's been a long time." She drew in a deep breath and eased it out. Then she took another sip of wine.

Feeling calmer, she asked, "What did you find out?"

Trace began to tell her what he'd discovered. "George Webster was convicted of a serious assault fourteen years ago. He was sentenced to five years in jail. He did four years and was released on probation."

"Only four years? But that was ten years ago! Where has he been all this time? Why hasn't he come to see us?"

Trace compressed his lips. "I believe he did. At least, he intended to. I found out that he was involved in a car accident the same night he was released."

Cassie gasped. "Is he...all right?"

Chapter Seventeen

Trace's expression turned somber. Icy fingers of fear clutched at Cassie's heart. Her hands tightened into fists. She braced herself for his next words.

"No. I'm sorry, Cassie. He stepped out onto the street and was hit by a car. He was killed instantly."

A tsunami of conflicting emotions overwhelmed her: disbelief, shock, devastation and then an all-encompassing sadness that weighed down her very bones.

"He was on his way home to us when it happened?" She gasped.

Trace nodded, his expression gentle. "Yes."

"How do you know?"

"It was in the police report. He'd been released from prison and had gone to a bar. He told someone there he was on his way home. To Broken. To his family."

A lump formed in Cassie's throat. Fresh tears burned behind her eyes. "All these years of not knowing..." And then another thought occurred to her. "Do you think my mother was told?"

Trace looked grim. "I can't say for certain, but it's standard procedure to notify the next of kin. As far as I can tell, that was your mother."

With growing horror and disbelief, Cassie took in the full import of what he'd said. "You mean, my mother knew? All this time, my mother *knew?*"

Trace merely looked at her, his gaze filled with sadness and compassion. "I'm sorry, Cassie."

Feelings of shock and disbelief flooded through her. She couldn't believe all these years her mother had known about her father and had said nothing. She slowly shook her head. "Why would she do that? Why wouldn't she have told us?"

"I don't know, but you were all still young when he died. Perhaps she thought you'd suffered enough having to deal with him leaving the first time."

Cassie stared blindly, her thoughts in a turmoil. "I grew up being terrified of the police," she said slowly "I was ten when the police came to our house and arrested my father. They took him away. I never saw him again."

She drew in a shaky breath and kept going. "I was so scared that day I walked into the police station to report Oscar missing. I remember sitting in my car, trying to summon the courage to go inside. I never consciously thought about why I had this fear of the police, but I'm pretty sure it was because in my mind I remembered my father was taken to the police station and never came back."

Trace regarded her with an expression that was filled with compassion. "I understand how you could have developed a subconscious fear of the police. You were just a child when he was sent to jail. And as you say, he never came back."

She nodded. "As I grew older, I knew it wasn't the fault of the police, but that's how it had become arranged in my ten-year-old mind. It was hard to overcome that instinctive fear."

"And yet you did it. You did it for Oscar. He would have been as proud of you as I am."

She wished she deserved his praise. She needed to come clean about the other reason she'd held back.

"It wasn't just about the fear I had of the police. There was also the shame I felt about my mother. I knew if I went to the police, other people would get involved, visit our house, talk to my mother. I didn't want to be talked about, made fun of behind other peoples' backs. I'd spent years living like that."

Her voice hitched. "My mother was the town joke. An enormous caricature of a woman people had to see to believe and then they'd laugh about it, like it was all some marvelous joke. Only, that was my mother they were making fun of. The teasing at school was merciless. It was hard to take. It made me so angry I wanted to punch people in the face. One of the reasons why I regularly escaped to the high school library."

Her chest was tight with emotion, but she was determined to finish. She looked up at Trace. "In the end, my concern for Oscar's welfare outweighed everything else. I found my way into the station. That's where I met you."

Trace's eyes filled with emotion. He reached for her hands and squeezed them. She reveled in his warmth and his strength.

"You're the bravest woman I know." He paused and then added, "Was your mother always so heavy?"

Cassie slowly shook her head. "No, at least, not like she is now. When I was a kid, she looked like everyone else's mom. It was only after my father was sent to prison that she started putting on weight. For a long time, she wouldn't come out of her room. I remember having to take her meals to her on a tray. She barely spoke. Cried all the time. I guess that's when it started. I was only a kid. Jeremy was three. Oscar was only a baby. I didn't know what was going on or what to do about it."

She dragged in a ragged breath. "So, I learned to ignore it. I pretended it wasn't happening. Until one day she was so big she couldn't even fit behind the steering wheel. From then on, she never left the house. We started getting our groceries delivered. Then she met Malcolm in an online chat room. A few months later, he moved in. For a while she seemed better, happier. He really seemed to care about her. She started getting out of bed and spending the day on the couch. She even took up embroidery again. It wasn't much, but it was an improvement."

Cassie sighed. "Who knows how she suffered during those years she was left alone to raise us. One of us with special needs. It couldn't have been easy. All that time her husband was in jail and then afterwards...he just disappeared.

"She never talked about how she felt about that, but we all knew not to raise the subject. My father was off limits. We were ashamed of him and as I got older and realized how the kids at school were making fun of my mother, I grew ashamed of her, too. I hated feeling that way, but I couldn't help it. I wanted her to be like all the other moms."

"No one would blame you for feeling like that, Cassie."

Trace's words were gentle and were said in a tone of finality, but she wasn't finished getting things off her chest.

"I wanted to go away to university to escape my sorry life and the daily humiliations, but I couldn't leave my brothers. They had no one. Mom hadn't yet met Malcolm. So, I did university online. The whole three years, except for my practical blocks. I didn't get to experience the fun and freedom of campus life, but my brothers were safe and cared for. So was my mother. By then she wasn't capable of looking after anyone, not even herself. So, I did it."

"That must have been a burden at times," Trace murmured.

Tears pricked her eyes. "Yes. But there was no one else to do it."

"You spent your youth being responsible and looking out for others. You're still doing that." He swiped the pad of his thumb tenderly across her forehead, brushing back a lock of hair. "When do you get to be *you*, Cassie Webster? A twenty-something, single woman. When do you get to set aside your responsibilities and have fun?"

She gave a short bark of laughter. "Fun? What's that? The best I manage is a drink at a local bar every now and then."

His expression grew thoughtful and then a smile turned up his lips. His eyes filled with excitement.

"What is it? What are you thinking, Trace?"

"I'm thinking it's time you took a break from your family and had some fun. Some real fun. How would you like to come to a party with me?"

She blinked in surprise. It was the last thing she expected him to say. "A *party?*"

"Yes. An engagement party. My half-brother Christopher is getting married. Remember I told you about him and Lexi?"

Cassie nodded without conviction, bemused. "Sure."

Trace reached for her hand. "It's going to be a big celebration. There'll be music and dancing and fun! What do you say?"

Cassie started to shake her head in refusal. Trace squeezed her hand. "Please say yes, Cassie. You owe it to yourself. Just this once. And I'd love to bring you as my date. Please, will you come?"

Her eyes went wide. "Your date?"

"Yes. Is that okay with you?"

His beseeching tone made it impossible to say no. "I guess. Yes, I'll come." She laughed.

The brilliant smile he sent her way was so full of warmth and tenderness she felt it all the way down to her toes.

Vaughan Barrington's smile felt strained as he handed the fruity cocktail, complete with a miniature decorative umbrella, to the flirty woman on the other side of the bar. He'd seen her sunbathing by the pool earlier. Tall and shapely, she was curvy in all the right places. With long blond hair, tanned limbs and teeth so white they were blinding, she was one of the most attractive women Vaughan had seen. Which was saying something.

In his part of town on the island paradise of Bali, attractive, wealthy tourists abounded. Sexy, tanned women in bikinis and men who could have fronted movie cameras as leading men were in abundant supply. It was like all the beautiful people in the world chose to holiday in Nusa Dua and most of them frequented his bar. Not that he was complaining. The eye candy helped the time go faster. A twelve-hour stint, on his feet all day serving drinks, and making idle conversation wasn't his scene, but he'd needed to be doing something or he would have gone mad.

His job as a bartender helped fill in the long hours that would have otherwise been spent thinking about the letter he'd received from the woman purporting to be his biological mother.

Elizabeth Craigdon...

After getting over the initial shock, his first reaction was denial. How could she be his mother? It didn't make sense... Now he was angry. Why had she waited so long to come forward? He was forty, for fuck's sake. The fact he had no answers to the questions that circled relentlessly in his mind made him even angrier and he hated feeling like that.

The first eleven years of his life had been shit. Passed from one awful foster home to another. But despite the hardship he'd faced, he hadn't let that get him down. He'd always been a glass half-full kind of guy, always looking for the positive.

Now he was angry all the time and it was Elizabeth Craigdon's fault.

His thoughts drifted to his adoptive family and a wave of yearning went through him. If the first eleven years had been insufferable, from the time he'd been taken in by Frank and

Evelyn Barrington, he'd felt like he was finally home. They'd showered him with unconditional love and support. Nothing was too much trouble. They'd raised him as one of their own and that didn't change even when they began having biological children. For the first time in his life, he'd felt like he belonged, and he credited his parents and his brothers and sisters with that.

No doubt they were worried about him. He'd emailed his father to let him know he was okay and needed some time away, but that had been more than a month ago. He hadn't contacted anyone since. The way he felt right now, he sure as hell couldn't leave. Not until he'd had a chance to work through his emotions, sort out how he felt. Came up with a plan of action regarding the woman who claimed to have given him life.

He wasn't sure how long that would take. It wasn't fair to his family to burden them with the news. They all believed, as he had, that his parents had died when he was young. That's why he'd ended up in the foster system. At least, that's what he'd been told.

He handed the leggy blond the cocktail and followed it with a flirty wink. She giggled and tossed him some money. More than enough to pay for her drink. He picked up the notes and opened the till. She leaned over the bar and stayed his hand.

"Keep the change." She smiled and winked.

Despite himself, he felt a response to her all the way down to his toes. With an effort, he shrugged nonchalantly and grinned at her again.

"Thank you kindly. You're welcome at my bar anytime."

She giggled again and tossed her hair and turned away with her drink. He watched the gentle sway of her shapely hips until she disappeared into the crowd. With a smile still curving his lips, he picked up the dishcloth and swiped it over the counter. Once again, he thought about his family. As much as he wasn't ready to have to answer a steady stream of questions, he didn't want them to worry about him.

I'll send Dad another email... Let him know I'm doing okay... With that decided, Vaughan greeted his latest customer.

"Hi, there. What can I get you?"

Cassie spent the day after Oscar's funeral at home. Though she couldn't yet bring herself to go through his things, she'd spent a lot of time in his room. It was exactly the way Oscar had left it that fateful Sunday night. The bed was unmade and there were clothes strewn on the floor. A half-eaten sandwich sat on a plate on his desk, dry and unappetizing. She picked it up and emptied the food in the garbage bin beside his bed.

With a sigh, she perched on the edge of his mattress. She picked up his pillow and buried her face in it. She breathed in deeply. It still bore the faint smell of his coconut-scented shampoo. She was almost overwhelmed by her sense of loss.

She'd lost count of the number of times she'd shouted at him to keep his room clean. Now she wished she'd accepted that not everyone was neat and tidy like she was, and that his messiness was just another part of who he was. She'd give anything to have him bounding back inside the house, grinning widely, ready to regale her with his latest adventure.

Earlier that morning, she'd given her mother and Jeremy the news about George Webster. Her mother admitted she'd been notified by the police all those years ago, but it was like Trace had guessed. She'd kept it to herself because what was the point of putting her children through that grieving process all over again? It had been hard enough the first time.

Though Cassie was still upset her mother had lied to her, she understood her reasons. Throughout the discussion, Jeremy remained outwardly unaffected. Cassie didn't judge him. Jeremy had been a toddler when their father had disappeared from their lives. It was hard to miss someone who'd never been there. Not in any real sense. Unlike Oscar.

Though Oscar and Jeremy frequently butted heads, Cassie had no doubt how much Jeremy had loved his brother. His death had hit Jeremy hard. He'd barely come out of his room since the discovery and though Cassie had gently suggested maybe Jeremy could use school as a distraction, her suggestion had been met with anger and disbelief.

"How can I think of school at a time like this?" he'd cried.

"You have exams coming up. Maybe throwing yourself into study will help keep other thoughts at bay. I'm not saying to stop grieving for your brother, but you can't keep hiding out like this."

Jeremy's eyes had flared with anger. "Says who?"

"It's not healthy, Jeremy. I want you to talk to a therapist, get some professional help. I've been looking into a few possibilities. We might all be able to go together, as a family."

Jeremy glared at her. "I don't want to have therapy! I can work this out by myself! Now get out! Get out and leave me alone!"

Cassie had quietly left the room. That had been a few hours ago. The door to his room had remained firmly closed. As far as she knew, he hadn't even ventured out to take a shower. She only hoped he was talking to Annie. The girl had dropped around after the wake and had stayed late, holed up together in Jeremy's room, but Cassie hadn't seen her that day. It wasn't healthy for him to keep himself shut off from the world. Just look what had happened to their mom...

Cassie was lucky she had Trace to help her through this. He was the one good thing to come from this nightmare.

Remembering their kisses, the heated touch of his lips. The way he held her close... She felt safe and protected from all the hurts of the world. He made everything feel more manageable, like there was nothing she couldn't do with him by her side. It was a heady, addictive feeling and one she'd never experienced. She yearned to feel it again.

With a quiet sigh, she set the pillow aside and stood. With a final look around the room, she went outside. Heading down the hallway, she paused outside Jeremy's room. She wished she knew how to help him, what to say. Only time would help him get over the grief of losing his brother, but there was no point in telling him that. He was hurting *now*. He needed a solution *now*.

A muffled sob on the other side of the door had pain clutching at her insides. She hesitated, remembering the last time they'd spoken. But this was her brother. She couldn't bear to stand by and do nothing. She eased opened the door and spied Jeremy curled up in fetal position on his bed. The curtains had been drawn, blocking out the afternoon light. In the dimness, Cassie made her way over to his side and perched on the edge of the bed.

"Hey, Jer. It's me. How're you doing?"

Jeremy buried his face into his pillow. His sobs got louder. Cassie's heart turned over. She felt so helpless. There was no point telling him things would get better, that he wouldn't always feel this way, that Oscar was in Heaven and no doubt having a great time...

She'd already tried to tell herself all those things and they'd sounded trite and pathetic. They hadn't made a speck of difference to how she felt. How could she expect they'd have any effect on her brother?

But she hated to see him so upset. Oscar was never coming home. They all needed to come to terms with that. Apparently, time was a great healer, but at this stage she couldn't imagine any of them ever being their old selves again.

With a sigh, she reached out and stroked the matted hair back from Jeremy's face. He looked just as bad as he had at the funeral. Whispering mindless words of comfort, she stroked his hair and spoke to him until the sobs finally subsided into hiccups. A long time later he turned and opened his eyes. The devastation in them snatched her breath.

"Oh, Jeremy!"

He sat up and threw himself against her. She brought her arms around him and held him tight. He cried again, big wet tears that soaked her shirt, but she held him until once again, he'd cried himself out.

"It's all my fault," he choked against her shoulder.

She frowned. "What do you mean?"

"Oscar! His death is all my fault!"

"Of course it's not your fault. Why would you say that?"

"But it is!" Jeremy insisted. "You don't understand."

He looked at her and his eyes were so filled with desperation it was almost more than she could bear. Jeremy averted his gaze and stared at the bedspread.

"Earlier that day we were hanging around at home. I asked Oscar if I could play with his PlayStation."

"The one he'd bought with the money he'd saved up from his part time job at Lahood's café?"

"Yes."

"But that was brand new. I wouldn't have thought he'd lend that."

Jeremy shrugged and kept his gaze focused away from Cassie's face. "So? Anyway, Oscar refused. I begged and pleaded and cajoled. I even threatened him. He wouldn't budge. So, I offered to do his chores that night in return for letting me play. Eventually he agreed."

Cassie frowned. "I don't understand how that had anything to do with Oscar's death."

Jeremy sighed heavily. "I haven't finished. See, I played with the PlayStation for over an hour, but then Annie called. She asked me to come over. So I did."

He scrubbed at his hair. Cassie could see the tension in his face. Whatever he was about to say, it wasn't going to be easy for him.

He sighed again. "Over at Annie's we mucked around for a bit, watched some TV. We joked and laughed and talked about what we were going to do when we left school. I lost track of time." His voice choked with emotion.

He looked up at Cassie with a stricken expression. "I forgot all about the chores."

Suddenly, Cassie knew where this was headed. Her stomach clenched with dread. Jeremy spoke again.

"Malcolm got home and went off at Oscar for not doing his chores. I don't know if Oscar told him I'd agreed to do them, but whatever he said or didn't say, Malcolm dragged him up to the shed. And that was the last we saw of him."

Fresh tears filled Jeremy's eyes. He looked devastated all over again. "Don't you *see?* It's all my fault! If I'd come home in time and done the chores like I'd promised, none of this would have happened!"

He collapsed against Cassie in another torrent of wrenching sobs. She cried quietly with him. When at last he calmed down, she spoke.

"You have to believe me, Jeremy. This isn't your fault. We don't know what happened to Oscar, but it had nothing to do with Malcolm. He's been cleared by the police."

Jeremy lifted his head. His eyes were red and swollen with tears. "But that's what made him run off in the first place! If he hadn't gotten into an argument with Malcolm, he'd still be here! Carrying on about nothing! Driving me insane!" His voice hitched. "I miss him, Cass. I miss him so much..."

As Jeremy dissolved into grief once again, Cassie battled to contain her own. No matter what she said, it would take a long time and a lot of counseling before Jeremy let go of his guilt. She vowed once again to do something about finding him a therapist, no matter how much he resisted. She wondered how Noelene Lahood had gotten on with the appointment she'd arranged for Joe. She made a mental note to call Joe's mother and get the details from her as soon as she could.

Chapter Eighteen

T race had barely taken a sip of his first cup of coffee for the day when Zac came bounding into the squad room.

"Kylie just gave me this," he said, handing Trace a manila envelope.

"What is it?"

"Looks like it's come from the lab."

Trace's heart skipped a beat. "The DNA results." He tore open the envelope and pulled out a single sheet of paper. It contained the results from DNA testing conducted on the red jacket purportedly found by Mandy Goodwin in Kevin Turner's house. Trace scanned the text, skipping over the preliminaries until he reached the most important part.

His heart thumped. "The jacket belonged to Oscar Webster," Trace said.

Zac nodded thoughtfully. "Okay."

"Yeah. The lab found several of Oscar's hairs around the collar. They also got matching DNA off a piece of used chewing gum that was rolled up in a wrapper and jammed into one of the pockets."

"So, the jacket's Oscar's."

Trace compressed his lips, feeling grim. "There's more. Skin cells were also recovered." He looked up at his brother. "They've been matched to Kevin Turner."

"Fuck." Zac reached for his jacket and slipped it on.

Trace pushed away from his desk. "Let's go."

On the way to Turner's house, Trace thought back to his interview with the man's girlfriend. It seemed Mandy Goodwin had been telling the truth. Now they had the evidence to prove it. Kevin Turner was going to regret lying to them.

Son of a bitch…

Trace's hands tightened on the steering wheel. He stared straight ahead, his jaw clenched. Zac threw him a sideways glance.

"Time to rattle Turner's tree. Did you sign the jacket out?"

Trace's gaze flicked to the red jacket that was in an evidence bag on the back seat of the cruiser. "Oh, yeah. I want to watch him squirm when we produce it and tell him what we've found."

Trace pulled up outside Turner's house. He was relieved to discover the previous week's crowd of angry townsfolk were nowhere to be seen. Grabbing the plastic evidence bag off the backseat, he and Zac walked up to Turner's front door. Trace knocked on the wooden panel and waited. A few minutes later, Turner appeared. He stared at them warily through the screen door.

"Detectives. What can I do for you?"

"We have a few more questions," Trace replied. "Can we come in?" Without waiting for Kevin to reply, Trace pulled open the door and shouldered past him.

Spluttering with outrage, Turner joined them in the front room. A couch and a matching armchair, a flat screen TV, a bookshelf stuffed with books and a coffee table comprised the furniture. An open pizza box with a half-eaten pizza sat on the coffee table, alongside a half-empty mug of coffee.

"Sorry to disturb your breakfast," Trace said, not sorry at all.

Turner glared at him. "What's this about?"

"We're here to talk to you about this." Trace produced the jacket from behind his back. He watched closely for Kevin's reaction. The small intake of breath, the flare of his nostrils, the widening of his eyes... If Trace didn't already have proof Turner had come into contact with Oscar's jacket, the man's reaction would have been enough to satisfy him this wasn't the first time Turner had laid eyes on the clothing.

"You know who this belongs to, don't you Kevin?"

Kevin paled. His mouth opened and closed, but no sound came out. And then he suddenly sat down on the couch, as if he no longer trusted his legs to hold him up. He buried his face in his hands.

Trace looked at his brother. Zac gave an imperceptible nod. Turner was about to confess. Trace's heart thumped with anticipation. He held his breath, waiting for Turner to speak.

"It's not what you think," Turner said in a stilted voice.

Trace's tone turned conversational. He sat down beside Kevin, purposely presenting his body language as casual and relaxed.

"Then how about you tell us what happened Kevin," he urged.

Turner drew in a deep breath and eased it out on a shaky sigh. "Oscar and I were friends."

"So, you lied when you told us you barely knew him," Zac stated flatly.

Turner nodded. "Yes. I used to see him walking past on his way to and from school. Mostly in the afternoons because he often rode with his sister in the mornings."

"How do you know?" Trace asked, keeping his tone conversational.

"He told me."

"Keep going," Trace encouraged. "You and Oscar were friends."

"He loved to stop and smell the flowers growing in my front yard. He loved all the bright colors, always wanted me to tell me their names. Sometimes I'd pick him a bunch and he'd bury his nose in them and take the biggest breath... He loved the perfumed ones the best. Especially the sweet peas. In the spring, I have a whole row of them growing along the front fence. He always used to stop and smell them."

"Did you ever invite him inside?" Trace asked.

"No, of course not. I'm a convicted sex offender. I'm not allowed to have kids inside my house."

"You're also not supposed to be talking to them," Trace reminded him, his voice hard.

Turner's face went red and he stared at the carpet. "You're right. And I didn't want to. I tried so hard to ignore him. Especially in the beginning. But he was persistent, you know. He'd pull up outside my fence and start calling out to me if he saw me. Sometimes I'd be on the front veranda, sitting out there enjoying the afternoon. Other times I'd be working in my garden. It takes a lot of effort to have a garden as good as mine."

"I'll take your word for that," Trace said. "Tell me about the jacket. How did that come to be in your house?"

Turner opened his mouth as if to protest, but Trace cut him off. "Don't bother to deny it, Kevin. Mandy brought it to us and told us where she'd found it. The lab just confirmed your DNA is on it."

Kevin closed his mouth. His shoulders slumped. "I know how it looks, but I swear, I didn't hurt that boy."

"Tell us what happened," Trace urged.

Kevin stared off in the distance. Both Trace and Zac held their breath. Finally, the man began to speak.

"That Sunday night, the night Oscar went missing, he came by my place."

"What time was this?" Trace asked.

"I don't know. It was after eight."

"Keep going," Trace encouraged.

"I was sitting on the front veranda after dinner, just taking in the night. He was outside my front fence. When he saw me, he called out to me. I didn't want to go over to him, but he was crying and upset. So, I went over to see what was wrong with him."

"Did he tell you?" Trace asked.

Kevin compressed his lips. "He kept talking about his stepfather."

"What about his stepfather?" Zac prodded.

"Just that he hated him. That he was sick of being told what to do. That he was going to run away."

"He said that?" Trace asked.

"Yes." Kevin drew in another deep breath. "He told me Malcolm had hit him. I could see a bruise forming on his cheek. He was crying so hard, saying he was never going to go back. I wanted to help him, but I didn't know what to do. You can appreciate in my situation..."

Kevin paused and looked away. He appeared to be struggling with what he was about to say next. Trace quietly urged him on.

"He asked me if he could stay with me. Of course, I told him no. He cried and begged and pleaded, but I stayed firm. I told him he had to go back home. That I couldn't help him. He cried so hard. I'll never forget the way he looked—betrayed and utterly devastated.

"See, we'd been bonding over the garden for months. He thought of me as a friend. I was fond of him too. I don't have too many friends. But there was no way I was going to risk breaching my parole by having him in my house. So, I turned him away. That's the last time I saw him."

Kevin's voice choked with emotion. Tears glinted in his eyes. He looked as upset as he sounded. Trace glanced at his brother. Zac nodded, giving Trace all the affirmation he needed. He believed Kevin's story and so did Zac. Of course, they'd know for sure when they had the DNA tests back. As a convicted criminal, Kevin's fingerprints and DNA were already in their system. It would be a simple matter to eliminate him, or otherwise, once the reports came back.

"What about Oscar's jacket?" Trace asked.

Kevin compressed his lips. "I remember seeing him wearing it, but I don't remember him taking it off. He was still crying when he left. I don't know where he went. He was already gone by the time I found the jacket hanging on my front fence. I took it inside, intending to return it to him the next time I saw him. I guess that's when my DNA got on it."

"Why didn't you tell us this the first time we came calling? Or the second?" Trace demanded.

Kevin shot him a scornful look. "You know about my record. What do you think?"

"You should have given us more credit," Trace murmured.

"Bullshit," Turner swore. "If I'd admitted to speaking with Oscar the very night he disappeared, you would have had me in handcuffs quicker than I could blink and you know it. Coupled with the jacket, you wouldn't have even looked for anyone else. I would have gone down for this, and you would have congratulated yourself on a job well done." His lip curled up with disgust. "I'm not that naïve, Detective Barrington."

Trace had the decency not to argue back. What Turner said was true. He would have gone to the top of Trace's suspect list that very day and though Trace liked to think he would have remained open to the possibility of other suspects, Turner's involvement would have made it easy not to look too hard at anyone else.

"We've also recovered DNA evidence from Oscar's body. Given your DNA profile is already on file, as soon as we identify who the DNA belongs to, it should be a simple enough matter to eliminate you...or not." Trace gave him a hard look.

"Then bring on the report. I have nothing to hide."

Trace nodded. "Let's hope you're right." He looked around. "Where's Mandy?"

"She took off right after she talked to you guys," Kevin muttered. "Said she couldn't bear the thought of living with a kiddy fiddler."

Trace had no response. He understood why Turner wouldn't be forthcoming about his criminal history with his girlfriend, but he also appreciated how said girlfriend might feel once she discovered the truth. It was a no-win situation. Not that Trace felt sorry for the man. No one had forced him to have sex with a minor. It was only right he live with the consequences.

Joe Lahood lay on his bed. The room was dark. The blinds had been drawn ever since Oscar's body had been found. Joe couldn't imagine ever wanting to be out in the sunshine again. In the days after Oscar's disappearance, Joe's parents had forced him to go to school, but ever since the funeral they'd left him alone.

All his life, they'd impressed upon him the importance of a good education. Of working hard and setting goals and making a success of his life. They'd emigrated from Lebanon with their parents with little more than the clothes on their back, determined to make a better life. Through sheer hard work and determination, they'd succeeded. They expected Joe to succeed as well. And he wanted to make them proud.

The problem was, they didn't know. They didn't know he was gay. The fact he preferred boys would devastate his parents. It would be inconceivable to them that their son could be gay. They might even disown him. And then what would he do? He was fourteen. Where would he go?

He'd heard them often enough commenting on TV shows that depicted homosexuals. The anger and scorn such shows elicited from them turned his stomach. It wasn't their fault. They'd been raised to think it was wrong, dirty, disgusting, immoral... There was no way he could tell them...

The only one who knew his secret was Oscar and now Oscar was dead. Stabbed through the heart. Gone, just like that. Joe missed him so much.

Tapping on his phone, he opened his camera roll. He scrolled through the pictures of Oscar, taken at school, in the park, in the bush. Oscar laughing, smiling, joking... He'd always been so much fun. Okay, so he was a scaredy-cat in the dark, but Joe could forgive him for that. The truth was, he'd been the best friend Joe had ever had and now he was gone.

Hot tears filled Joe's eyes and flooded over. The therapist his mom had taken him to had encouraged him to think about Oscar and remember the good times they had. Doctor Parker assured him Oscar's death wasn't his fault. Sometimes bad things happened to good people. No one understood why. It was just the way things were. That didn't mean Joe had cause to feel guilty. He'd been a good friend to Oscar. The best....

The problem was, Joe hadn't been completely honest with Doctor Parker. If she knew the truth, there was no way she'd sit there and tell him it wasn't his fault. Because his friend's death *was* Joe's fault. He knew that...and so did Oscar.

Cassie hung out the last load of washing and brought the basket back inside. It was late afternoon. The house was still and quiet. Her mother and Malcolm had gone in his truck to the cemetery. Jeremy was in his room. She'd checked in with her principal about how her senior students were faring without her and had been assured that all was in hand. She also inquired about Joe. She hadn't seen him since the funeral. His devastation over the loss of Oscar weighed on her.

Jacquie advised her Joe hadn't been back to school since the funeral. Cassie understood his reluctance. Jeremy felt the same way. She hoped Joe's parents had gotten an appointment with the therapist. She was reminded that she still hadn't arranged anything for Jeremy. Guilt pricked at her conscience.

With renewed determination, she set the laundry basket on the counter and crossed the kitchen to dig out her phone from her handbag. She scrolled through her contacts until she found the number for Lahood's café. Noelene answered the phone.

"*Café on Main.* Can I help you?"

"Noelene. It's Cassie Webster."

"Oh. Cassie. Is this about Joe? I'm sorry, but I can't get him to leave his room. I—"

"No, no. I'm not calling in an official capacity. And don't worry about Joe. He'll be fine. He just needs some time to come to terms with what happened. We all do."

"That's what Doctor Parker said." She paused and then added in a tone thick with emotion, "We're all so sorry for you, Cassie. If there's anything we can do to help…"

"As a matter of fact, there is. You mentioned Doctor Parker. Is she the child psychologist Joe is seeing?"

"Yes. Doctor Zoe Parker. She has an office in the city. I got her name from a friend of mine. I also did some research on the Internet. She comes highly recommended."

"How is Joe doing with her?"

"It's early days. He's only seen her twice, but I'm hopeful she'll be able to help him. She seems to have helped plenty of kids in the past."

"That's good to know. I… I'd like my brother, Jeremy, to get some help. He's… He's really struggling with Oscar's death."

Noelene gave Cassie the contact details for the doctor. "I'm so sad for all of you." Noelene sounded on the verge of tears. "Please, give my best to your mother. I can't imagine what she's going through."

Cassie swallowed against the lump that had lodged in her throat. She cleared her throat and managed to thank Noelene for her concern. Slowly, she ended the call.

Her thoughts went to Trace, who'd also expressed such caring and concern for her and her family. *He gave me purple sweet peas!* No one had ever done something so special for her. She'd been incredibly touched. His beautiful gesture had only made her like him more. As well as being very attractive, he was a good and decent man—and with every sweet gesture, it only reinforced her certainty he was a man she could fall for.

I might have already fallen for him…

The thought appeared from nowhere and was completely unexpected, but she couldn't deny it was true. The days and nights since Oscar's funeral had been filled with sadness and grief and she hadn't let herself think of Trace. But now that she'd given herself permission, it seemed she could think of no one else.

The way his eyes crinkled when he smiled... His strong, solid presence... The air of calmness about him, like nothing would ever faze him... No doubt he'd learned that skill at the academy, but it sure had a way of making her feel better. Then there was the way he kissed...

The memory of his lips on hers nearly overwhelmed her. The heat, the softness, the passion... They'd kissed at Oscar's funeral when she'd been overcome with grief, and yet she wasn't sorry it had happened. In fact, she yearned to kiss him again.

She thought about the invitation he'd extended to attend his half-brother's engagement party. Though a good part of her found the thought of going out and enjoying herself so soon after Oscar's death repugnant, a tiny part of her wanted to go on a date with Trace. She wanted to forget about the pain of the past couple weeks, even if it were just for a night. Being in Trace's company would make that possible. She felt good when she was around him and though she felt a little apprehensive about meeting his family, she was sure she'd still enjoy the night. With Trace by her side, how could she not?

Chapter Nineteen

Trace let the door of the station close behind him and headed toward the side door. He was halfway across the room when the young constable behind the desk called out to him.

"Trace. I have some mail for you."

He changed direction and collected two letters. Murmuring his thanks, he tore open the first envelope. It was a signed statement from the prosecutor's office in relation to a burglary investigation Trace had been involved in. The case was due in court in a couple of weeks. The second letter had come from the DNA lab. With his heart picking up its pace, Trace walked into the squad room and sat down at his desk.

Sliding his thumb along the envelope, he broke the seal and pulled out three pieces of paper. The first one was the forensic report prepared in relation to Oscar Webster. Trace scanned the contents, his heart beating faster.

Foreign DNA had been found in saliva they had discovered in a swab taken from Oscar's lips. The same foreign DNA matched the DNA they'd found on the single black human hair Samantha had discovered caught in Oscar's hair. With growing excitement, Trace flipped to the next page. It was a forensic report on Oscar's phone.

Technicians had already downloaded Oscar's texts and had forensically examined his call log, but nothing had come of that. Trace hadn't held out much hope they'd find anyone's fingerprints but Oscar's on the phone, but he'd submitted it for analysis just the same. Now he was glad he had.

The report stated that fingerprints not belonging to the victim had been lifted from the device. Trace raised his arm in the air to cheer, but then he read the next line. Neither the prints nor the DNA profiles matched anyone in their database, including the recently submitted sample from Malcolm Russell.

That also means it wasn't Kevin Turner…

He made a mental note to call Turner and give him the good news.

Deflated but not surprised, Trace flipped to the final page. It was a report on the analysis of the sleeping bag. Trace was the first to admit the sleeping bag hadn't been on his radar. Joe had talked about how Oscar liked to go camping in the bush. He'd even shown Trace their last camping spot. Trace had assumed the sleeping bag belonged to Oscar. Now he realized he should have paid it more attention.

According to the report, hairs belonging to both Oscar and to an unknown person had been found on it and though the foreign hairs didn't match anyone in their system, they'd all come from the same person and were a match to the saliva sample.

Trace sat back in his chair and sighed. He needed to ask more questions about the sleeping bag: Namely, who it belonged to. What they now had was progress, but it didn't give them the answers Trace so desperately needed. Okay, so their perp had left something of himself behind. They now had his DNA profile. They knew he was male, but he was unknown in their system. That made him the hardest type of criminal to find.

Scrubbing his hands through his hair, he tried to overcome his frustration. One step forward and two steps back. That's how the investigation felt right now. They could eliminate Kevin Turner and Malcolm Russell, but eliminating those men didn't bring them any closer to finding the killer.

He wished he had better news for Cassie and her family. He couldn't imagine the toll this was taking on them. Not knowing... Maybe never knowing who had done this to their son and brother. It was heartbreaking.

Trace felt the weight of their disappointment. He was disappointed too. But this was only a minor setback. They had more to go on than they had before. They had a DNA profile of their killer. Now they just had to find him. Trace would start with the sleeping bag.

He reached for his phone, intent on calling Cassie. His thoughts strayed to Christopher's upcoming engagement party. He hoped Cassie still wanted to go. He was worried she might have second thoughts. Might be feeling guilty. Might think it was too soon.

If only she knew how good it would be for her to forget about all this for a while... Even for one night...

He dialed her number and waited for her to answer.

Cassie had just finished preparing dinner—lamb chops and seasonal vegetables—when her phone rang. She checked the screen and her pulse jumped.

Trace.

"Hi," she said, hoping she didn't sound as breathless as she felt.

"Hi."

"H-how are you?" she stammered, blushing. They hadn't spoken since the funeral. She wondered if he was thinking about their kiss, like she was. In fact, she'd been thinking about it—about *him*—way too much.

"I'm fine. Listen, I just received a report on the DNA found on Oscar's body."

Her heart clenched. *Okay, no not thinking about their kiss…* Her hand tightened on the phone. She strove to keep her voice even. "Oh?"

"Yes. The good news is the killer left behind enough DNA that we should be able to identify him."

Cassie's heart leaped into her throat. Before she could speak, Trace continued.

"The bad news is, there's no match in our system, which means at this stage we're unable to say who it is. One thing we *can* say with complete certainty, it isn't a known perpetrator. That means Kevin Turner is in the clear."

Cassie's breath *whooshed* out. Until then she hadn't realized she'd been holding it. "I see," she managed. "So where does that leave us?"

"We keep knocking on doors. We keep asking questions. Someone must know something. It's probably not what you want to hear, but most police investigations are solved through good old-fashioned police work." He paused and then added, "I'm not going to let this go, Cassie. I gave you my word. I'll find whoever did this to your brother."

She swallowed past the lump in her throat. "Thank you. I believe you."

She heard the relief in his voice. "I'm glad," he said softly. Then he cleared his throat. "Listen, the sleeping bag Oscar was found in... Was that his?"

"No. I don't know who it belonged to. We don't own any sleeping bags."

"What about when Oscar went camping with Joe?"

"I can't say for sure, but I think Oscar borrowed a sleeping bag from Joe."

"I see."

"Why?" Cassie asked. "Do you think the sleeping bag's important?"

"I'm not sure."

Before Cassie could question him further, Trace spoke again.

"Are we still on for Christopher's engagement party Saturday night?"

She blinked at the sudden change in subject. "Yes, of course. That's if you still want to take me."

"Of course. I want you to come. I wouldn't have asked you otherwise. I think it will be good for both of us. God knows, we both need a break."

He said the words lightly, but she heard the tension in his tone. Until then, she hadn't given too much thought to how difficult this must be for him. The pressure on the police to solve the murder—any murder—must be horrendous. She was desperate for answers. No doubt it was the same for all the relatives of victims of homicide. But that didn't make it any easier for those charged with providing the answers...

"You're right," she agreed softly. "A break would be good for both of us. Let's go and have fun."

Trace ended the call to Cassie and stared unseeingly at his desk. Whenever Oscar went camping, he borrowed a sleeping bag from Joe. His best friend. The same best friend he often turned to when he was upset. A feeling of dread started to spread in Trace's gut. He picked up his phone and made another call.

"Café on Main, this is John."

"John. It's Trace. How are things?"

"Trace. All good. School's out. I'm busy serving up milkshakes and French fries. What can I do for you?"

"I won't keep you, but I was just wondering if I could speak to Joe?"

"Joe? No, I'm sorry. He and Noelene went into the city. Joe has an appointment with that therapist and tomorrow they're going shopping. Joe needs new shoes and a tracksuit. Kids. They grow so fast."

"What time will they be home?"

"I'm not sure. Not until late tomorrow afternoon is my guess. I know what Noelene's like when she's let loose in the shops with the credit card. Is there something I can help you with?"

"I was just wondering if you own any sleeping bags?"

"Sleeping bags? Sure."

"Do you know what brand they are?"

"Wouldn't have a clue."

"What about the color?"

"Nada. You'd have to ask Noelene. She bought them over the Internet. Or Joe might know. He uses them more than anyone."

Trace tamped down his disappointment. "No worries. Let Noelene know I need to speak with her. Get her to call me when she can."

"Will do. Sorry Trace, but I have to go. I have hungry teenagers backed up to the door."

"Of course. I understand. I'll let you go."

Trace ended the call and dropped his phone into his shirt pocket. Stacking his hands behind his head, he leaned against the back of his chair and slowly blew out his breath. He didn't want to consider the possibility that Joe Lahood might be involved in Oscar's death, but Trace had promised Cassie he wouldn't give up until Oscar's killer was found. That meant pursuing every angle, no matter how unpalatable.

But Joe and his mother were unavailable and he needed them to confirm his hunch before he could proceed. No matter that he itched to get the information. For now, he'd have to wait.

The last call he made was to Kevin Turner. In a conversation that lasted less than a minute, Trace told Turner he was off the hook.

Evelyn Barrington surveyed her surroundings and was quietly pleased. The backyard of Barrington Estate had been transformed into a magical fairy garden in anticipation of her son's engagement party. Multitudes of sparkling white fairy lights had been strung through the trees. Huge swathes of gauzy white fabric twisted to form bunting, stretched between tall Greek columns and used to delineate the perimeter and create the feeling of an open-air marquee.

Large displays of fresh flowers stood in huge urns at all four corners of the marquee. The same displays, in slightly smaller form, decorated each of the thirty tables. It had started out as an intimate gathering, but very quickly the guest list had surpassed two hundred. The final count was just under two hundred and fifty.

Evelyn couldn't be more pleased for Christopher and Lexi. When he'd turned forty-one she'd almost given up hope he'd find his special someone, but those fears had been put to rest the moment she'd been introduced to Lexi. She was everything Evelyn had been praying for. Sweet, kind, gentle, smart. And with a heart of gold. She suited Christopher perfectly.

Even better, she came with a ready-made family of adopted and foster kids—eight in total and counting. Christopher had taken to fatherhood like a duck to water. Seeing him now, no one would believe only a short time ago he'd been a sad and embittered man, angry about the hand he'd been dealt and the disdain with which he'd been treated by his biological father.

But it seemed that was all behind him now and Evelyn had Lexi to thank for that. The woman had been a godsend, perfect in every way for her son. As she put the finishing touches to the table decorations, her husband of thirty years came up behind her and put his arms around her. She squeaked in alarm.

"Frank! You startled me."

"Just thought I'd steal a kiss while I can. With so many people arriving, I might not set eyes on you again before the night's over." He made good on his threat and kissed her soundly on the cheek.

She smiled and turned in his arms. "You look so handsome in your tuxedo. Black on black Armani is *so* sexy."

He wiggled his eyebrows suggestively. Evelyn laughed. They'd been together for many years; had raised nine children. And yet, they still loved each other as much, maybe more, than they had when they'd met all those years ago. She'd been an employee in his company, a single mother doing her best to support herself and her son. They'd met by chance in the staff cafeteria and as they liked to say in the movies, the rest was history.

"You've done a wonderful job, Evie. The place looks great."

Evelyn smiled and looked around her. "Thank you. Only the best for our son."

"Of course. I'm just pleased we finally have a child prepared to make the walk down the aisle. It sure took him long enough."

She laughed in agreement. "Absolutely. Let's hope this is the start of a stampede. Every single one of our nine children are old enough to take the leap."

"Yes. Wouldn't it be great if Christopher's nuptials kick off a cascade of engagements and weddings? I mean, I don't want them to get married just for the sake of it, but I sure would love to see them all find their soul mate. Just like I did."

His words filled her with a surge of warmth. She kissed him tenderly on the lips. "Thank you, my love. I feel the same."

"Are all the kids coming tonight?"

"Yes, all except Vaughan. I'm glad he sent you another email to let us know he's okay, but I wish he'd tell us where he was. Or leave us a phone number where we can contact him." She sighed.

"Yes, I wish for that too," Frank replied. "At least we can contact him via email, although he did say he's not checking it all that often."

Evelyn frowned. "What do you think made him up and leave like that? He didn't say a word to anyone. Not even to any of the other kids."

"I'm not sure. He didn't say anything to me either. But he did put in a request for six months' leave of absence from Barrington Mining."

"So, he must have been planning to leave," Evelyn mused. "Why didn't he tell us at his fortieth birthday party?"

"I don't know. But I don't think there was too much planning involved. He put in his request for leave only the day before it was due to commence."

Evelyn sighed again. "Well, I guess we ought to be thankful he's staying in touch—even if that's only an email once a month."

Frank kissed her again. "I'm sure he's fine. And now's not the time to get into the doldrums. We have a party to host and a son to celebrate."

"You're right. And one thing I'm looking very much forward to is meeting Trace's date."

Frank started in surprise. "Trace is bringing a date?"

"Apparently. He called me last week and asked if it was okay."

"Good for him. It's been a long time since Trace brought a woman to a family function."

"Yes. That's what makes me think this woman must be special."

Frank chuckled. "You have that look in your eyes, Mrs Barrington."

She widened her eyes innocently. "What look?"

He laughed again. "You don't fool me, Evie. Don't tell me you're planning another wedding already? We haven't gotten Christopher down the aisle yet!"

She widened her eyes. "I'm not planning anything. Just... looking forward to meeting the woman Trace is bringing to the party. That's all."

Frank gave her a knowing look, not falling for her innocent act for an instant. She gave him a cheeky wink and then linked her arm in his. Together, they went to meet their guests.

Cassie smoothed her dress with her hands and wished she could quell the nerves in her stomach as easily as the creases in her skirt. She'd spent an inordinate amount of time choosing her outfit and had finally decided on a deep purple satin number as a nod to her little brother. It was off the shoulder with a low V neck and cinched in at the waist. Oscar had always loved the color and the way the material felt.

"So soft Cassie!" he'd say, on the rare occasions she wore it. "As soft as rose petals, but without their sweet smell."

She'd laugh and spray herself with perfume. Sometimes she'd spray some on him. He'd always laugh and tell her how nice it smelled. She smiled at the memory and then slowly, her smile faded.

She still couldn't believe Oscar was gone. That he'd never come bounding through the house again. Never stroke the soft satin fabric of her dress. Never talk about how sweet she smelled. It still felt so surreal—the murder, the ongoing investigation. Even to some extent her burgeoning relationship with Trace.

Trace.

"Are you okay?" he asked, helping her out of the taxi.

At his suggestion, they'd traveled to the function together. Now his eyes were clouded with concern. His tender expression filled her with warmth. It was a nice change from the usual to be the one someone worried about.

She offered him a shaky smile. "Yes. I'm fine. This dress reminds me of Oscar, that's all." Understanding filled Trace's eyes.

"His favorite color, right?"

She swallowed the lump that suddenly lodged itself in her throat, again pleased he'd remembered. "Right."

He looked gorgeous in a midnight black suit and sparkling white dinner shirt. He'd teamed it with an expensive-looking gold tie. His dark hair was damp, like he'd not long stepped from the shower. It had been combed back roughly from his face. He was clean shaven and when he moved, a whiff of his spicy cologne reached her nose.

With nerves still bouncing in her stomach, she gave him another shaky smile. He winked, which only made the butterflies intensify. Then he held out his arm and she linked hers through his and together, they walked inside the house. Though she wasn't entirely convinced she was ready to let down her hair and party, she was determined to set aside the sadness and grief that had consumed her for the past weeks and enjoy herself. Starting now.

The house could only be described as a mansion and looked like it had been decorated straight out of the pages of *Home Beautiful* magazine. As she and Trace crossed the wide foyer and entered the main part of the house, they passed room after room. Living rooms, dining rooms, sitting rooms, music rooms, games rooms, rooms she wasn't even sure she could identify their purpose except to say they were beautifully appointed, yet somehow still managed to look comfortable and inviting.

"Your home is beautiful," she breathed.

"Not my home anymore. It belongs to my parents."

She flushed. "Of course, but you grew up here."

"Yes. And I had a happy childhood. But despite all this," he indicated the grandeur that surrounded them, "we grew up very grounded. You might find that hard to believe, but my parents were adamant we never forgot how privileged we were. We were also encouraged to make our own mark in the world, do something worthwhile with our lives."

Cassie smiled. "Well, it worked with you at least. You became a police officer. A very noble profession."

His answering flush was endearing. "I guess. I didn't think about how noble it was. I just wanted to help people. Being a cop was one way I could do that."

"Your parents must be proud."

Once again, a flush heightened the color in Trace's cheeks. Cassie found his humility endearing. It said so much about the man. He'd grown up in a family wealthy beyond her wildest imaginings and yet he remained grounded and modest and humble. It was a credit to both him and the parents who'd raised him that way.

"Speaking of parents..." Trace murmured.

As he led Cassie through the house and out onto a wide covered patio, they were suddenly surrounded by people. A tall white-haired man in his sixties and a slightly younger white-haired woman broke away from the crowd and came toward them. A fresh rush of nerves fluttered inside Cassie's stomach.

"Mom, Dad. I'd like you to meet Cassie Webster."

"It's a pleasure to meet you, Mr and Mrs Barrington. And thank you for having me here. You have a beautiful house."

The words came out in a rush. Heat burned across Cassie's cheeks. She averted her gaze and prayed for the moment to be over. Trace's mother merely laughed.

"It's lovely to meet you too," she said graciously. "And please, call me Evelyn."

"I'm Frank," Trace's father said. "Welcome to Barrington Estate."

"I'm honored to be here to celebrate such a momentous occasion," Cassie added. "You must both be so pleased."

"Yes, we certainly are," Evelyn agreed. "Have you met Christopher and Lexi yet?"

"No," Cassie said.

"We only just arrived," Trace explained.

"Well, make it your business to introduce your lovely date to the rest of your family," Evelyn said pointedly.

Trace merely nodded. "I intend to Mom."

Evelyn smiled. "Well, great." She turned to Cassie. "It was lovely to meet you, Cassie. I hope you enjoy the party."

"Thank you, Evelyn."

With that, Trace's parents turned and blended back into the crowd. Trace blew out his breath.

"Well, that's the parents out of the way. Now let's go and find my brothers and sisters."

"Are they all here tonight?"

"All except Vaughan."

Cassie recalled the brother who had seemingly dropped off the face of the earth. She felt a pang. "Has anyone heard from him recently?"

"Yes. Dad called me last night. He received another email from Vaughan. Not much in it, other than to say he was doing okay and not to worry."

"Did he say where he is?"

"No."

"Sounds like he doesn't want to be found right now," she mused.

Trace's lips tightened. "Yep."

"Maybe you should respect his need for privacy?"

Trace chuckled. "Yeah, except you don't know the Barringtons. We like to poke our nose into each other's business. There's no such thing as privacy. Not knowing where Vaughan is and what he's doing is driving us all mad. Not because we're busybodies, but because we care. We just want to know he's all right. Most of all, we want to know what caused him to take off like that, without a word to anyone. It doesn't make sense."

"Was there something going on at work?" Cassie asked.

"Not that I know of. He works with Dad at Barrington Mining. He's a top-level executive, involved in all the important decisions."

"Do you think his taking off might have had something to do with that?"

Trace sighed. "I don't think so. I'm sure Dad would have known something about it, if that were the case."

Cassie saw the despondent expression in Trace's eyes and sought to cheer him up. "Hey, don't look like that. We're at a party. The first party I've been to in... Goodness, I can't remember the last time I went to a party."

"I thought you told me that day we first met that it had been your birthday only a couple weeks earlier?" Trace teased.

Cassie thought back. "You're right," she said slowly. "The photograph of Oscar. It was taken at my birthday." She gave him a small smile. "You have a good memory."

He merely winked. Reaching for her hand, he tucked it into his and led her through a crowd of partygoers. His hand was warm in hers, his fingers strong and lean. She liked the way it felt, holding hands. Like they were a couple.

"Where are we going?" she asked, bemused.

"You'll see," was his reply.

Chapter Twenty

Frank Barrington sipped at his single malt scotch and regarded his youngest daughter over the rim of his glass. The engagement party was in full swing outside. The sound of merrymaking could be heard faintly through the open windows that framed one side of his study. Hannah had pulled him aside and asked for a private word. She was concerned about an accident that had occurred at the Hunter Valley mine.

"Tell me what happened," Frank said.

Hannah pushed her long hair out of her eyes and sighed. "I don't have all the details. The investigation by WorkSafe is still going on. All I know is there was a collision."

"Any fatalities?"

"No, thank God. The driver of the excavator suffered a broken bone, some lacerations, and bruising. It could have been a lot worse."

"Absolutely. How much damage to the equipment?"

"We're still assessing that. At least a million dollars and that doesn't take into consideration the downtime."

Frank eyed her steadily. "What do you think happened?"

Hannah compressed her lips. "I've spoken to everyone involved. Some of their accounts are a bit hazy. No one seems to be able to agree on what happened. I'm afraid we might never get to the bottom of it."

Frank looked at her grimly. "We need to do better than that. If we don't find out what happened, there's no guarantee it won't happen again. Accidents are costly for all of us, Hannah."

She flushed under his criticism, but gamely held his gaze. "I understand."

"Good. We're all a bit stretched with Vaughan gone. I need you to step up and do your job."

"Yes Dad. I understand. You know you can count on me."

Frank nodded. "I wouldn't have appointed you my manager if I didn't have faith in you. Thank you for bringing this to my attention. You need to dig deeper and find out what's going on up there. I want a full report in due course. But for now, go and enjoy the rest of your brother's engagement party."

Cassie and Trace kept walking across the expansive lawns and gardens until they arrived at a makeshift bar, complete with wooden countertop, barstools, stainless steel refrigerators and beer on tap. Trace turned to her with a smile.

"What are you drinking?"

Cassie smiled. "I'll have a Sauvignon Blanc, please."

"Coming right up."

Trace gave her order to the smartly dressed bartender and then asked for a beer. A few moments later, armed with their drinks, they looked around for somewhere to sit. Trace led her to a wooden bench big enough for two that stood beneath an ancient Moreton Bay fig. The bench had been built around the enormous twisted and gnarled tree roots, so cleverly done that it looked like it was growing out of them. It had been stained dark from countless seasons of falling leaves and looked like it belonged there.

"This is wonderful," Cassie commented, taking a seat. "Like something out of a novel. I feel like I'm in Terabithia."

Trace frowned. "Terabithia? Where's that?"

Cassie slammed her hand against her mouth in a pretense of abject horror. "You've never heard of Terabithia?"

"No. Should I have?"

"It's a book, and a movie. But the book came first and it's *sooo* much better than the movie. They always are."

Trace grinned. "Okay, so a book about Terabithia." He pretended to think for a moment and then shook his head. "No, can't say I've ever heard of it."

"The book was written by Katherine Paterson way back in 1977. It's actually called *Bridge to Terabithia*. Disney made it into a movie in 2007."

Trace continued to look nonplussed. Cassie shook her head and grinned ruefully. "Trace Barrington, I'm afraid your childhood was sadly lacking. Growing up not knowing about the wonders of Terabithia... I feel so sorry for you."

He laughed and pulled her close. At the same time, he planted a kiss on her mouth. It seemed so natural, neither of them thought about it until after it happened. Then heat exploded across Cassie's cheeks and Trace's face flushed.

"I'm sorry, Cassie."

"Don't be. In fact, I'd like to do it again."

His eyes lit up on a grin and he looked so sexy it stole her breath. "You would?"

She nodded and the heat spread to other places—to her breasts, her stomach and lower...

Slowly and with heated intention in his eyes that sent her pulse ricocheting through the stratosphere, Trace stood and drew her up with him. He pulled her into his arms and brought her up snug against him. His hands cupped her ass. Her arms came around his neck. His head lowered.

Their lips touched and it was as soft as butterfly wings. Sweet, sensual, seeking... And then it was like a tinder had been struck. Trace deepened the kiss, cupping her face, holding her head in place. There was no need. She wasn't going anywhere.

Fire ignited between them. She clung to Trace's shoulders. His tongue pressed against her lips, seeking entrance. She eagerly opened her mouth and their tongues twined. She kissed him like she couldn't get enough.

And that was true...

It seemed like she'd waited her entire life for this man. He was everything she could have dreamed of. They'd met under the worst of circumstances, but even in the midst of her worst nightmare, she'd found herself turning to him for reassurance, and later, for comfort when her whole world fell apart.

And he'd been there for her, every step of the way. Okay, so he was yet to find Oscar's killer, but he'd assured her he wouldn't give up until he had. She hadn't been lying when she'd told him she believed him.

The sound of someone loudly clearing their throat intruded on her pleasure. She suddenly realized the sound was close. *Very* close. She opened her eyes and saw two impossibly good-looking men standing beside them, matching grins and open curiosity on their faces.

She dropped her arms and stepped back, her face flaming. Trace blinked at her abrupt departure and looked around him. When he spied the men, he quietly cursed.

The older one winked. "Don't stop on our account. We were enjoying the show, weren't we Wade?"

The one named Wade laughed, his eyes gleaming with mischief. "Sure were, Christopher. And here I thought you and Lexi were the star attractions of this show. Obviously Trace here didn't get the memo."

"Cut it out fellas," Trace grumbled. He glanced at Cassie. She could tell he was almost as embarrassed as she was. And then Trace reached for her and drew her in close against his side.

"Christopher, Wade. This is Cassie Webster."

Wade grinned unrepentantly. "Nice to meet you, Cassie."

"Hi, Cassie. We're pleased you were able to share in our celebration. Come, I'll introduce you to my fiancée, Lexi."

With that, Christopher drew her away from Trace and headed back into the crowd. Cassie threw a helpless glance over her shoulder toward Trace. He merely smiled and shrugged. Christopher continued walking. His hand on her arm guided her through the throng until he finally came to a halt beside a woman who looked luminous with happiness. There was no other way to describe her.

She wore a shiny royal blue satin dress that brought out the color of her eyes. Right now, they sparkled with mirth. Her full lips were red and parted. Her thick chestnut hair hung in long ringlets down her back, exposing her graceful neck. She was a beautiful woman in every sense, but what made her even more stunning was the utter joy and serenity she radiated.

As Christopher drew Cassie forward, she felt like she'd stepped into a bright circle of light. It felt so real, she was taken aback. She looked up at Christopher to determine if he felt it too. She found him smiling at his fiancée with so much love and tenderness, she had her answer.

"Lexi, honey. This is Cassie Webster. She's Trace's date."

Lexi's eyes widened only slightly and then she bestowed the same beatific smile on Cassie.

"It's so lovely to meet you, Cassie."

"C-congratulations on your engagement," Cassie stammered.

"Thank you. It's wonderful that you're here to share in our celebration."

Lexi spoke like she really meant it, which Cassie found a little odd, given they didn't know each other. Lexi continued to regard Cassie with an open and kind expression.

Perhaps she really does mean it... Perhaps she really is that good and kind...

Cassie felt a rush of warmth. She was a stranger to this woman and yet Lexi made her feel included. Like she belonged there at this incredible celebration where uniformed waiters walked around bearing platters of amazing food. Where a string quartet played quietly, off to one side. Where the who's who of Sydney society chatted and laughed and danced on a makeshift dance floor. Where the spectacular grounds looked like they were something out of a movie...

Suddenly, Cassie felt overwhelmed. There was such a vast difference between her life and Trace's. At least in the way they'd grown up. He might be a cop in a small country town, but *this* was who he really was. *This* is where he came from. This is where he shared meals, conversation, celebrations... He was so far out of her league it was staggering.

She moved through the rest of the party in slow motion, smiling and managing conversation with all the people Trace introduced her to. All the time, the realization kept being hammered home: There was such a vast canyon between them as far as social standing went.

She'd fallen in love with Trace, the cop. But the reality was, he was the son of a billionaire. He'd grown up in a mansion, for Pete's sake! For all she knew he'd been surrounded by servants seeing to his every need...

It was incomprehensible. Completely foreign to everything she'd ever known. She'd come to care for him deeply and was now at a loss about where those feelings could lead.

How can I be in love with someone who is so different from me? He's never had to worry about money. I count every penny... How can this work?

Her thoughts left her feeling despondent and confused. Trace seemed to sense her change in mood. He looked at her with such concern she felt even worse.

"Is everything all right, Cassie? You've been very quiet these past couple of hours."

The party was winding down. They were seated on chairs that had been arranged with conversation in mind and located a distance from the dance floor. Though Trace had tried to get her on her feet, she'd begged off. She was a passable dancer, but right now she wasn't in a dancing mood. In fact, the sooner she got out of there and home to her modest house in Broken, the better.

"I'm fine," she said.

"You don't look fine," he said gently. "Are you thinking about Oscar?"

It was his tenderness that did her in. Tears burned behind her eyes. Her lips trembled with the effort to contain her emotions. Trace looked even more concerned.

"Cassie? Oh, honey! I'm so sorry! It's too soon, isn't it? This is all my fault!"

She waved a hand in front of her face in an effort to control her emotions. It would be beyond embarrassing to break down here. They were at a party! She stood and turned her back on him, quickly putting distance between them. She headed to a dimly lit part of the garden. Trace followed behind her.

"I'm sorry," she said when he reached her.

"*I'm* the one who's sorry," he said softly. "I was thoughtless. I should never have asked you to come."

"No," she said, unwilling to let him think that was the cause of her distress. "I'm glad you invited me. I needed a night away from everything that's been going on." She paused and then added, "This isn't about Oscar."

His forehead creased. "Then what's the matter? Why are you so upset?"

She drew in a deep breath and silently debated the wisdom of coming clean. No doubt she was being silly, but her concerns were real. She decided he deserved to know how she felt. After all, if she couldn't be honest with him, then what was the point?

"We come from such different backgrounds," she said slowly, "I just can't see how it could work between us."

Trace's expression was filled with astonishment. "*That's* why you're upset? Because I come from money, and you don't?"

He sounded so incredulous her cheeks flamed. "It's a big deal, Trace. It's something that could cause friction in the future."

He looked nonplussed. "How? I'm sorry, I don't understand what difference it makes. I'm still the same person I was before you arrived here and were given a firsthand glimpse into the life I had as a child. So what if I come from money? That doesn't change who I am. Just like I don't care that you come from more modest means. I couldn't care less about wealth and social status. I'm a cop, for Pete's sake. If I cared about money, don't you think I would have chosen a better paying job? I could make three times as much as a doctor or a lawyer or an executive at Barrington Mining."

His breath came fast. Cassie stood there, hardly knowing what to say. Before she could respond, he spoke again. This time, his tone was calmer.

"I care about you because you're a good person, Cassie. Not because of how much money you do or don't have. I'd like to think you felt the same way about me."

She tuned out after his first comment. "You care about me?"

"Yes. I care a good deal. I wasn't looking for a relationship and really, I've been taken as much by surprise by this as you have, but I guess we don't get a say in when we meet someone special." He paused and shook his head. "This issue you have with money... Does it really change the way you feel about me? Is it that important that you'd walk away from what we have?"

A tingling warmth began to spread through her veins. Her lips turned up in a smile. "You care about me?" she repeated.

"Yes!" His tone was tinged with frustration. "But I need to know... My parents' wealth... How important is that to you?"

Cassie felt like she was floating on air. She could barely remember why she'd been so upset about the disparities in their backgrounds. He was right. The way he was raised, that didn't change the person he was. The kind of person she'd fallen in love with.

"Cassie?" A shadow of fear crept into his eyes.

She hastened to reassure him. "I'm sorry, Trace. I've been so silly. Of course it's not important! For a while I was overcome with the extreme differences in our social status, but you're right. That doesn't matter at all. It's who you are, your character that's important. I've fallen in love with *you*, not your family, your money, your status."

His eyes widened with disbelief. "You've fallen in love with me?"

She grinned. "Yes. Is that okay?"

He *whooped* with joy. "More than okay."

With that, he put his arms around her and lifted her off the ground. He spun her around and *whooped* again. She couldn't wipe the smile off her face. When he finally lowered her back to the ground, he slid her deliberately down his long body. She felt every hard inch of him. Desire ignited inside her. Their lips met in a scorching kiss and she forgot everything but him. When they finally came up for air, they were both breathing hard.

"Come back to my place," he whispered.

She nodded. "Yes."

Chapter Twenty-One

Cassie clung to Trace's hand and tried to calm her nerves. Despite her earlier eagerness to go home with him, now that they were on their way—cocooned together in the dimness of a taxi—reality was setting in fast. It had been a long time since she'd slept with anyone, let alone someone as magnetic and sexy as Trace. Before heading to the party, she'd taken the time to shave, shampoo and moisturize, but she was suddenly assailed by doubts.

What if he doesn't find me attractive? What if my naked self doesn't measure up? What if...

She clenched her jaw and did her best to push the negative and increasingly panicky thoughts aside. Of course he found her attractive. He wouldn't have kissed her like that, invited her home, if he didn't. It was just that the last time she'd been intimate with a man had been more than two years ago and she was feeling a little out of practice.

She'd met Ryan in a bar in Broken. He was cute and funny and sweet. He came from Ireland and had the sexiest accent.

Best of all, he was a backpacker just traveling through, headed north to Queensland for the sugarcane harvest. There had been no expectations of anything more than a one night stand on both their parts and that had suited Cassie just fine.

But with Trace everything was different. In the first instance, she hadn't started out intending to fall in love—intending *anything* with him. She'd needed him to find her brother. That was it. But somewhere along the line, she'd grown closer to him and had begun to rely on him in ways she hadn't expected. Despite the nightmare she was living and not knowing where her brother was, she'd started thinking about Trace at odd times, wanting to talk to him, to be with him. And here they were, headed for his place to make love.

A fresh wave of butterflies swarmed her stomach. She drew in a deep breath and eased it out. Trace glanced at her and tightened his hold on her hand.

"It's okay if you change your mind," he said. "I'm happy to drop you home."

She loved that he'd given her a way out, but that's not what she wanted. She was nervous about getting naked with him, but that was only because of her own insecurities. It had nothing to do with him. Her hand tingled under his touch. Her heartbeat thumped with anticipation. Desire sent a heated flush coursing through her body. She was wildly attracted to him and couldn't wait to feel his naked skin against hers.

"I'm not going to change my mind," she assured him. "I'm just nervous." She ducked her head, grateful for the darkness that hid her embarrassment. "It's been a while for me," she finally admitted.

He squeezed her hand. "It's been a while for me too. I'm not sure what impression you have about me, but I'm not in the habit of inviting women home. I'm very choosy about my bed partners. I gather you're the same."

She smiled, relieved. "Yes. I guess you could say that."

"I'm glad," he said softly. "That makes me feel even more privileged that you said yes."

The nerves in her stomach eased. She felt so much more comfortable now at the thought of getting naked with him. She lifted his hand to her lips and brushed a kiss across his knuckles. She heard his swift intake of breath. There was a corresponding leap in her pulse.

As the taxi crested a rise, the lights of Broken appeared in the distance. Cassie had never given any thought to where Trace lived. Given he worked in Broken, she assumed he lived there too, and she was right. Trace gave the driver directions.

On the edge of town, in a newer and nicer part of Broken, the driver turned into the paved entryway to a gated estate. Trace pulled a remote out of his pocket and activated a button. The double wrought iron gates slid open on well-oiled tracks. The sweep of the taxi's headlights picked up neat garden beds, mature trees and a complex of eight identical townhouses that backed onto the greens of Broken Golf Course.

"Do you play golf?" she asked, breaking the silence.

He grinned. "Yes. Do you?"

"No. But I'd like to give it a go. Cruising around in a golf cart sounds like my idea of fun."

"I'm sure that's something I can arrange." He winked and the sheer sexiness of it sent another wave of desire rushing through her.

"The last one on the right thanks mate," Trace said.

The taxi pulled up as asked. Trace fished out his wallet and handed the man a handful of notes. "Keep the change."

Trace turned to face her. "This is us."

Us. She loved the way that sounded. She'd never been an "us" with anyone. The handful of dates she'd been on couldn't be construed as any one special relationship. She'd never been part of a couple. Now she discovered she liked the idea. Or maybe it was the idea of being a couple with Trace that was so appealing.

He unlocked his front door and stepped aside to allow her to precede him. She walked down a short corridor and into a spacious open plan living room and kitchen. It was neat and tidy without being obsessively so. A couple of golfing magazines were on the couch, like they'd been left there when the reader had finished with them. A coffee mug stood on the side table nearby. There were dishes on the drying rack and the tea towel hadn't been hung up. A pile of library books—novels, by the look of them—were on the counter near an old-fashioned wall phone.

The place had a comfortable and relaxed feel to it. The décor was masculine—dark leather sofa, chrome and glass coffee table, a plain hessian rug—but it still held a certain appeal. Family photographs in various sized frames stood on the top of a low bookshelf that was overstuffed with books.

"You like to read?" she asked.

"Yes. Thrillers, mostly. Although I occasionally venture into sci-fi and fantasy too. How about you? Are you a reader?"

She laughed. "Of course. Remember *Bridge to Terabithia*? I can't imagine a life without books."

"Paperback or hard cover?"

"Both. Although I must confess, I splurged on an e-reader for my birthday and...I'm loving it!"

His hand came over his heart. At the same time, he looked appalled. "*Digital* books? Oh, Cassie! You're breaking my heart!"

She giggled at the teasing light in his eyes. "I know! Sacrilege, right? But, hey! You can't deny they're convenient. And a darn sight cheaper too."

He nodded in defeat. "You're right. I agree. They're all that and more. But there's something about the look and feel of a real book... It's indescribable."

As he spoke, he slowly drew closer until he stood a mere hair's breadth away. The intensity in his gaze sent fireworks exploding through her veins. He reached out and traced a finger down her cheek, pausing to tuck an errant strand of hair behind her ear. Her heart stopped and then took off at a gallop. Desire pounded in her chest. And then he bent his head and touched his lips to hers.

Soft, like butterfly wings, he kissed the corners of her mouth, nibbling from one side to the other. The lightest touch, but fire trailed in its wake. He kissed his way across her cheek and lower to nuzzle her neck. She tilted her head back to give him greater access. He moved to her ear and flicked at her lobe with his tongue. Unable to stand there a moment longer, she buried her hands in his hair and dragged his mouth back to hers.

Passion unleashed, they kissed and tasted, tongues dancing, lips ravishing, heartbeats racing hard. The world tilted on its axis. Breathless, she clung to his shoulders. On a moan of surrender, his arms came around her, pressing her close. And still they kissed.

After long moments, they drew apart, both breathing hard. With their foreheads pressing against each other's, they slowly regained control. Without speaking, Trace reached for her hand and entwined his fingers with hers. He turned and started across the living room to the hallway and into his bedroom, tugging her gently behind him.

His room was furnished in a similar style to the living room: minimalistic, big dark furniture, a plain navy-blue bedspread, no cushions. The single large window looked out onto the night. Trace walked over to it and drew the curtains.

"No sense in giving any early morning golfers a sight they won't forget," he teased.

She smiled hesitantly. Now that the moment was upon them, her stomach once again fluttered with butterflies. As if sensing the return of her nerves, Trace gave her a reassuring smile.

"Hey, it's not too late to change your mind. We're not going to do anything you aren't comfortable with. Okay?"

His calm and steady tone reminded her of what she'd seen in him. He was a good and decent man. He was also the sexiest man she'd ever gotten it on with. All of a sudden, she was overcome again by a yearning to see him naked, to run her hands over the firm planes of his chest. To taste his skin. To taste *him.*

In answer to his question, she reached up and loosened his gold tie. She slid it from around his neck and tossed it to the floor. His eyes darkened with emotion. Desire glinted in their depths. But he stood in silence and let her touch him. Next her fingers went to the buttons of his fancy pleated shirt. She slid each one from the hole until there were none left and then she spread his shirt wide.

His skin was firm and tanned, his pectorals well defined. A smattering of dark hair covered his chest, only emphasizing its length and breadth. He was built like a professional sportsman—a footballer, a basketball player, a boxer. His washboard stomach and slim hips only highlighted his physical perfection. Unable to help herself, she flattened her palm against his chest.

He sucked in his breath at her touch, but otherwise remained still and quiet. Her fingers trailed over his muscles, defining each one. When her fingernails grazed his nipples, once again she heard his swift intake of breath. The tiny brown nubs pebbled in response.

Feeling empowered, she pushed the shirt all the way off his shoulders. It landed on the floor behind him. She reached for his belt. With her gaze on his, she undid the buckle and slid the belt from the loops. She tossed it aside with a lazy grin and then started in on his pants. The top button slid easily from its hole and the zipper slid down with ease. Her fingers brushed the huge bulge behind it. She shivered on a wave of desire.

He might have been turned on by her actions, but she was turned on too. Her chest was tight with yearning. Her nipples ached to be touched. Heat burned between her legs.

Trace moved his hips and the pants slid lower until they were pooled around his feet. He stepped out of them and stood there, tall and proud, wearing nothing more than his underwear. Form-fitting cotton briefs clung to his hips and cupped his huge erection. At the sight of it, Cassie's mouth went dry. Hesitantly, she reached out and touched him.

He was hard as a rock and bigger than she ever thought possible. Another rush of heat-filled desire rushed through her veins. She cupped his cock and gently squeezed and then raked her nails over his erection. All the time he stood stock still and let her do what she wanted.

She looked up at him and nearly gasped at the fire burning in his eyes. "I want to touch you," he rasped.

In answer, she reached up and lifted her hair off her neck and then presented her back to him. His fingers felt hot against her skin as he fumbled for her zipper. And then it was sliding down, lower and lower, until her dress gaped in the front. She held it close, feeling a sudden shyness, until the zipper was all the way down. With gentle fingers, Trace turned her to face him.

She clutched the dress to her chest and did her best to ignore his heated stare.

"Look at me, Cassie."

She was powerless to resist his gentle command. After all, he was nearly naked at her hand. Besides, she wanted to gauge his reaction when he looked at her. Drawing in a deep breath, she let the dress fall. The shiny fabric slithered over her hips and pooled on the floor at her feet. She stepped out of it and stood there, letting him look his fill.

"You're so beautiful," he breathed.

And standing there in front of him, with raw emotion flooding his face, she felt beautiful.

Trace's fingers weren't quite steady when he reached out and traced a finger along the curve of Cassie's black lace bra. He paused when he reached her nipple. The little bud was hard. His cock leaped as blood pounded through his veins, but he intended to take this slowly and so once again he ignored the desperate need that had been pulsing through him all night.

He moved his attention to her other breast, cupping the soft fullness through the lace. This time he bent his head and suckled her hard nipple in his mouth. He heard her swift intake of breath and smiled as she arched into him. The lace was rough against his tongue. No doubt it was also rough against her nipple. He wondered if she liked it that way.

Slowly, he reached around her back and undid the clasp of her bra. Her generous breasts sprang free. He tossed the bra aside and looked his fill. Her nipples were dusty pink, her breasts large and round. Unable to help himself, he cupped them in his hands and buried his face against them. She smelled of something sweet and exotic—like frangipani or oriental lilies. Whatever it was, she smelled delicious. He wondered how she would taste.

That thought sent another hot rush of blood surging to his cock. He wanted nothing more than to bury himself inside her, but he held on to his self-control. He wanted their first time together to be special, more wonderful than she'd ever experienced. He already knew it would be the best for him.

Never had he felt so strongly about a woman. Sure, he'd had a few brief relationships and he'd liked those women well enough, but he knew what he'd felt for them didn't compare to what he felt for the woman in his arms. He was in love with Cassie Webster and he couldn't be happier.

If he could have arranged to meet her under different circumstances, he would have. The loss of her brother in such a violent way was devastating. But he couldn't be sorry that Oscar's disappearance was what had brought them together. He hoped her little brother was happy for them.

Bending, he lifted her in his arms and set her down gently on his bed. He followed her down, covering her body with his. He kissed his way across her breasts and over her taut stomach. Sliding his fingers beneath the waistband of her panties, he inched them lower over her hips. Little by little he exposed more creamy flesh, along with her mound of soft curls. She lifted her bottom to aid him and her panties soon went the same way as their other clothes.

Not giving her time to feel embarrassed, he buried his face between her thighs. He breathed in her scent, her soft silky skin and then kissed the inside of her thighs. Slowly, he made his way back to her core and kissed her innermost lips. His tongue stole out and stroked her and she arched against him on a gasp.

"Trace!"

He came up on one elbow and grinned at her. "You don't like that?"

She stared at him, her gaze intense. "I like it way too much."

With that he increased his attentions, stroking her over and over again. When she was moaning and writhing beneath him, he moved his body up and once again covered hers. He kissed her passionately on the lips, his tongue stealing into her mouth. Stroking and tasting the soft, warm recesses, it was like kissing her nether regions all over again.

Her breath came fast. So did his. She clung to him, digging her nails into his shoulders. His cock was so hard he felt like he might explode and still he kept kissing her. When he couldn't stand it another minute, he pulled away. Gasping for breath, he reached over to his bedside table and pulled out a condom. Tearing it open with his teeth, he quickly sheathed himself and moved back between Cassie's thighs. His cock nudged at her wet entrance. Poised to thrust forward, he stared down at her, his gaze locked tightly on hers.

"Do you want me?" he rasped.

"Oh God, Trace. *Yes!*"

Chaper Twenty-Two

Trace plunged forward in one hard thrust, filling Cassie completely. She gasped from the sheer size of him. Forcing herself to relax, she gave over to the sensations he stirred inside her. Her desire had already reached fever pitch before he entered her. Now that he was inside her, hot and huge, it was all she could do not to explode.

The tension visible on his face and shoulders told her what an effort this was for him to hold back. He was waiting for her to find her fulfillment first. The knowledge sent a rush of warmth flooding through her. Though her experience in the bedroom was limited, she'd never been with a man who so unselfishly looked out for her needs. It was a refreshing change. It was wonderful.

With her arms around his neck, she moved in rhythm with his body, riding the waves of pleasure. Over and over, he thrust into her. The anticipation, the growing need, the white-hot desire kept building. She clung to him, her breath coming fast and then all of a sudden, she was there. On the precipice and toppling over; gasping with relief; her muscles contracting around him.

As her body went limp from the most explosive orgasm she'd ever experienced, Trace continued to pound into her. She held onto him, urging him on, watching the tension in his face, feeling it in his shoulders. Faster and harder until suddenly he reached his climax. He poured himself inside her. On a yelp of triumph and relief, he collapsed against her, breathing hard.

It was a long time after that he shifted his weight and Cassie was able to breathe normally again. She turned her head and looked at him. It had been wonderful for her and she was pretty sure it had been good for him too. She peeked at him and caught him looking at her. She blushed to the roots of her hair.

He shot her a wry smile. "After all we've done, and you're *blushing?* God, you're adorable."

His words only brought more heat to her face. She tried to duck her head, but he was having none of it. He took her by the chin and turned her to face him. He planted a kiss on her mouth.

"That was amazing. Better than I've ever had in my life," he said.

He looked so sincere she couldn't help but believe him. "Thank you," she whispered. "I feel the same way."

He *whooped* and hugged her to his side, grinning from ear to ear. Then he pressed a kiss against her hair. He slowly drew back and reached for her hand, threading their fingers together.

"I love you Cassie Webster," he whispered. "How do you feel about that?"

She froze in shock and then came alive, leaning over him and covering his face with kisses.

"*You love me?* You really love me? Oh my God! I love you too! I can't believe it, but it's true. In all my wildest imaginings... I never dreamed something like this could happen... That amidst the pain and devastation of losing my brother, I'd find the man I love... My soul mate... My forever."

Trace shouted out in triumph and dragged her back into his arms. His kiss was full of heat and passion and it wasn't long before both of them were breathing hard again. This time, Cassie straddled his hips and guided his cock into her entrance. She rode his hard length, moving fast, needing him deep inside her.

When he reached up and cupped her breasts and pinched and teased her nipples, her desire reached fever pitch. When her body shuddered and shook as she climaxed, she cried out her relief. She dragged in deep breaths in an effort to calm her racing heart.

Not giving her any time to relax, Trace gripped her hips and moved her up and down his cock. More frantic now, he picked up his speed, the tension in his arms and on his face told her he was close. And then he was there, on a shout of triumph, spilling into her, finding his release.

Slowly, their pulses returned to normal. They fell asleep in each other's arms, both with smiles on their faces.

It was late. The last time Jeremy had checked his phone it had been two thirty-nine in the morning. It had been more than a week since Oscar's funeral. He still couldn't sleep. He was tired, so tired. His eyes were gritty and sore. His head thumped from lack of sleep, but no matter how he tried, every time he closed his eyes he was beset with nightmares. Oscar crying out to him, shouting for help. Oscar yelling at him for not doing the chores. The worst one was where Oscar stared at him silently, recriminations in his eyes.

Jeremy thumped his pillow and flopped back down on it and closed his eyes in the hope sleep would come. There was no one he could talk to. Cassie wasn't home. She'd gone to some fancy party with that detective. Jeremy could tell she liked him and from the way the cop's eyes followed her when he thought no one was looking, he liked her too. Jeremy didn't mind that they liked each other. He was happy Cassie had something else to focus on, but he wished she was here now, to reassure him, to stroke his hair, to sing quietly until he drifted off to sleep, like she used to do when he was a kid.

Sometimes he wished he was still a kid, when he had nothing more to worry about than doing well in school, pulling his weight around the house and getting along with his brother. How he longed for those uncomplicated days! His mother might have been the joke of the town, too fat to leave the house, but she'd been that way as far back as he could remember, and he'd learned long ago not to let the cruel taunts affect him.

But now he wished his mom was able to come into his room and hug him tight. He needed a hug so badly. To have someone tell him everything was going to be all right. In his heart he knew that wasn't the case. After all, Oscar's killer was still out there. But just this once, for a smidgen of time, he wished he could pretend.

From the other side of his closed door, he could hear his mother snoring. It sounded like she'd fallen asleep on the couch. Who knew where Malcolm was? Jeremy didn't care. He hated him.

It was Malcolm's fault Oscar was dead. Okay, so he might not have killed him, but he might as well have. If Malcolm hadn't gone off at Oscar that night, Oscar wouldn't have taken off. He wouldn't have been all alone in the bush with a murderer.

With a weary sigh, Jeremy opened his eyes. There was no point pretending he was going to sleep. It would be another night like all the others, spent staring through the dark toward the ceiling, wishing things were different. Wishing he'd been the one who died.

He'd wanted so badly to find his brother, to bring him home safe and sound. But it hadn't worked out that way. Oscar was dead. Murdered. He was never coming back.

Jeremy's gaze bounced off the walls. He stared at the sliver of moonlight that leaked from under the curtains. It shed a thin silver beam onto his desk and landed on Oscar's laptop. The computer had been in Jeremy's room since the day Oscar went missing. Oscar had loaned it to him so he could play on Oscar's PlayStation. It now seemed so juvenile, so meaningless. What was a game when his brother was gone forever?

A wave of sadness overwhelmed him. Tears burned in his eyes and slowly leaked down his cheeks. He missed Oscar so much! It wasn't fair! Why did his brother have to die?

It hadn't been easy living with an autistic brother. Jeremy admitted there were times when he was jealous of Oscar. He was so good looking, with great skin, great teeth, great hair. Everything Jeremy didn't have. On top of that, everyone loved Oscar. He always got all the attention from their mom, their sister, their friends. There had been many times when Jeremy felt invisible. Like he didn't exist at all. But now he wished with all his heart that Oscar was still there. He'd give anything to have him home.

The beam of moonlight got wider as a gentle breeze eased its way inside and lifted the bottom of the curtains. Once again, Jeremy's gaze was drawn to Oscar's laptop. On a sudden urge to feel closer to his brother, he threw off the covers and went and sat at his desk. In the darkness, he opened the laptop.

The login screen loaded instantly and the space to enter the password started to blink. He didn't even have to think about it. Oscar always used the same password. He'd been using it from the first day. It didn't matter how many times Jeremy told him to change it.

"Why should I change it, Jeremy? I like this one."

In the end, Jeremy had given up explaining to his brother about security and hacking and all that other stuff. Now he was glad Oscar hadn't taken his advice. He typed in the letters: Oscar321. The computer started loading the home page. Jeremy hovered over the photo's icon, but instead clicked on mail. It was too soon to be looking at photos of his brother and the life he'd enjoyed before it had been so cruelly and irrevocably stolen.

Oscar's email program began to open on the screen. Jeremy blinked in surprise. There were hundreds and hundreds of unread emails from Oscar's classmates.

I knew my little brother was popular, but this is something else…

He felt a pang of regret that Oscar wasn't there to see it. Pulling the laptop closer, Jeremy started reading them. Most of them were from kids at school, sending Oscar messages of support. There were a few from his teachers and other staff, even one from the principal telling Oscar they were all concerned about him and urging him to come home.

Jeremy scrolled down the list of emails and found a few older ones. A flurry of emails sent by Joe a few weeks before Oscar was murdered caught Jeremy's attention. He used the down arrow and read through one and then another and another and another. There were so many, all filled with the same heart-wrenching yearnings to be understood.

Then Jeremy's mind snagged on something else: the blue sleeping bag. It had belonged to Joe. At the time, Jeremy had been too upset to think about it. Oscar and Joe had camped out plenty of times. Oscar always borrowed a sleeping bag from Joe. He didn't own one himself. Jeremy just assumed Oscar had kept it from the last time the two had camped out.

And maybe that was the case, but what Jeremy had just discovered about Joe filled him with unease. The emails had all been read by Oscar. He wondered how his brother had reacted. He'd said nothing to him about Joe's revelations. Perhaps Oscar had spoken to Cassie?

The problem was, Cassie wasn't there to ask. With a sigh, Jeremy closed the laptop and threw himself back on his bed.

There was no way he'd sleep now, but what else was he meant to do? All he could do was close his eyes and count the minutes until morning. Then he'd go down to the police station and talk to Cassie's detective. The contents of Joe's emails might be nothing, but Jeremy didn't want to leave any possibility to chance. All he wanted was to get justice for his brother. He'd do whatever it took to achieve that.

Cassie tried to stay focused on her senior history class, but that was proving difficult. It was Monday, her first day back after her leave of absence. It had been tough facing everyone again, knowing they knew about her brother, but it had also been good to get back into a routine and focus on her students.

She was grateful this was her last class for the day. She was beat.

After spending the rest of the weekend with Trace, sharing breakfast, learning his likes and dislikes, exploring each other's bodies all over again and even playing a round of golf, she'd returned home late Sunday night feeling a mixture of elation and guilt that hadn't abated overnight. The overriding thought was concern that she was rushing into something without thinking it properly through.

How can I be falling in love at the same time my brother's murderer roams free?

A fresh wave of guilt washed over her, weighing her down. All that time she'd been cocooned in Trace's arms, she'd been happy, and yet nothing had changed. Her brother was still dead, brutally murdered and the culprit had yet to be found. Just as important, Jeremy was still locked up in his room.

She felt guilty that she hadn't done more about getting him some help, but she'd called the psychologist and had been put on a waiting list. She made a mental note to call Doctor Parker again and insist she see her brother—either that, or she would provide Cassie with the name of another reputable doctor who might be able to help.

Then there was Joe. His name had come up several times earlier that morning during the weekly staff meeting. He'd returned to school but was still acting out, picking fights, being rude and disruptive. At lunchtime he'd punched a boy in the face and had knocked out several teeth. He'd be lucky if the boy's family didn't press charges. The principal, Jacquie Harper, had advised the staff he'd been given enough chances and would be suspended this time.

The news had filled Cassie with sadness. The reason for Joe's bad behavior stemmed from the tragic loss of his best friend. She voiced the possibility that Joe be shown some leniency.

"He's been given so many chances," deputy principal, Suzanne Crofter said.

A few of the staff nodded in agreement. Cassie tried again.

"It's just that he's been through so much and... He's getting help. His mother told me he's seeing a child psychologist. Shouldn't we try and encourage positive behavior, support him, try and understand him, rather than punish him?"

"What would you have us do, Cassie?" Suzanne said tiredly. "He knocked out Roy Ashworth's teeth. The assault was completely unprovoked. Joe admitted that."

Cassie sighed, weighted down with sadness. There were no winners here. She understood the need to enforce rules and to have consequences for bad behavior, but she wished... She wished things were different. That they could go back to the way they were before... Before her brother had been brutally murdered... Before his best friend was forced to suffer through the terrible knowledge his friend was gone forever...

Suzanne's expression softened. "I understand how you feel, Cassie. We're not trying to demonize Joe. Neither are we unsympathetic to his circumstances. But he's going to be suspended and that's the end of it."

"I know it's your first day back, but perhaps you'd like to sit in on the meeting with Joe and his parents?" Jacquie suggested. "You can be the good cop to my bad."

In the end, Cassie had accepted the offer. She wanted the chance to reassure Joe that even though he was being suspended, she was still on his side. She thought it important that he realize he still had some of the teachers rooting for him and that she understood what he was going through.

The sound of the bell signaling the end of the day filled Cassie with relief. She'd made plans to have dinner with Trace that evening. They were going out to eat. Their first date, not counting the engagement party. But first she needed to get through the meeting with Joe and his parents.

As her students filed out at the end of the day, she gathered her things together, picked up her handbag and closed her classroom door.

Cassie headed to the staffroom and poured herself a coffee. She had a few minutes before Joe's parents were due to arrive and she intended to use the time clearing her head.

As much as she looked forward to seeing Trace again, Joe deserved her full attention. Though she didn't countenance bad behavior, and especially when it resulted in someone getting hurt, she felt a great deal of sympathy and compassion for Joe's situation, and she wanted to make sure he and his parents knew that.

She took another sip from her coffee and tried to control her breathing. Though she wasn't feeling nervous about the upcoming meeting, she also didn't want to break down at the mention of Oscar. She wanted to be strong for Joe so he would know he could count on her if he needed help. Falling apart in front of him wasn't an option.

A few minutes later, Jacquie appeared in the doorway of the staffroom. "John and Noelene Lahood are here. Joe is with them. They're waiting in the room next to my office."

Cassie nodded in acknowledgement and poured the rest of her coffee down the sink. She rinsed and dried her cup and put it back on the shelf. Wiping her hands, she gathered herself together and headed to the room beside Jacquie's office.

Joe looked terrible. She hadn't seen him since the funeral and she was taken aback by his appearance. Dark shadows formed crescent shapes beneath his eyes. His skin was pale, his cheeks hollow. He looked like he hadn't slept or eaten since Oscar had disappeared.

"Hey Joe," she greeted him quietly.

He barely lifted his head. She turned her attention to his parents. "John, Noelene. It's nice to see you again."

Their somber gazes glanced off her before returning to the floor. Cassie understood this wasn't fun for them either. They were proud of their son and they took his education seriously. They believed a good education could make the difference between a successful life and a mediocre one. In their eyes, a suspension could set Joe back in more ways than one. It was as much a punishment for his parents as it was for him. Cassie hoped her boss understood that.

Jacquie took the seat next to Cassie and smiled at the Lahoods. "Thank you for coming in. I'm sorry it's for such an unpleasant reason."

Joe stared at the floor, along with his parents. Shame and defeat permeated the air. Cassie looked at Jacquie. The principal gave her an imperceptible nod.

Cassie cleared her throat. "We understand what you're going through Joe. And we sympathize with you. We really do. I know better than anyone how you feel. But you can't hit another student, no matter how upset and angry you are."

Noelene lifted her head. Her eyes were dark with distress. "We've spoken to him about his behavior. We've told him it's unacceptable. He's been grounded for a month."

Seated beside his wife, John Lahood made a sound of disgust in the back of his throat. "What good is grounding the boy? He knows he's done the wrong thing. Right, Joe?"

All eyes turned to Joe. His shoulders were hunched forward. When he looked up at Cassie, his eyes were filled with angry tears. Her heart clenched.

"What was the fight about, Joe?" she asked quietly.

Joe clamped his mouth shut and continued to stare at the floor. His gaze glanced off his parents and was quickly averted. His face grew flushed. His hands clenched into fists. Anger and resentment came off him in waves, but still he remained silent. Once again Cassie communicated silently with her boss. Jacquie cleared her throat.

"Joe, would it be better if we spoke to you alone?"

Joe continued to stare at the floor. After a long moment, he nodded. Jacquie turned to his parents.

"Mr and Mrs Lahood, would you mind stepping outside for just a moment?"

Joe's parents looked at each other in surprise and then looked at their son. "Is that what you want Joe?" Noelene asked.

Joe nodded again, his gaze averted from everyone.

After his mother and father left the room, Cassie drew her chair up closer to the boy and spoke to him quietly.

"We want to hear your side of the story. You're not the kind of boy who goes around punching people in the face. Roy could have been seriously injured. Is it because you're upset about Oscar? Is that why you lashed out at him?"

Joe remained stubbornly silent. Cassie glanced at Jacquie and tried again. "Talk to us, Joe. We want to understand. We want to help you deal with whatever you're going through. What happened to Oscar was terrible. We're all dealing with it the best way we can. You don't have to go through this alone, Joe. I—"

"It had nothing to do with Oscar." Joe's sudden announcement took Cassie by surprise. Recovering quickly, she spoke again, wanting to keep him talking.

"Okay. Well, that's good. What happened then? What was it about?"

"Roy Ashworth is an asshole."

Beside her, Jacquie made a noise of disapproval. Cassie shot her a look. The principal remained silent.

"Why do you say that Joe?"

Joe narrowed his eyes. "He just is."

"Did he do something to upset you?" Cassie asked.

Jacquie leaned forward. "Mrs Crofter said you told her the attack on Roy was unprovoked. Is that right?"

Joe remained silent for so long, Cassie despaired of him giving them an answer. Just when she was about to suggest they bring his parents back in and wind up the meeting, Joe spoke again.

"He called me a faggot."

Both Cassie and Jacquie started in surprise. It was the last thing Cassie had expected him to say.

"Roy said that?" Jacquie asked.

Joe nodded. Tears glinted in his eyes. Hunching over even further, he let out a sound filled with so much despair Cassie's heart broke. He covered his face with his hands and sobbed. Cassie stood, unable to sit there a moment longer without offering him comfort. She patted him on the shoulder. He lifted his head and stared at her, his eyes wet with tears, his expression filled with devastation.

She wanted so badly to hug him, but that was against school rules. Instead, she patted his shoulder again. Jacquie murmured something about going to fetch his parents. Quietly she left the room. Joe continued to cry, his obvious pain shooting shards of agony through Cassie's heart. This boy had been such a good and loyal friend to her brother. She hated to see him so upset.

She was just about to ignore the rules and give Joe a proper hug when he turned and threw himself against her, burying his face against her stomach. His arms went around her middle. She looked down as his shirt sleeve fell away and then blinked in surprise at the sight of Oscar's watch on Joe's wrist.

No, I must be mistaken… Joe must have one the same…

An Apple watch, silver face, navy-blue band. She couldn't remember Oscar telling her he and Joe had the same watch, but that was the only explanation. She remembered Trace telling her Oscar hadn't been wearing it when he was found. She'd thought that was unusual at the time. Oscar always wore his watch. He'd saved up a long time to buy it, just like he had the PlayStation. He was so proud he owned such a nice watch.

As Joe soaked her skirt with his tears, she looked at the watch again. It looked exactly like Oscar's... A feeling of foreboding crept through her veins.

I need to ask Joe about it… I need to make sure the watch is his and that it doesn't belong to my brother…

Chapter Twenty-Three

Trace flicked through the precious few pieces of evidence they'd managed to gather on Oscar Webster's murder and cursed under his breath. The sum total of the case file comprised of crime scene photographs, witness statements—most of which had taken them nowhere—and the forensic reports. They had fingerprint and DNA evidence, but no one to match it to. It was one of the most frustrating positions to be in: They had hard evidence linking the killer to their victim, but they were still unable to identify the perp and charge him with Oscar's death.

He still hadn't heard from Noelene Lahood and had finally called the café again. John had answered and said Noelene wasn't there. Trace left a message for her to call him back. If he didn't hear from her by that afternoon, he'd visit the café and see if he could catch her there.

After spending the remainder of the weekend with Cassie, Trace was desperate to find justice for her brother. There was nothing Trace could do to bring Oscar back, but he could track down the prick who had stolen her brother's life. He wanted to do that for her. To be the one who brought her closure. To be her hero.

He scoffed.

Who am I kidding? I'm no one's hero. I'm just a bloke trying to live my life the best way I can… A bloke who's fallen head over heels for a woman when I had least expected to and now I'm kind of scared…

He and Cassie barely knew each other. Was it possible to fall in love so quickly? To know with utter certainty she was the one? And what about her? She was still dealing with the tragedy of losing her brother. Was it fair to expect her to be thinking clearly? She'd told him she loved him, but was that more a reaction to the terrible strain she'd been under these past weeks, or did she really feel that strongly about him?

The last thing he wanted was to get his heart broken, but he also knew nothing worthwhile came without risk. That's the way life worked. The greater the risk, the greater the reward… Or so they said. He'd never been in love before, so he didn't have any experience with how he was supposed to feel—but if it were anything like the constant butterflies that filled his belly whenever she was near, the need to see her, touch her, kiss her; thinking about her all the time; wanting to look after her, protect her, keep her safe…then he'd fallen hard.

Is this what love feels like…?

He thought about asking Christopher. He was the only Barrington sibling who knew what it felt like to be in love and boy had it changed him. Trace's oldest brother was hardly recognizable from the bitter and twisted, angry and resentful boy and man they'd grown up around. Lexi Greenaway had worked her magic on him and so had the love he so obviously felt for her.

It had been clear to everyone at the engagement party. Even Cassie had commented on how in love the happy couple looked. Trace agreed. He was pleased for his brother. Love for Christopher had been a long time coming. Now Trace wondered if cupid had struck him with a similar arrow.

The thought sent a rush of nervous excitement surging through him. Tonight, he was taking Cassie to dinner. Afterwards, he'd invite her back to his place. Hopefully she'd spend the night. Even better would be if he could bring her some positive news on the investigation front.

He looked up as the door to the squad room opened. One of the constables who often manned the front desk walked toward him.

"There's a kid outside asking for you, Detective."

"Who is it?"

"He wouldn't give his name. Said he won't talk to anyone but you."

Trace considered the comment, his curiosity piqued.

"Okay." He pushed back from his desk and followed the constable out to the reception area.

Jeremy Webster stood there, looking scared. His acne stood out in stark contrast to his pale cheeks.

Though Trace had initially harbored suspicions of Oscar's brother, Jeremy's alibi that he was with his girlfriend until late that night had checked out. Of course, it was always possible Jeremy had detoured to the bush, come upon his brother and knifed him in the heart before turning up at home, but Trace didn't think so. His gut told him Jeremy had nothing to do with his brother's murder.

Trace greeted him with a friendly smile. "Hi Jeremy. How are you?"

The boy's expression remained somber, his eyes intense. "I need to talk to you. In private."

Trace frowned. Had Jeremy come to confess or to share details he'd kept private before? Surely not. Trace nodded and led Jeremy to the same interview room he'd taken Cassie to a few weeks earlier.

Has it only been a matter of weeks? It feels like I've known her forever…

Trace pulled out a seat and Jeremy did the same. The boy clasped his hands tightly together and rested them on the table between them. Then he dropped them to his lap. Scratched at his ear. Picked at a scab on his face.

Trace tried to put him at ease. "How have you been?"

Once again, Jeremy ignored his question. "I came here to see you yesterday, but they told me you were on a day off. I guess you were with my sister."

Trace tried to detect a censuring undertone in Jeremy's words but found nothing. He remembered exactly how he'd spent a good deal of yesterday with Jeremy's sister and fought back a blush. "You're right. We were together. We talked a lot. And played golf. I like her. I like her a lot. And she likes me. Are you okay with that?"

Jeremy shrugged. "Yeah. I guess. She's a good person. She deserves to love and be loved. Just promise me you won't ever hurt her."

Trace kept his gaze steady on Jeremy's. "I'll do my very best." Trace cleared his throat. "So, you said you needed to talk. What can I do for you Jeremy?"

Jeremy's gaze dropped to the table. He started picking at a hangnail. Then he looked back at Trace. "The sleeping bag... The blue one Oscar was in... I... I'm pretty sure it belongs to Joe Lahood."

Trace blinked in surprise and then came on alert. He leaned forward. "What makes you think that?"

"It looks just like the sleeping bag Oscar's borrowed from Joe before."

"Why have you taken so long to tell me this?"

"I don't know. I didn't think too much of it at first. Oscar and Joe often went camping together. Joe always brought Oscar a sleeping bag to use. We don't have any. When I saw it, I thought it might have ended up in our shed after one of their trips and that he'd taken it with him the night he ran off. But then I found something else."

The gravity of Jeremy's tone, coupled with the expression on his face told Trace whatever Jeremy had found was important enough that it had brought him here to the police station.

"What did you find, Jeremy?"

The boy drew in a deep breath. He looked sideways, scratched at his chin and then finally appeared to reach a decision.

"I logged into Oscar's laptop and started reading his emails."

"Okay," Trace replied.

"I wasn't trying to snoop. I... I just wanted to feel closer to Oscar. I miss him so much!"

The boy's voice cracked with emotion. Tears shone in his eyes. Trace gave him a moment to compose himself before gently encouraging him to continue.

"There were a lot of emails from the kids at school, even some of the teachers. Wishing him well, telling him to come home, asking him if he was okay. But then I looked back further, to the time before Oscar disappeared, and I found a heap of emails from Joe."

"What did they say?"

"I didn't read all of them and what I did read made me feel so uncomfortable I skipped through a lot of them, but the thing is, Joe came out to Oscar. It was the first time he'd come out to anyone."

Trace frowned. "Came out? As in, came out as a homosexual?"

"Yes! They started out talking about sex and girls and that kind of stuff and then Joe asked Oscar if he'd ever thought about having sex with a guy. I could tell from Oscar's responses that he was a bit confused. Joe explained what it meant. Oscar told him no, he'd never thought about having sex with a guy. There was a bit more to and fro, talk about other things. Then a few days before Oscar disappeared, Joe told him he was gay."

"How did Oscar react?" Trace asked.

"I don't think he really knew what it meant. He didn't say much about it. Just something like that was okay."

Trace looked at Jeremy. "Why are you telling me this?"

Jeremy's face crumpled. "I don't know! I don't know if it's important or not, but I can't just sit around in my room doing nothing! I want to find out who killed Oscar and I want to make sure he's put away for life! Oscar didn't deserve any of this and he sure as hell didn't deserve to die!"

"You're right," Trace agreed quietly. "I appreciate you coming forward with this, especially the bit about the sleeping bag. It might just be the break we're looking for."

Jeremy's expression brightened. "Really? You think it might help?"

Trace nodded. "Tell me, do you think Joe might have had something to do with Oscar's death?"

"I don't know. I really don't. I want to say no, that Joe and Oscar were best friends. They did everything together. When Oscar ran off, the first person Cassie called was Joe. That's where she thought Oscar would be. With Joe. When Joe said he hadn't seen Oscar all weekend, we were a bit surprised. It was unusual for them not to have caught up at least once over the weekend. Still, I can't imagine that Joe would hurt my brother. They loved each other."

As if suddenly becoming aware of what he'd just said, Jeremy blushed to the roots of his hair.

"I don't mean... What I mean is... They didn't love each other like *that*. They were best friends. That's all."

Trace brought the interview to an end and thanked Jeremy for coming in. Then he returned to his office. If what Jeremy said was true and the sleeping bag belonged to Joe, it was even more important that Trace talk to him. There was always the possibility that Oscar had merely taken the sleeping bag from the shed where it had been left behind from a previous camping trip, but Trace's gut was telling him different and he recalled Malcolm had said Oscar hadn't been carrying anything the night he'd left the shed.

Joe Lahood had confided in Oscar that he was gay. Trace could only imagine how difficult that had been for Joe. He was fourteen and living in a small country town. There weren't too many resources available to help kids deal with such issues. And if Joe had felt he couldn't talk to his parents about it... He might have bottled up his emotions for a long time.

Still, that didn't mean he had anything to do with Oscar's murder. Like Jeremy said, the boys were best friends. They had strong feelings for each other. A friendship that had been forged from the time they were in kindergarten.

But the sleeping bag Oscar had been found in belonged to his best friend and black hairs from an unknown person were on both Oscar's person and the sleeping bag. If the hairs belonged to Joe, it meant he'd been in close contact with Oscar during the hours before his death and yet Joe had said he hadn't seen his friend since they'd been together at school on the Friday afternoon.

The hairs in the sleeping bag could be explained away. After all, the sleeping bag was Joe's. But how did one of his hairs get caught in Oscar's hair if they hadn't been in close contact? And what about the saliva that had been swabbed from Oscar's mouth? The DNA from the saliva matched the hair sample. It had been left by the same person.

Then there was the location where Oscar's body had been found. Though he'd been hidden in a ravine, he'd been found in the bush. The same bush where he and Joe had been camping on numerous occasions, even if they'd never stayed out all night...

Before Trace could know for sure, he needed to get a DNA sample from Joe. That meant contacting his parents and getting consent. He glanced at the clock. Three o'clock. He wasn't sure when school got out, but he figured it must be soon. He pulled out his phone and dialed Cassie.

It was her first day back. He'd spoken to her earlier and she'd assured him she was doing okay. The call rang out and eventually went to voicemail. He left a message asking her to call him.

Then he called the Lahoods' café. Once again, the phone rang out. He was just about to hang up when it was answered by a harried-sounding woman.

"Yep?" she shouted.

"It's Detective Trace Barrington. I'm looking for John or Noelene Lahood."

"They're not here."

"Okay." Trace knew the café was open every day until seven o'clock. "Do you know when they'll be back?"

"Hopefully not long. They left to attend a meeting at the high school."

Trace thanked the woman and ended the call. If the Lahoods were meeting someone at the school, there was a fair chance Joe would be with them. Trace could ask them about the sleeping bag and obtain consent for the DNA sample there and then. It would save him time instead of waiting for them to stop by the station.

After telling his boss where he was going, Trace grabbed a swab kit and a handful of evidence bags and jumped into the police cruiser. He headed for the high school. On the way, he tried Cassie's number again, but once again it went through to voicemail. He left her another message, this time letting her know how much he was looking forward to their date.

He turned into the high school carpark. Cassie's Honda was parked next to another car he didn't recognize. There was also a delivery truck with *Lahood's Café on Main* emblazoned across the door. Trace grabbed the swab kit and an evidence bag from the back seat and headed toward the administration block.

As he walked, he braced himself for the upcoming confrontation. He didn't think Joe's parents would become aggressive, but they'd certainly be taken aback, and they'd catch on quickly to the reason for his request. He wouldn't be asking for a sample if he didn't regard their son as a suspect. And after obtaining the sample, he fully intended to ask Joe and his parents to accompany him to the police station to undergo a formal interview.

As he walked into the office area, Trace heard the murmur of voices from behind a closed door at the end of the corridor. He knocked on the door and then opened it. He found himself in what was obviously the staffroom. A long table ran down the middle of the room. Rows of chairs stood against either side. A small kitchenette, complete with a sink, dishwasher and microwave took up most of one wall.

A middle-aged woman dressed in a smart charcoal-gray suit and sensible heels stood with John and Noelene Lahood. The woman—Trace guessed to be either the principal or her deputy—turned as he approached. She blinked in surprise.

"I'm sorry. Can I help you?" she asked, coming toward him.

"I'm Detective Trace Barrington." He nodded toward Joe's parents. "Hello, John. Noelene. How are you?"

They mumbled a response. The woman stuck out her hand. "Detective, I'm Jacquie Harper, the principal. Is there something I can do to help you?"

"Yes. I need to speak to Joe Lahood and his parents." Once again, he looked at John and Noelene. "Is Joe here?"

"Yes," the principal responded on their behalf. "He's meeting with one of the teachers. Cassie Webster. We're in the middle of a private meeting. Do you mind waiting until we're finished?"

Though she couched it in terms of a question, Trace heard the steel in her tone. Whatever he needed to discuss with Joe and his parents, she was going to ensure her meeting was dealt with first.

He acknowledged her request with an inclination of his head. He wasn't in a hurry. He could wait.

<div style="text-align: center">~~~</div>

When Joe's sobs had subsided to the occasional hiccup, Cassie returned to her seat. It still concerned her that Joe wore a watch that was identical to Oscar's. Deliberately keeping her tone casual, she pointed to his wrist.

"That's a nice watch, Joe. It looks just like the one Oscar owned. Where did you get it?"

Fear flashed across Joe's face. That expression was gone so fast she wasn't sure if she'd imagined it. He stared at the floor. "Oscar gave it to me."

Cassie's heart stopped and then blood rushed through her veins as realization set in.

"Please don't lie to me, Joe."

He shot her a belligerent look. "I'm not."

"Oscar worked hard to save up the money to buy that watch. There's no way he would just give it away."

Anger flared in Joe's eyes. "Are you calling me a liar?"

Cassie strove to remain calm. Suddenly, she understood clearly that the person who could tell her what had happened to her brother was sitting right in front of her. She drew in a breath and leaned toward him.

"Of course not, Joe. But I know my brother... He... He loved that watch. It was his most prized possession. As his best friend, you must know that."

Joe sneered. "So, you *are* calling me a liar. Figures. No one believes me about anything. Not my parents; not the police; not you. Everyone hates me. They hate what I am. Even Oscar. My best friend. Well, I showed him what happens when you reject Joe Lahood."

Cassie gasped at the ugly expression on Joe's face, as well as his words. She needed to keep him talking.

"W-what do you mean?" she stammered.

"I *mean*, he knew how I felt about him, how much I loved him! And he rejected me! Do you have any idea how that *feels?*"

Cassie stared at him in confusion, not at all sure she understood. The wild and unfocused look in Joe's eyes sent a frisson of fear running down her spine. Her heart started thumping, but she worked hard to appear cool and calm. And then Joe pulled out a wicked-looking knife and she was more terrified than she'd ever been in her life.

"Joe, please. What are you doing?"

His lips curled up in disgust. "What do you think I'm doing? I don't know why I expected *you* to understand. After all, you're his sister. You're just the same as *him*."

He waved the knife in front of her face. She shrank back against the chair. As the blade flashed past, she glimpsed a reddish-brown stain on it.

Blood?

Her fear intensified, but she knew her only way out of this was to remain calm and do everything she could to distract him.

"Joe, listen to me. I know you're hurting. I know you're upset. You and Oscar were best friends. Now he's gone. There's no one who understands you. But resorting to violence is never the answer. Joe, please put the knife down. Slowly, right now. Put it down on the floor."

She could tell he was listening and held her breath as he stood there deciding what to do. She tried again.

"Put the knife down, Joe. I know you don't want to hurt me. Just like you didn't want to hurt Oscar. He just didn't understand. But I do. I promise, Joe. I do."

Joe's face crumpled. Cassie eased out her breath, relief flooding through her. And then Joe tensed and his eyes burned with anger. His arm holding the knife came up and then started down in a fast arc toward her.

A scream tore out of her throat. Eyeing the dangerous blade as it came perilously close to her body, she knew she only had a split second to take the action that might very well save her life.

Trace waited in the corridor outside the staffroom. The hallways were silent. Everyone had gone home for the day. In the distance, he heard the sound of a vacuum cleaner. Then a chilling scream rent the air. Trace spun around and ran in the direction it had come from, behind one of the other closed doors.

Cassie… She's in there with Joe…

With his heart in his throat, he barged into the room and was suddenly brought up short. Cassie had her arms around Joe and was holding him tightly. The boy was sobbing hysterically, his face buried against her shirt. On the floor was a lethal-looking knife. The sight of it made Trace's blood run cold. Cassie looked up and saw him and mouthed that she was okay.

John and Noelene Lahood filled the doorway, looking scared and confused. The principal pushed past them in a panic and then came to a surprised halt. Cassie continued to murmur mindless words of comfort to the distressed boy.

As the enormity of what almost happened began to sink in, Trace's legs felt weak. He'd faced many tense situations as a detective, but none that involved the woman he loved. Wrapping his handkerchief around his fingers, he carefully picked up the knife. As he slid it into one of his evidence bags he thanked God that Cassie was safe and that another Webster hadn't fallen prey to Joe Lahood.

Chapter Twenty-Four

It gave Trace no pleasure to arrest Joe Lahood and take him back to the station. Cassie and Joe's parents followed behind them. Trace left Joe in an interview room and came to explain the process to the others. While he would have felt better if Cassie had stayed away, she'd insisted on being there for Joe. His parents looked so shell-shocked Trace was afraid they'd fall apart. In the end, he inwardly conceded that Joe needed someone who could offer him some support.

Joe looked small and defeated, sitting on one side of the table. In the presence of Cassie and Joe's parents, Trace explained the process to him, including the fact the interview would be recorded and that he was under no obligation to answer any questions.

"Do you understand?" Trace asked.

Joe nodded.

"I need a verbal response from you Joe," Trace said quietly.

"Yes, I understand."

Trace drew in a deep breath and started the interview. "Tell me about Oscar. How long have you been friends?"

"Since kindergarten. He was my best friend."

Trace teased out other information. How the boys were always together. How they spent their free time. How they liked camping.

"But Oscar would never stay out overnight," Joe added.

"I want to take you to the night Oscar disappeared. Do you remember what you were doing that night?" Trace asked.

"Yes. I was at home."

"What were you doing?"

"Nothing much. Watching TV."

"Did you talk to Oscar?"

"Yeah. He called me and told me he needed to see me. He asked me to meet him outside."

Trace cursed under his breath. The call must have been made from a landline. "What time was this?" Trace asked.

Joe shrugged. "About eight o'clock. Mom and Dad hadn't been home from the café for very long. They were having dinner. I ate earlier."

"So, you met Joe outside. Did you say anything to your parents?"

"No. They were in the dining room. I slipped out the back."

"And was Oscar waiting for you?" Trace asked.

"Yes."

"What did he say?" Trace asked.

"He was crying and really upset. He kept talking about Malcolm and how much he hated him."

"Did you ask him what had happened?" Trace asked.

"Yes. He told me he and Malcolm had gotten into a fight over not doing his chores and Malcolm had punched him in the face."

Trace glanced at Cassie. Her face was pale and drawn. He couldn't imagine how hard this was for her. A wave of love and admiration washed over him. He forced his attention back to the interview.

"Did you believe him?" Trace asked.

"Yes. His cheek was red and puffy. A bruise was forming."

"What happened next?" Trace asked.

"Oscar kept crying and going on about how much he hated his stepfather. At one point he said he wanted to kill him."

Cassie's quiet gasp filled the sudden silence. Trace fought against the urge to comfort her. Instead, he asked another question.

"Did you think he was serious?"

"I don't know. Maybe. Yeah. He was so upset. He kept saying it over and over. *I want to kill him! I want to kill him!* Eventually, I told him I had a knife."

This time a cry of disbelief came from Joe's mother. Her husband put his arm around her and they huddled together. Noelene started crying quietly.

"What happened next, Joe?" Trace asked.

Joe drew in a deep breath. "I returned to the house and took the knife out from under my bed. Then I went back outside and showed it to Oscar."

"Where did you get the knife, Joe?" Trace asked.

"I bought it from a camping store ages ago."

"What did Oscar do when he saw the knife?" Trace asked.

"He was shocked at first, but then he got all excited. He wanted to hold it, touch the blade. I told him to be careful. It was sharp."

"What happened next?" Trace asked.

"Oscar kept going on and on about killing Malcolm. He wanted to stab him to death, but he was scared he might not have the courage to do it. We decided to go and hide out for a while in the woods to get away from everyone and make plans."

"I thought Oscar was scared of the dark. Didn't you tell me earlier that Oscar had never stayed out all night?"

"Yes. And he *was* scared of the dark. But I told him we needed to go somewhere where no one would overhear us. We didn't want anyone listening in on our plans."

"Your plans to kill Malcolm," Trace confirmed.

"Yes."

"What happened next?" Trace asked.

"I went back inside and collected two sleeping bags—the same ones Oscar and I always use when we go camping. I also fetched a torch. I snuck back outside without my parents seeing and we headed into the bush."

"Did you take the knife with you?" Trace asked.

"Yes. I tucked it into the waistband of my jeans."

"Did Oscar know you still had the knife?"

"Yes. He asked me to bring it."

"So, the two of you headed into the bush from your place. Is that right?" Trace asked.

"Yes. My house backs onto the same National Park. There are a lot of other trails there too."

Trace guessed this was why the sniffer dogs hadn't caught Oscar's scent. "What happened after that?"

"We walked deeper into the bush than we'd ever been, way further than our usual spot. I didn't want anyone to stumble upon us. We spread our sleeping bags on the ground. Oscar was scared, but I distracted him by talking to him about all the ways we could kill his stepfather. He kept asking me questions and looking concerned. I could tell he was starting to back away from the idea. That's when I told him I'd do it for him instead."

Cassie gasped and Noelene cried out again. Trace kept his poker face. "What did Oscar say when you offered to kill Malcolm for him?"

Joe smiled at the memory. "He couldn't believe it! He kept asking me over and over again. 'Are you sure you're going to do it for me? Are you going to kill Malcolm? Are you really going to do it?' I assured him I meant what I said."

"And did you?" Trace asked.

Joe slowly nodded. "Of course. There's nothing I wouldn't do for Oscar. I loved him."

"Did you tell Oscar that?" Trace asked.

"Yes." Joe stared at the floor. "That's when it all went to hell."

"How do you mean?" Trace asked.

"I told Oscar exactly what I told you: There wasn't anything I wouldn't do for him. That I was in love with him. I always had been. We were lying on top of our sleeping bags, side by side. I rolled over and put my arms around him and... tried to kiss him."

The shocked silence in the room lingered until Trace broke it with another question: "How did Oscar react?"

Joe's mouth twisted. "He shouted at me and tried to push me off him. We were both about the same size. We wrestled for a bit. I was so angry and hurt. All I could think was that he'd rejected me. I remember feeling the knife where it was tucked into my waistband. That's when I reached down and pulled it out and stabbed it into Oscar's heart."

Once again, the silence was complete except for Noelene's quiet weeping. Trace hazarded a glance in Cassie's direction. She was pale as death. Silent tears ran down her cheeks.

"What happened next, Joe?" Trace asked.

Joe now spoke like he was sleepwalking, numb and in a monotone he said: "I rolled him into one of the sleeping bags and hid him in a ravine. It took a lot of effort, but I half-dragged, half-pushed him until I got him all the way down. Then I covered him with leaves and branches and anything else I could find."

Trace reached down beside him and produced the knife he'd bagged at the school. The same knife Joe had threatened Cassie with. "Is this the knife you used, Joe?"

Joe glanced down at the table. "Yes."

Noelene's howls of grief grew louder. John comforted her as best he could. Trace pushed forward with the interview, wanting to get it over with.

"What about your clothes, Joe? They must have been covered in blood. What did you do with them?"

"I snuck back home and hid them in my closet, under a pile of clothes."

"Are they still there?" Trace asked, holding his breath.

"Yes."

"I'm going to need you to show me those clothes, Joe."

"Okay."

Trace drew in a deep breath, feeling like he'd been put through the wringer. He could only imagine how the others felt. He was concerned about Cassie's pallor and the shallowness of her breathing, but he needed to see this through to the end, including charging Joe with Oscar's murder.

In short order, he asked for and received permission for a DNA sample and explained to those present what would happen next. Then he asked Joe's parents to accompany them to the charge room. With a sympathetic look in Cassie's direction, he left her where she was. There would be time enough to offer her comfort later, when Joe was behind bars. Though the prospect gave Trace no pleasure, Oscar's killer deserved to be punished. That's just the way it was.

It was a week since Joe's confession. On the strength of the prosecution's case, Joe had been refused bail and was now awaiting trial. Sitting through his police interview had been the most trying time of Cassie's life. She still couldn't believe Joe was responsible for Oscar's death.

She sighed as she stared out of the large living room window that framed the rear portion of Trace's house.

"Here, Cass. Chilled just how you like it."

Trace handed her a glass of white wine. She accepted it from him and murmured her thanks. He leaned over and kissed her gently on the mouth.

"What's that for?" she asked.

"Just because."

She smiled. "Because why?"

"Because I can. Because I want to chase the shadows from your eyes. Because I want to make you smile." The teasing light in his eyes faded. "And because I love you so much it hurts and I hate seeing you so sad."

"You're right. I am sad, but I'm also happy—if that makes sense. Out of all this heartache and tragedy I found you."

He kissed her again. "That's a lovely thing to say."

"You're a lovely man."

He grinned. "Have I told you lately how perceptive you are? And how much I love your forgiving heart? No one would have blamed you for being angry at Joe and yet you seem to have found your peace."

She nodded. "You're right. I've made my peace with Joe. What's the point in remaining angry and bitter? That's not going to bring Oscar back. I'd rather focus on the positive. Like you, and the fact that at least now we know what happened and Oscar's killer can be punished, as he should be."

"We got the DNA report back on the blood on Joe's knife. It was Oscar's," Trace said quietly. "We also have Joe's DNA and fingerprints on Oscar's phone, along with a positive identification of a hair belonging to Joe that was found on Oscar's body. According to Joe's lawyer, he's going to plead guilty to murder, which will save you all from having to sit through a trial. Oscar will get justice and we can all put this tragic event behind us."

Cassie was filled with relief, then her heart swelled with love. She set down her glass and put her arms around Trace and hugged him tightly.

"Thank you for the part you played. Without you, we might never have known what happened."

"I was just doing my job. And I don't mind saying, you'd make a fine detective too. Have you ever given thought to a career change?"

"Not a chance." Cassie grinned and then tilted her head up. At the same time, Trace's head came down. Their lips met in the sweetest of kisses that tasted of forever.

THE END

Get a free book when you sign up for Chris Taylor's newsletter at: http://www.christaylorauthor.com.au

If you enjoyed Trace and Cassie's story, don't forget to leave a review at your favorite digital retailer. Every review is really appreciated and helps with visibility so other readers and can find and enjoy my books.

Broken Spirits is the next book in the Barrington Family Series. Keep reading for a sneak peek:

CHAPTER ONE

Doctor Zoe Parker peered through the windscreen at the black clouds that threatened overhead. She'd been driving for hours and had only pulled up once at a service station to refuel and use the bathroom. She hadn't even stopped to eat. Just a couple of chocolate bars was all she'd had since she'd left Sydney. Now she was in the middle of nowhere with a storm about to hit.

Great. I really didn't think this through, did I?

A flash of lightning followed a few moments later by a deafening crash of thunder made her jump. She'd always feared the power and ferocity of a storm. It was bad enough to suffer through them from the safety of her sturdy house. Now she was out in the elements, with only the thin layer of metal of her Toyota to protect her. She'd left in such a hurry; she hadn't bothered to check the weather report. Now it looked like she was headed straight for a storm.

At least she'd taken the time to call Josie Barrington and had arranged to stay with her for a few nights. They'd been friends since university. They'd both graduated as child psychologists and had since opened their own private practices. Zoe worked in the exclusive eastern suburbs. Her office was situated on the ground floor of her two-story townhouse in Vaucluse. Her parents lived in nearby Point Piper.

Five years earlier, Josie had relocated to the country, where she'd married the love of her life. Chase Barrington was a cop in their local town. Zoe had gone to their wedding and the baptisms of their two adopted kids. Chase was everything a woman could want in a man: Kind, considerate, intelligent, funny and oh-so good looking. Josie was living the perfect life. Every now and then, usually after one too many glasses of wine, Zoe envied her friend.

Especially at times like this. Escaping the pressures of her life—even for just a few days—had seemed the perfect antidote, but now she was hurtling full throttle into what promised to be a doozy of a storm. The sun had disappeared long ago. It wouldn't be long before she was surrounded by the night. Alone. In a storm. In the middle of nowhere.

It was a good analogy for her life. At least, that's how she felt. Batted and buffeted from all sides. Too many scared and unhappy kids. Especially since the pandemic. The number of kids seeking help had skyrocketed. She couldn't keep up with the demand. As much as she hated saying no to a desperate parent, there were only so many hours in the day. Lately she'd been working fifteen hour days and it still wasn't enough. No wonder she needed a break.

Of course she hadn't said anything to Josie about her present state of mind. No need to worry her friend. Zoe was sure things would settle down eventually. She just needed to get away for a few days. Rest. Relax. Recharge. The thought of kicking back with Josie, catching up over a glass of wine... All she had to do was get through the storm brewing up ahead and everything would be fine.

According to the GPS, she had another half an hour before she reached her destination. Watervale was a sleepy country town with a population of less than five thousand. It was just the kind of place Zoe needed. No busy city traffic, no noisy, impatient blasts from car horns. No crowds, no smog, no interruptions. Just fresh, clean country air and good company. There was nothing like catching up with an old friend and Josie Barrington nee Munro knew her better than most. Zoe couldn't wait to get there.

Biting her lip, she stared out at the oncoming storm again. The winter sky billowed with dark, angry clouds, even heavier and blacker than the last time she'd taken notice. She shivered and turned up the heat. Over the last little while the temperature had plummeted. No doubt in anticipation of the oncoming storm. And then a strange noise registered against the wind.

Zoe frowned and listened harder. The noise was coming from her car. She thought about pulling over and then dismissed the idea.

What do I know about cars? A flat tire is about the extent of what I could diagnose…

It didn't sound like a flat tire and the steering was working just fine. She was sure the noise was coming from the vicinity of the engine. She checked her gauges. The temperature hovered around halfway, like it usually did.

At least it's not over heating…

Another loud rumble of thunder reminded her of the encroaching storm. The only thought in her mind was to get to Watervale before it struck and unleashed its fury on her poor unsuspecting Toyota. She just hoped there was no hail in it. She pressed down on the accelerator. The car leaped forward, but a louder, more ominous sound from the engine accompanied it.

Feeling more apprehensive, but determined to reach her destination, she kept driving, ignoring the sound, until with a loud belch and a cloud of smoke, the car shuddered to a stop.

Great. Now what?

Tamping down her panic, she pulled out her mobile phone. She wasn't too far from Watervale. She'd call Josie and tell her what had happened and let her know she was going to be late. She'd also get the number for a tow service. Surely even a town the size of Watervale had one. She tapped in Josie's number and put the phone up to her ear, waiting for the call to dial out.

Nothing.

She looked at the screen and cursed.

No mobile service. Great.

Blowing out her breath, she closed her mouth shut against another irritated curse.

How the hell do people live out here where there isn't even reliable phone service?

There was no point in wasting time thinking about that now. She tried to remember how far back the last town was. It was at least half an hour ago since she'd passed through it. In between were ten miles of steep and winding road through the mountains and verdant rain forest. Twenty minutes earlier, she'd been admiring the lush greenery, the smooth tree trunks, the soaring canopy. Now the thought of walking up and down that steep, twisting road filled her with dread.

She'd dressed for comfort in blue jeans and a white T-shirt, but vanity had insisted she add a pair of high heels. Probably not the most practical choice for driving, but they looked great and were comfortable enough, if not exactly sturdy. Of course, she'd never dreamed she'd be walking cross-country in them. On top of that, there was a nasty storm about to hit.

She thought back to how many cars she'd passed in the last little while. The sad reality was, she couldn't remember the last time she'd seen one. Either travelers had opted to stay indoors and wait out the storm, or there just weren't that many motorists on the quiet country road.

She suspected the latter. Not that either option was going to help her now. No passing cars meant no one to stop and ask for help. The way she saw it, she had two options: She could either get out and walk to the nearest farm or stay put until the morning and then reassess her options. Another crack of lightning was followed quickly by a bellow of thunder. She shivered.

She didn't relish the idea of spending the night in her Toyota. It came with all the mod cons like Bluetooth, leather seats and parking assist, but there wasn't a whole lot of room to stretch out on the backseat. When the salesman had been extolling its virtues, neither of them had imagined the necessity for spending the night in it. Now that might be about to become a reality.

She peered through the windscreen again. She estimated she had another hour or so of daylight. If she could call it that. The sky was now almost purple-black with a greenish tinge that often indicated hail. Her stomach sank.

Please God. Not hail… Not on my little Toyota…

Apart from the potential damage to her car, she was also concerned about being deafened inside the mostly metal vehicle. She'd never sat through a hailstorm while trapped in her car and she didn't relish the idea of doing so now.

She vaguely remembered passing a mailbox about a mile back. A mailbox meant a farmhouse. Even if there was no one home, it was better than taking shelter in her car. Mind made up, she collected her handbag off the front passenger seat, climbed out of her car and locked it with the remote. Though she was fairly sure the car wasn't going to start again without the assistance of a mechanic, she wasn't willing to take the chance someone might come along and steal it.

Looking to her left and right, she debated about which way to go. To the right was Watervale. She'd be closer to her destination if she headed in that direction. But the mailbox was behind her. At least she knew how far away that was. She had no idea if that was the last mailbox between here and Watervale.

Better the devil you know…

Squaring her shoulders, she slung her handbag over her shoulder and started off. She hadn't gotten further than half a mile down the road when the storm struck. Huge droplets of rain fell on her bare head, soaking her within minutes. It was like the heavens had opened and dropped a month's load of rain at once. She stopped and looked back the way she'd come.

Do I go back? Or do I go forward?

She estimated she was about halfway between the two. Going back meant spending the night in her car. Going forward, she risked that the mailbox was nothing more than an ancient remnant of a life someone used to have. There might not be a farmhouse at all.

She pushed her wet hair off her face. The long strands clung to her cheeks. Rivulets of water continued down her face and trickled across her neck. Her T-shirt was soaked, her expensive high heels kept slipping off her feet. And she was still stuck in the middle of nowhere.

When she'd struck out for Watervale earlier that morning, she'd envisaged a long drive through the country with the promise of a warm bed, good food, wine and conversation at the end of it. The last thing she'd expected was for her car to break down in the middle of a storm. And yet here she was. Soaked through and shivering from the cold.

With nothing for it but to keep plowing on, she slipped and slid her way down the road and prayed for an end to her journey. The bitumen road stretched out in the distance. The rain kept pounding down. Finally, she rounded a bend in the road and to her relief, spied the dilapidated mailbox. Picking up her pace, she hurried toward it.

High grass grew on either side of the driveway. Calling it a driveway was too kind. It was no more than a narrow dirt track leading into the farm and right now it was a mass of puddles. There was no way around it. She was going to have to walk right through them.

With a sigh, she paddled through the muddy water, feeling the icy coldness soak into her feet all over again. It splashed up the legs of her jeans. She grimaced. When she'd splurged on the designer duds a few months earlier, she never imagined she'd be putting them through this. Ditto for the high heels.

As she walked through the blinding rain, a building appeared in the distance. Her heart leaped. There were no lights showing through the grimy windows, but she was willing to take her chances someone might be home. Either way, it was more solid shelter than that afforded by her car. With her feet now aching from the rough terrain, she limped the final few yards.

The closer she got, the more obvious it was the farmhouse was abandoned. The white paint on the walls was cracked and peeling. The corrugated iron roof was rusted. A front verandah leaned alarmingly to one side. The yard was overgrown with weeds. The whole place looked sad and neglected.

Refusing to be daunted, she continued forward. As she mounted the steps and gingerly crossed the rickety veranda, she was momentarily halted by a sudden awareness of her vulnerability. She was out in the middle of nowhere, with no car and no mobile phone service. Night was fast approaching. Soon it would be too dark to see anything.

Still, she'd come this far. She wasn't going to let her courage desert her now. Besides, her initial impressions of the place were correct. She was certain the place was abandoned.

Perhaps I can break in and use the landline? If there is one... Or maybe I don't have to break in at all... Maybe the door will be unlocked... It's not really trespassing if no one knows I'm here... Is it?

She worried her bottom lip with indecision. Another crash of thunder and lightning made up her mind. Before she could knock on the door, the sound of barking reached her ears. She turned just in time to see a large black dog hurtling toward her. Her heart stopped. She wasn't afraid of animals and she prided herself on having a special affinity with dogs, but that didn't mean she wasn't scared out of her wits.

She held up one hand placatingly. "It's all right, boy. Calm down. I don't mean any harm."

The dog eventually quieted, although he continued to regard her with suspicion. His presence gave her some hope there might be someone home. Giving the dog a wide berth, she moved back toward the door. She rapped on the wooden panel. Like the house, it had seen better days.

To her surprise, the door was snatched open almost immediately. A large, imposing man with icy brown eyes and a chiseled jaw stood on the other side, glaring at her. Animosity came off him in waves. Zoe blinked, taken aback. She pushed wet hair out of her eyes.

"H-hi."

Before he had a chance to respond, another flash of lightning lit up the sky. It was followed almost immediately by a crash of thunder. Zoe squealed in alarm and jumped. "Do you...mind if I come in?"

Lincoln Barrington stared at the woman who stood on his front veranda. She stood almost as tall as him, with a gaze that held an air of superiority, even while she was obviously startled by the storm. His gaze scanned over her. Expensive designer clothes soaked and spattered with mud. Designer handbag, high heels that were likewise damaged. Even soaked through and covered in mud, she had that polished look about her that spoke of old money.

No doubt in her own environment she might even be intimidating to most people. Too bad he wasn't most people. Still, she might have pulled it off if she didn't look so disheveled. Thick golden hair that was swept off her high forehead and perhaps had once been pulled back into a bun, was now loose and long, wet, errant strands stuck to her face. She pushed them away impatiently. Blue eyes that were now clouded with uncertainty and the tiniest hint of fear. He wondered what she was doing there in the middle of a storm and then dismissed the thought. He didn't give a damn who she was or where she'd come from. All he cared about was getting rid of her as soon as he could.

He glowered at her. "You're trespassing."

The woman gaped at him. "Um... I-I'm sorry. I..."

"I suggest you turn around and clear out. Go back to wherever you came from. I'm not in the mood for visitors."

Another crack of thunder and the rain intensified. It was deafening on the tin roof. Lincoln scowled. Whatever patience he might have had was now at an end.

"Did you hear me? I told you to leave."

She continued to stare at him without comprehension and then an angry flush stained her cheeks. "But... But it's pouring! You can't expect me to—"

"Looks like you're already soaked through. What's the problem? You can't get any wetter."

As he said the words, he wished he didn't notice how her T-shirt had plastered itself to her skin. Her round breasts were clearly outlined under the fabric. The cold air had pebbled her nipples. Their hard nubs strained against her shirt. Lincoln's cock hardened instinctively. His body's unwanted reaction only served to fuel his temper. He narrowed his eyes at his unwelcome visitor. It was a glare he'd perfected over years of military training. He could only hope it had the desired effect now.

CHAPTER TWO

Zoe stared at the man in shock. Anger coursed through her. Everything she'd heard about country charm and hospitality had bypassed this man in spades. He couldn't have been more unwelcoming. She half expected him to produce a shotgun and make sure she understood his order for her to depart as quickly as she'd arrived.

She swiftly catalogued his features: Bleary, bloodshot eyes, dark whiskers that covered his chin, a rumpled flannelette shirt only half-tucked into well-worn jeans. Broad shoulders and a wide chest that tapered to narrow hips. Fit and athletic build. The sleeves of his shirt were rolled up to expose strong forearms and bunched biceps. Even in winter, he sported a tan.

As the silence dragged out, the air between them crackled. Everything about him exuded danger. Still, he spoke in educated tones and even his dishevelment couldn't conceal the intelligence in his chocolate-brown eyes. He was no homeless wanderer, but that didn't mean she could trust him. The fact he was glaring at her now with such overt hostility did nothing to put her at ease.

Zoe's heart thumped. And then she looked down and saw the dog. He stood quietly to one side, his tongue lolling to one side. He watched his master with interest, waiting for a cue. Zoe took comfort from the animal's presence. No man who owned a dog could be all bad.

Perhaps he's just having a difficult day?

She'd come this far. She wasn't about to turn and leave without at least filling him in on her predicament. Besides, it was still raining hard.

She plastered a smile on her face. "I'm sorry. How rude of me. I'm Zoe Parker." She extended her hand toward him, but he ignored it. She concealed a flash of annoyance. She didn't care who he was or why he was so antagonistic, the least he could do was show some manners.

The dog moved to sit quietly beside him, reinforcing her assumption the man was his master. The man absently reached down and patted the dog on the head. Some of Zoe's tension eased.

She cleared her throat. "My car's broken down about a mile from here. I tried to call for a mechanic, but there was no phone service. I guess you know that." She offered him a strained grin, but once again he remained unresponsive. She forged on. "Anyway, I was wondering if maybe you had a landline. I'd be happy to pay for the call." She opened her handbag and fished inside for her wallet. Before she could find it, he spoke.

"I don't have a landline. I have no use for being able to get into contact with anyone or them contacting me. That's why I'm here."

She blinked in surprise. His voice was harsh with emotion. Anger once again glinted in his hard gaze.

"Oh. I see. Well..." She offered him a shrug and another pleasant smile, hoping he'd take the hint and come up with another suggestion out of her current predicament. Instead, he remained silent.

She tried again. "Do you know how far away the next farm is? Maybe they have a landline?"

"It's twenty miles away, right outside Watervale."

She gaped. "T-twenty miles? Oh, dear. That's...a long way."

Just then, another crack of thunder made her jump. Her heart skipped a beat and then took off at a gallop. She'd never been good around storms.

"It's not so far," the stranger said in a dismissive tone. "But you'd best get a move on. That storm's not going anywhere soon and from the look of it, it's going to get even wilder."

With that, he turned and went back inside, shutting the door firmly closed behind him and his dog. Zoe blinked, taken aback by his abrupt departure.

Has he really just left me standing here? What an ignorant, rude, insufferable man!

Of all the people to come across in the middle of nowhere, right when she needed help. What about all the stories she'd heard about country hospitality and how country people were the salt of the earth. This man was salty all right, but not in a good way. He was crusty from the inside out.

With no other choice, she stepped back into the rain. The icy water hit her in the face, snatching her breath. She seethed with anger. This was all his fault. She'd never come across someone so insufferably rude and uncaring. It was obvious he had a beef against society and everyone in it. She'd return to her car and prepare to spend the night cramped in the back seat. At least she'd be dry. Well, *she* wouldn't be dry. There was no way her soaked clothing would dry out in this weather. But she hoped the interior of the car would be.

With that thought in mind, she straightened her shoulders and set her sights on the mailbox a hundred yards or so in front of her. As she drew closer, she noticed it looked just as tired and worn as the farmhouse. The white paint had peeled and cracked. She could just make out the name "Abundance" in faded black lettering.

Abundance? Really?

She made a sound of disgust in the back of her throat. She wasn't sure what "abundance" referred to, but it definitely wasn't an abundance of kindness and compassion or concern. She couldn't remember ever meeting someone so obnoxious.

She made it past the mailbox and was just about to turn back onto the road when one of her high heels got stuck in the thick black mud. The action abruptly halted her progress and she would have fallen had she not managed to maintain her balance just in time. Carefully, she lifted her foot and was grateful when the sandal finally came free. Sticky, wet, mud coated her six hundred dollar shoes.

"Shit," she grunted.

She dared not think of the condition of her sandals. No doubt they were ruined. She quietly mourned the loss of them and more particularly the money she'd wasted. Still, at least they protected her feet. The dirt road was now a muddy concourse and was littered with sharp rocks and stones. Her feet would be cut to pieces without protection.

She gritted her teeth and concentrated on putting one foot in front of the other and ignored the cold trickle of water that leaked under the top of her T-shirt and ran down her spine. She'd get through this. She might have been feeling overcome with the sheer volume of needy clients these past few months, enough that she'd arranged for this sabbatical on short notice, but she wouldn't be defeated by a bit of rain – or mud, for that matter.

She squeaked in fright at the sound of another crack of thunder. She was tired and hungry after driving for so long and was on the verge of tears, but there was no way she was going to let this situation get to her. A fresh wave of determination surged through her. With her shoulders back and head held high, she forged through the deluge, counting each step that would bring her closer to the warmth and security of her car.

Lincoln stood by the front window and stared at the woman's departing back. She looked like a drowned rat, battling her way through the rain. She slipped and slid in the mud, almost losing her balance. He narrowed his eyes. Served her right. Rex tilted his head at him and whined. Lincoln was immediately filled with guilt and that left him feeling even more irritated.

"Don't look at me like that, Rex. It's not my fault her car's broken down."

No doubt she was some city slicker who didn't have the first idea about how to go about fixing it. Well, that wasn't his problem. He'd long since stopped being the kind of person who gave a damn about other people. Three tours of Afghanistan had seen to that.

Rex merely gave him another doleful look. Determined to ignore him, Lincoln walked back into the kitchen and went to the stove to stir the stew he'd fixed for dinner. The smell of cooking meat, onion, herbs and garlic wafted toward him. His stomach growled. He'd spent most of the day chopping firewood, replenishing stocks in the woodshed that had been let to run low. He didn't know the last time someone had been there. Certainly not over the winter.

He'd only arrived at the farmhouse a couple of nights earlier and hadn't yet taken the time or found the inclination to wipe away dust or brush off the cobwebs. It was enough that the old place had been available. He didn't care about the fact it was in desperate need of a thorough cleaning. All he needed was somewhere to escape for a while and contemplate the sorry state of his life.

Another clap of thunder sounded outside the kitchen, followed by a fresh deluge of rain. Rex whined and made a beeline for the kitchen table and disappeared between the chair legs. He'd always been scared of storms. Lincoln thought of the woman he'd sent packing and frowned. The road would be a quagmire by now. It didn't take much for the heavy black soil to start picking up underfoot. It would be tough going for anyone, let alone a woman who wore outlandishly impractical shoes.

Once again, his conscience pricked him. With a muffled oath, he cursed. This wasn't his problem. *She* wasn't his problem. Still...

What if she were one of my sisters? Would I want some boorish man treating her like this? Turning his back on her? Sending her out all alone in the middle of a storm. She needs help...

With another curse, he turned the heat down on the stove and went to fetch his heavy waterproof coat. He tossed a look in Rex's direction.

"Stay here," he ordered.

Pulling the collar up around his ears and jamming his battered Akubra on his head, he reluctantly went in search of her.

Zoe had nearly made it back to the car when one of her heels sunk so far into the black mud it snapped off when she tried to tug it out. With a gasp of disbelief, she stared at the sandal, or what was left of it, in her hand. With nothing left to do but slip it back on, she hobbled awkwardly to her car, squelching all the way.

Before she reached the door, the sound of an engine reached her over the pouring rain. She looked over her shoulder and spied an oversized monster of a farm truck bearing down on her. Dark gray as the storm clouds and with a wide shiny chrome grill, she watched it come toward her with a mixture of gratitude and alarm.

What if it's another surly farmer? What if this one's armed? Do I really want to be at the mercy of a stranger?

She was in the middle of nowhere in the pouring rain with no phone service. She'd never felt so vulnerable. The approaching driver was almost upon her. Fear clutched her insides. She could see the driver was male. Dark haired, broad and bulky... Her heart skipped a beat.

He could be anyone. A serial killer, a rapist, a drug dealer...

With a sound of impatience, she forcibly curbed her imagination and waited for the truck to come to a stop. As it pulled alongside her, the driver eased down his window and a familiar head popped out.

"Oh. It's you," she muttered. She was filled with equal parts relief and annoyance.

The man who hadn't even bothered to introduce himself earlier gave her a curt nod. "Get in."

Zoe reared back in indignation. No one ordered Zoe Parker about. No one. The stubborn streak that had led her astray in the past kicked in and wouldn't let go. She eyed him balefully.

"No, thank you. I'm fine. As you can see, I've made it back to my car just fine."

"You're soaked through and this storm shows no sign of abating. Get in."

Something about his brusque manner irritated her beyond measure. She was sure she could survive a night in her car. So what if she was already shivering from the cold? She'd do her best to dry off and change into something else in her car.

She lifted her head and stared him down. "Thank you for your kind offer, but like I said. I'm fine."

The man cursed long and loudly. Zoe blinked.

"Are you trying to drive me crazy, lady? Look, the truth is, I don't want to help you and I don't give a damn if you freeze to death out here, but I have a mother and I have sisters. Three, in fact. I'd hate to think if any of them were in the same situation, that someone wouldn't help them out. So, get in before I change my mind. I'll take you back to the farmhouse."

Zoe chewed on her bottom lip. It would be nice to be safe and dry inside four walls rather than be at the mercy of the elements in her little car, but the thought of spending another minute in the company of someone so obnoxious...

He swore again and scrubbed at his hair. "I promise you'll be safe. For all my outward appearances, I'm not an ax murderer, or whatever else you think I am." He looked away. "My grandfather owns the farm. He moved into town a few years ago. It's mainly used by my family for hunting trips and such. I came out here for some peace and quiet. To get away from things for a while. To think…" he added quietly.

His gaze returned to hers and she was taken aback by the pain she glimpsed in their dark depths. It was quickly concealed by a half-hearted attempt at a smile that didn't reach his eyes.

"Come and shower off and get dry. I have dinner cooked. There's a spare room with a passably comfortable bed in it. You're welcome to use it for the night. In the morning, I'll see about getting your car fixed."

She thought about his offer. It was definitely tempting and though he came across as all brusque and bad mannered, instinctively she felt she could trust him. Of course she barely knew him and she could be reading him all wrong. She could end up dead before morning. But she didn't have many choices unless she was prepared to spend a long damp night in her car.

"Make up your mind, lady. I don't have all night."

Right on cue, her stomach growled. She couldn't remember the last time she'd eaten. The day had all but disappeared. Soon it would be completely dark. Another icy trickle made its way along her spine. She shivered and then came to a decision.

"Okay. I'll come with you. But just for the night. I won't… impose any longer than I have to."

His only response was a curt nod. He leaned across the gearstick and opened the passenger side door.

"I just need a minute to get my suitcase. It's in the back of the car."

Acutely aware of his scrutiny, she hobbled lopsidedly on her broken heel and popped the lid of the boot. Reaching inside, she pulled out her Yves Saint Laurent branded suitcase. Slamming the boot shut, she held onto the handle of her suitcase and hobbled back to him, praying she didn't drop it in the mud. Like her stilettos, her suitcase had cost a fortune.

The insufferable man stayed where he was, watching her make her way awkwardly back to his truck. Her hair was plastered to her face. Her clothes were saturated. No doubt she looked like a drowned rat. On top of that, she couldn't even walk properly. She caught a flicker of a smile on his face and her anger flamed higher. He didn't even bother to climb out and help her.

The bastard… I bet he's enjoying this…Too bad I don't have any other option…

The thought of a hot shower and a warm meal was much too tempting, along with her reluctance to spend a night out in the storm. With an effort, she forced her temper down. She'd treat him with utmost courtesy, like her upbringing demanded. There was no way she'd stoop to his standard.

Huffing and puffing and with a huge groan, she managed to get her suitcase over the high side of the back of the truck. Then she hoisted herself up onto the seat. He barely glanced in her direction as he ordered her to put on her seatbelt. Biting back a snarky comment, she bit her tongue and did as she was asked. They rode the way back to the farmhouse in silence.

It was all Lincoln could do not to hold back his laughter when he saw the woman struggling to walk on her broken shoes. With one heel significantly higher than the other and the ground heavy with black mud, it was an amusing sight. Still, he could tell from the tense set of her shoulders and the way she had her jaw clenched that she wouldn't appreciate any comment. Especially not from him. And that was fine. He only had to put up with her for the night. A shower, a meal and a bed. That didn't have to include conversation. He could handle that. He'd been in far worse situations.

A sudden flashback from the warzone filled his consciousness. The intensity of it snatched his breath. His chest went tight and his heart pounded. He squeezed his eyes shut against the fiery images and did his best to slow down his breathing. The woman beside him shot him a strange look.

"Are you all right?" she asked.

Lincoln steadied his breathing with an effort and gave her a curt nod. "Of course."

He turned the truck around and headed back the way they'd come, effectively bringing an end to the conversation. She sat quietly beside him, her arms crossed over her chest, her lips taut. He slid her a sideways glance. Even looking like a drowned rat, there was no denying she was beautiful. Full lips that looked softer than rose petals. Clear, golden skin. Her wheat-colored hair was plastered to her face. He wondered what it would look like when it was dry. Soft and silky, golden like sunshine...

He cursed under his breath. *For Christ's sake. What the hell am I doing?*

She was an unwelcome guest, here for one night only. He'd offer her the basic courtesies and then see her on her way. He could go back to his solitude and return to licking his wounds with no one around to interfere or judge him. And that's just the way he wanted it.

He came to a stop outside the farmhouse. The woman climbed out and wobbled unsteadily. Straightening her shoulders, she hobbled to the back of the truck. She reached over the high side for her suitcase. Her hand flailed at least two inches short of the desired target.

Once again, Lincoln suppressed a grin. "I'll get it," he muttered.

She shot him a grateful look. "Thank you."

With that, she stumbled up the steps and across the verandah. Resting her hand against the wall, she tugged off her high heels and dropped them to the ground. They fell in a mud-caked thud. Her shoulders slumped. No doubt she was bemoaning the destruction of what looked like had once been a very expensive pair of sandals. Rex barked twice and then wagged his tail on the other side of the gauze door, eyeing the woman eagerly.

Lincoln grimaced. Even his dog had taken her side and she'd been there less than a few minutes.

Great.

As Lincoln carried her suitcase inside and set it on the floor of the spare room, he reminded himself it was only for the night. He looked at the mattress and thought briefly of rummaging around for sheets and a blanket, but then decided against it. Let her fend for herself. He wasn't putting himself out any further.

Walking down the short corridor, he reentered the kitchen and found her bending low and talking to his dog.

"And aren't you a nice boy. What's your name? You look so cute."

Rex lapped up the attention, his eyes gleaming, his tail wagging double time. Lincoln made a sound of disgust in the back of his throat.

"His name's Rex. And he isn't cute. He's a black barb. A dingo-kelpie cross. He'll tear your throat out if he's of a mind to."

The woman took a few steps backward and looked slightly alarmed. Lincoln felt another flash of guilt. Okay, so Rex might not be quite as ferocious as Lincoln had made out, but so what? The woman was an interloper. He'd offered her shelter for the night. That didn't mean he had to like it.

He moved over to the stove and lifted the lid on the stew. The meaty aromas immediately filled the room. Rex barked and Lincoln nodded.

"Yes, mate. There's enough for you, too."

With that, Lincoln spooned out a generous portion into Rex's bowl and set it aside to cool. Lincoln stared out the window over the sink. Night had set in. Rain continued to patter gently against the glass. From the corner of his eye, he saw the woman rub her hands up and down her arms and shiver. He had yet to light the fire.

"Dinner's almost ready, but you should take a shower first. You're dripping all over my kitchen floor. Bathroom's down that way." He indicated with his head. "I put your suitcase in the spare room."

She merely nodded and turned away, headed in the direction of the bedrooms. The house was modest – two bedrooms and a single bathroom. He was sure she wouldn't have any trouble finding her way around.

"There's a linen cupboard in the hallway. Dig around and help yourself. I don't care what you use," he called to her retreating back.

She turned and murmured her thanks. Lincoln cursed under his breath. He'd gone out of his way to be rude to her and yet she continued to treat him with respect. It pricked at his conscience and he hated when people made him feel like that. He reminded himself she was there for one night only. Morning couldn't come soon enough.

Broken Spirits is available for preorder at all digital retailers. It is due for release in late February, 2022.

Other books by Chris Taylor

The Munro Family Series (in order)

The Profiler

The Investigator

The Predator

The Betrayal

The Deception

The Negotiator

The Christmas Vigil (A novella)

The Ransom

The Defendant

The Shooting

The Maker

The Sydney Harbour Hospital Series (in order)

The Perfect Husband

The Body Thief

The Baby Snatchers

The Final Bullet

The Debt Collector

The Lab Test

The Stolen Identity

The Cliff-top Killer

The Likeable Fraudster

The Sydney Legal Series (in order)

An Accidental Murderer

At the Hand of her Father

A Woman Scorned

Lies and Deception

Ordinary Evil

The Ties that Bind

The Perfect Crime

A Toxic Inheritance

Malicious Love

The Craigdon Family Series (in order)

Callum

Joel

Isabella

Nicholas

Sophia

Flynn

Noah

Logan

Elizabeth

The Barrington Family Series (in order)

Broken Lives

Broken Promises

Broken Bonds

Broken Spirits

Broken Minds

Broken Vows

Broken Hearts

Broken Dreams

Broken Homes

The Fairfax Family Series (in order)

A Cattleman in Disguise

A Cattleman's Quest

A Cattleman's Daughter

A Cattleman's Secret Baby

To Catch a Cattleman

The Doctor and the Cattleman

To Rescue a Cattleman

A Cattleman's Heart

For the Love of a Cattleman

Bachelors and Brides Series (in order)

Matilda

Austin

Farrah

Benjamin

Verity

Denver

Ebony

Tyrone

Willow

Books by Chris Taylor Writing as
Bella Christian

This Is Where It Ends Series (in order)

Jessie's Story

Ryan's Story

Holly's Story

Sarah's Story

Veronica's Story

Love audiobooks? Check out Chris Taylor Books on audio

iTunes   Amazon   Audible

Join Chris Taylor's Facebook reader group/fan page and be among the
first to receive news of book releases, read and review books
prior to release
and other amazing offers.

Join Now!

Acknowledgments

As usual, no book comes into being without a lot of help and support by my friends and family. A world of thanks must go to my wonderful editor, Pat Thomas. Thank you for everything that you do to make my stories even more amazing than I could ever dare to dream. To former Detective Superintendent Michael Kilfoyle, once again thank you for lending my story credibility. Any mistakes are wholly my own.

To Justin Mendez and all of the team at 100 Covers, thank you for the fantastic book cover. To my sister, Nicole Guihot and to my friends, Ally Thomson and Sue Ricardo, thank you for your excellent editorial comments, proof reading skills and suggestions. I hope you like the final result.

To the fantastic writer organizations such as Romance Writers of Australia, Romance Writers of America and Novelists Inc for all the help, support and encouragement they offer new and aspiring writers, including me.

To my readers, thank you for your support and love for my stories. Your encouragement and enjoyment make this journey all worthwhile.

And lastly, to my friends and family, especially my husband and children. Thank you for putting up with late dinners and even later conversations as I've emerged day after day from the sometimes scary but always enthralling world I've created on my computer.

About the Author

Chris Taylor grew up on a farm in north-west New South Wales, Australia. She always had a thirst for stories and recalls writing her first book at the ripe old age of eight. Always a lover of romance and happily-ever-afters, a career in criminal law sparked her interest in intrigue and suspense. For Chris to be able to combine romance with suspense in her books is a dream come true.

Chris is married to Linden and is the mother of five children. If not behind her computer, you can find her doing the school run, taxiing children to swimming lessons, football, ballet and cricket. In her spare time, Chris loves to read her favorite authors who include Richard North Patterson, Sandra Brown, Kathleen E Woodiwiss and Jude Devereaux.

You can find out more about Chris and get a free book when you sign up for her newsletter at her website:
http://www.christaylorauthor.com.au

Join Chris on Facebook at:
https://www.facebook.com/christaylorauthor/